Italo Calvino

THE BARON IN THE TREES

Translated by Archibald Colquhoun

A Harvest Book
A Helen and Kurt Wolff Book
Harcourt Brace & Company
San Diego   New York   London

Library of Congress Cataloging-in-Publication Data
Calvino, Italo.
The baron in the trees.
Translation of Il barone rampante.
"A Helen and Kurt Wolff book."
I. Title.
[PZ3.C13956Bar8]   [PQ4809.A45]
853'.9'14   76-39704
ISBN 0-15-610680-9 (Harvest: pbk.)

Printed in the United States of America
T V X Z AA Y W U

THE BARON IN THE TREES

Other Books by Italo Calvino

THE BARON IN THE TREES

} 1 {

It was on the fifteenth of June, 1767, that Cosimo Piovasco di Rondò, my brother, sat among us for the last time. And it might have been today, I remember it so clearly. We were in the dining room of our house at Ombrosa, the windows framing the thick branches of the great holm oak in the park. It was midday, the old traditional dinner hour followed by our family, though by then most nobles had taken to the fashion set by the sluggard Court of France, of dining halfway through the afternoon. A breeze was blowing from the sea, I remember, rustling the leaves. Cosimo said: "I told you I don't want any, and I don't!" and pushed away his plateful of snails. Never had we seen such disobedience.

At the head of the table was the Baron Arminio Piovasco di Rondò, our father, wearing a long wig over his ears in the style of Louis XIV, unfashionable like so much else about him. Between me and my brother was the Abbé Fauchelefleur, the family almoner and tutor of us two boys. We were facing our mother, the

Baroness Corradina di Rondò, nicknamed the Generalessa, and our sister Battista, a kind of stay-at-home-nun. At the other end of the table, opposite our father, sat, dressed in Turkish robes, the Cavalier Avvocato Enea Silvio Carrega, lawyer, administrator and waterworks supervisor of our estates, and our natural uncle, being the illegitimate brother of our father.

A few months before, Cosimo having reached the age of twelve and I of eight, we had been admitted to the parental board; I had benefited by my brother's promotion and been moved up prematurely, so that I should not be left to eat alone. "Benefited" is perhaps scarcely the word, for really it meant the end of our carefree life, Cosimo's and mine, and we were homesick for the meals in our little room, alone with the Abbé Fauchelefleur. The Abbé was a dry, wrinkled old man, with a reputation as a Jansenist; and he had in fact escaped from his native land, the Dauphiné, to avoid trial by the Inquisition. But the rigor of character for which he was so often praised, the severe mental discipline that he imposed on himself and others, was apt to yield to a deep-rooted urge toward apathy and indolence, as if his long meditations with eyes staring into space had but brought on him a great weariness and boredom, and in every little difficulty now he had come to see a fate not worth opposing. Our meals in the Abbé's company used to begin, after many a prayer, with ordered ritual, silent movements of spoons, and woe to anyone who raised his eyes from his plate or made the slightest sucking noise with the soup; but by the end of the first dish the Abbé was already tired, bored, looking into space and smacking his lips at every sip of wine, as if only the most fleeting and superficial sensations could get through to him; by the main dish we were using our hands, and by the end of the meal were throwing pear cores at each other, while the Abbé every now and again let out one of his languid ". . . Oooo bien! . . Oooo alors."

Now, at table with the family, up surged the intimate grudges that are such a burden of childhood. Having our father and mother always there in front of us, using knives and forks for the chicken, keeping our backs straight and our elbows down—what a strain it all was!—not to mention the presence of that odious sister of ours, Battista. So began a series of scenes, spiteful exchanges, punishments, retaliations, until the day when Cosimo refused the snails and decided to separate his fate from ours.

These accumulating family resentments I myself only noticed later; then I was eight, everything seemed a game, the battle between us boys and grownups was the same as in all families, and I did not realize that my brother's stubbornness hid something much deeper.

Our father the Baron was a bore, it's true, though not a bad man: a bore because his life was dominated by conflicting ideas, as often happens in periods of transition. The turbulence of the times makes some people feel a need to bestir themselves, but in the opposite direction, backwards rather than forwards; so, with things boiling up all around him, our father had set his heart on regaining the lapsed title of Duke of Ombrosa, and thought of nothing but genealogies and successions and family rivalries and alliances with grandees near and far.

Life at our home was like a constant dress rehearsal for an appearance at court, either the Emperor of Austria's, King Louis', or even the court of those mountaineers from Turin. When, for instance, a turkey was served, our father would watch us like a hawk, to see if we carved and boned it according to royal rules, and the Abbé scarcely dared touch a morsel lest he make some error of etiquette, for, poor man, he had to add his own rebukes to our father's. And we saw now a deceitful side of the Cavalier Carrega; he would smuggle away whole legs under the folds of his Turkish robe, to munch them bit by bit later, at his ease, hidden in the vineyard; and we could have sworn (although we never succeeded in catching him in the act—his movements were so quick) that he came to table with a pocketful of stripped bones, to be left on the table in place of the hunks of turkey he whisked away. Our mother the Generalessa did not worry us, as even when serving herself at table she used brusque military manners, "*So! Noch ein wenig! Gut!*" and no one found fault with her: she held us not to etiquette, but to discipline, supporting the Baron with parade-ground orders, "*Sitz ruhig!* And wipe your nose!" The only person really at ease was Battista, the nun of the house, who would sit shredding her chicken with precise deliberation, fiber by fiber, using some sharp little knives, rather like surgeon's scalpels, which she alone had. The Baron, who should have held her up to us as an example, did not dare look at her, for, with her staring eyes under the starched coif, her narrow teeth set tight in her yellow rodent's face, she frightened him too. So it can be seen why our family board brought out all the antagonisms, the incompatibilities, between us, and all our follies and hypocrisies too; and why it was there that Cosimo's rebellion came to a head. That is why I have described it at some length—and anyway it is the last set table we shall find in my brother's life, that's sure.

It was also the only place where we would meet the grownups. The rest of the day our mother spent in her apartments, doing lace and embroidery and petit point; for in truth it was only in these traditionally womanly occupations that the Generalessa could vent her warrior's urge. The lace and embroidery were usually in the designs of geographical maps; our mother would stretch them over cushions or tapestry and stick in pins and tiny flags, showing the disposition of battles in the Wars of Succession, which she knew by heart. Or she would embroider cannons, with the trajectories from the muzzle and the line of flight and the signs of anglings, for she was highly competent in ballistics, and also had at her disposal the entire library of her father the General, with treatises on military lore and atlases and tables of fire. Our mother was a Von Kurtewitz—Konradine, daughter of General Konrad von Kurtewitz, who, twenty years before, had commanded the Empress Maria Theresa's troops, which had occupied our area. A widower, the General had taken her around with him from camp to camp; there was nothing exciting about that, for they traveled well equipped, put up at the best castles, with a suite of servants, and she had spent her days making lace on a cushion. All the stories people told of her going into battle with him were legends. She had always been an ordinary little woman with a rosy face and a snub nose, in spite of that inherited zest for things military, which was perhaps a way of showing up her husband.

Our father was one of the few nobles in our parts who had been on the side of the Empire in that war; he had greeted General von Kurtewitz with open arms, put our retainers at his disposal, and even shown his great devotion to the Imperial cause by marrying Konradine—all this with an eye to that duchy; and he was considerably put out when the Imperial troops soon moved on, as usual, and the Genoese came down on him for taxes. But he had gained a good wife, the Generalessa, as she began to be called after the death of her father on the Provence expedition (when Maria Theresa sent her a golden collar on a cushion of brocade), a wife with whom he nearly always got along, even if she, born and bred in camps, thought of nothing but armies and battles and criticized him for being just an ineffectual schemer.

But at heart they were still living in the times of the Wars of Succession, she with her artillery, he with his genealogical trees; she dreaming of a career for us boys in some army, no matter which; he, on the other hand, seeing us married to a grand duchess and electress of the Empire . . . With all this, they were excellent parents, but so absent-minded that Cosimo and I were usually left to our own devices during our childhood. Who can say if that was a good thing or a bad? Cosimo's life was so uncommon, mine so ordinary and modest, and yet our childhood was spent together, both of us indifferent to the manias of adults, both trying to find paths unbeaten by others.

We clambered about the trees (those innocent games come back to me now as a first initiation, an omen; but who could even have thought it then?), we followed the mountain streams, jumping from rock to rock, exploring caves on the seashore, and we would slide down the marble banisters in the house. It was one of these slides that caused the first serious rift between Cosimo and our parents, for he was punished—unjustly, he declared—and since then harbored a grudge against the family (or society? or the world in general?) which was to express itself later in his decision of that fifteenth of June.

As a matter of fact, we had already been warned against sliding down the marble banisters, not out of fear that we might break a leg or an arm, for that never worried our parents—which was, I think, why we never broke anything—but because they feared that since we were growing up and gaining weight, we might knock over the busts of ancestors placed by our father on the banisters at the turn of every flight of stairs. Cosimo had, in fact, once brought down a bishop, a great-great-great-grandfather, miter and all; he was punished, and since then he had learned to brake just before reaching the turn of a flight and jump off within a hair's-breadth of running into a bust. I learned this trick too, for I copied all he did, except that I, ever more careful and timid, jumped off halfway down, or slid the rest bit by bit, with constant little brakes. One day he was flying down the banisters like an arrow when who should be coming up but the Abbé Fauchele-fleur, meandering from stair to stair, with his breviary open in front of him, and his gaze fixed on space like a hen's. If only he had been half asleep as usual! But no, he was in one of those sudden moods that occasionally came over him, of extreme atten-tion and awareness. He saw Cosimo, and thought: Banisters, bust, he'll hit it, they'll blame me too (at every escapade of ours he used to be blamed also for not keeping an eye on us), and he flung himself on the banister to catch my brother. Cosimo banged into the Abbé, dragged him down the banister too (the old man was just skin and bones), found he could not brake, and hit with double force the statue of our ancestor Cacciaguerra Piovasco the Crusader; they all landed in a heap at the foot of the stairs—the Crusader in smithereens (he was plaster), the Abbé and Cosimo. There followed endless recriminations, a beating, his being locked in our room on bread and cold minestrone. And Cosimo, who felt innocent because the fault had not been his but the Abbé's, came out furiously with the phrase: "Fie on all your ancestors, Father!"—a portent of his mission as a rebel.

Our sister felt the same at heart. She, too, though the isolation in which she lived had been forced on her by our father after that affair of the Marchesino della Mela, had always been a rebellious and lonely soul. What happened with the Marchesino, none of us ever really knew. How, as the son of a family hostile to ours, had he ever got into the house? And why? It could only be to seduce, no, rather to rape our sister, said my father in the long quarrel which ensued between the families. We boys, in fact, could never succeed in picturing that freckled simpleton as a seducer, least of all of our sister, who was certainly much stronger than him, and famous for beating the stable hands at competitions of physical strength. And then, why was it he who shouted for help, not her? And how did the servants who rushed to the scene, led by our father, come to find him with his breeches torn to strips as if by the talons of a tiger? The Della Mela family refused even to admit that their son had made an attempt on Battista's virtue or to agree to a marriage between them. So our sister was eventually confined to the house, dressed up as a nun, though without taking any vows even as a tertiary, in view of her rather dubious vocation.

Her evil schemes found expression in cooking. She was a really excellent cook, for she had the primary gifts in the culinary art: diligence and imagination; but when she put her hand to it, no one ever knew what surprise might appear at table. Once she made some paté toast, really exquisite, of rats' livers; this she never told us until we had eaten them and pronounced them good; and some grasshoppers' claws, crisp and sectioned, laid on an open tart in a mosaic; and pigs' tails baked as if they were little cakes; and once she cooked a complete porcupine with all its quills—who knows why, probably just to give us all a shock at the raising of the dish cover, for even she, who usually ate everything, however odd, that she had prepared herself, refused to taste it, though it was a baby porcupine, rosy and certainly tender. In fact, most of these horrible dishes of hers were thought out just for effect, rather than for any pleasure in making us eat disgusting food with her. These dishes of Battista's were works of the most delicate animal or vegetable jewelry; cauliflower heads with hares' ears set on a collar of fur; or a pig's head from whose mouth stuck a scarlet lobster as if putting out its tongue, and the lobster was holding the pig's tongue in its pincers as if they had torn it out. And finally the snails; she had managed to behead I don't know how many snails, and the heads, those soft little equine heads, she had inserted, I think with a toothpick, each in a wire-mesh; they looked, as they came on the table, like a flight of tiny swans. Even more revolting than the sight of these delicacies was the thought of Battista's zealous determination in preparing them, of those thin hands of hers tearing the little creatures to pieces.

It was as a protest against this macabre fantasy of our sister's that my brother and I were incited to show our sympathy with the poor tortured creatures, and our disgust, too, for the flavor of cooked snails—a revolt really against everything and everybody; and from this, not surprisingly, stemmed Cosimo's gesture and all that followed after.

We had devised a plan. When the Cavalier brought home a basket full of eatable snails, these were put into a barrel in the cellar, so they should starve, or eat only bran and so be purged. When we moved the planks covering these barrels an inferno was revealed: snails moving up the staves with a languor which was already a presage of their death agony, amid remnants of bran, streaks of opaque clotted slime and multicolored excrement, mementos of the good old days of open air and grass. Some of them were right outside their shells with heads extended, and waving horns; some all curled up, showing a different pair of antennae. Others were grouped like village gossips, others shut and sleeping, others dead, with their shells upside down. To save them from meeting that sinister cook, and to save us from her ministrations too, we made a hole in the bottom of the barrel, and from there traced as hidden a trail as we could, with bits of chopped grass and honey, behind barrels and various tools in the cellar, to draw the snails toward a little window facing an uncultivated grassy field.

Next day we went down into the cellar to see the results, and we inspected the walls and passage by candlelight—"One here! ... And another there! ... And just see where this one got to!"

Already there was an almost continuous line of snails moving from the barrel over the flagstones and walls toward the little window, following our trail. "Quick, snaily-wailies! Hurry up, out!" we could not help shouting at them, seeing the creatures moving along so slowly, now and then going around and around in circles over the rough cellar walls, attracted by occasional fly-droppings and mildew. But the cellar was dark and cluttered; we hoped no one would notice them, and that they would all have time to escape.

But that restless creature, our sister Battista, used to spend the nights wandering around the house in search of mice, holding a candelabra, with a musket under her arm. That night she went down into the cellar, and the candlelight shone on a lost snail on the ceiling, with its trail of silvery slime. A shot rang out. We all started in our beds, but soon dropped our heads back onto the pillows, used as we were to the night hunts of our resident nun. But Battista, having destroyed the snail and brought down a hunk of plaster with her instinctive shot, now began to shout in that strident voice of hers: "Help! They're all escaping! Help!" Half-dressed servants hurried to her, our father came armed with a saber, the Abbé without his wig; the Cavalier did not even find out what was happening, but ran off into the woods to avoid the fuss and went to sleep in a haystack.

Everyone began hunting the snails all over the cellar by the light of torches—no one with any real will, but stubbornly, so as not to admit being disturbed for nothing. They found the hole in the barrel, and at once realized we had made it. Our father came with the coachman's whip and seized us from bed. Then, our backs, buttocks and legs covered with violet weals, we were locked into the squalid little room used as a prison.

They kept us there three days, on bread, water, lettuce, beef rinds and cold minestrone (which, luckily, we liked). Then, as if nothing had happened, we were brought out for our first family meal at midday on that fifteenth of June; and what should the kitchen superintendent, our sister Battista, have prepared for us but snail soup and snails as a main course! Cosimo refused to touch even a mouthful. "Eat up or we'll shut you in the little room again!" I yielded and began to chew the wretched mollusks (a cowardice on my part which had the effect of making my brother feel more alone than ever, so that his leaving us was also partly a protest against me for letting him down; but I was only eight years old, and then how can I compare my own strength of will, particularly as a child, to the superhuman tenacity which my brother showed throughout his life?).

"Well?" said our father to Cosimo.

"No, and no again!" exclaimed Cosimo, and pushed his plate away.

"Leave the table!"

But Cosimo had already turned his back on us all and was leaving the room.

"Where are you going?"

We saw him through the glass door as he picked up his tricorn and rapier.

"I know where I'm going!" And he ran out into the garden.

In a little while we watched him, from the windows, climbing up the holm oak. He was dressed up in the most formal clothes and headdress, because our father insisted on his appearing at table this way in spite of his twelve years of age—powdered hair with a ribbon around the queue, three-cornered hat, lace stock and ruffles, green tunic with pointed tails, purple breeches, rapier, and long white leather gaiters halfway up his legs, the only concession to a mode of dressing more suitable to our country life. (I, being only eight, was exempted from powdered hair except on gala occasions, and from the rapier, which I should have liked to wear.) So he climbed up the knobby old tree, moving his arms and legs along the branches with the sureness and speed which came to him from years of our practicing together.

I have mentioned that we used to spend hours and hours on the trees, and not for ulterior motives as most boys, who go up only in search of fruit or birds' nests, but for the pleasure of getting over difficult parts of the trunks and forks, reaching as high as we could, and finding a good perch on which to pause and look down at the world below, to call and joke at those passing by. So I found it quite natural that Cosimo's first thought, at that unjust attack on him, was to climb up the holm oak, to us a familiar tree spreading its branches to the height of the dining-room windows through which he could show his proud offended air to the whole family.

"*Vorsicht! Vorsicht!* Now he'll fall down, poor little thing!" anxiously exclaimed our mother, who would not have turned a hair at seeing us under cannon fire, but was nevertheless in agony over our games.

Cosimo climbed up to the fork of a big branch, where he could settle comfortably, and sat himself down there, his legs dangling, his arms crossed with hands tucked under his elbows, his head buried in his shoulders, his tricorn hat tilted over his forehead.

Our father leaned out the window. "When you're tired of being up there, you'll change your mind!" he shouted.

"I'll never change my mind," exclaimed my brother from the branch.

"You'll see as soon as you come down!"

"I'll never come down again!" And he kept his word.

} 2 {

COSIMO was in the holm oak. The branches spread out—high bridges over the earth. A slight breeze blew; the sun shone. It shone through the leaves, so that we had to shade our eyes with our hands to see Cosimo. From the tree Cosimo looked at the world; everything seen from up there was different, which was fun in itself. The alley took on a new aspect, and so did the flower beds, the hortensias, the camellias, the iron table for coffee in the garden. Farther away, the tops of the trees thinned out and the kitchen garden merged into little terraced fields propped by stone walls; the middle ground was dark with olive trees, and beyond that the village of Ombrosa thrust up roofs of slate and faded brick, and down at the port ships' masts. In the distance was the sea where a boat was idly sailing—and beyond, a wide horizon.

And now out into the garden, after their coffee, came the Baron and the Generalessa. They stood looking at a rosebush, pretending not to take any notice of Cosimo. They were arm-in-arm first, then soon drew apart to talk and gesture. But I moved under the holm oak as if I were playing on my own, though really to try and attract Cosimo's attention; he was still feeling resentful of me, and stayed up there looking away into the distance. I stopped and crouched down under a bench so as to go on watching him without being seen.

My brother sat there like a sentinel. He looked at everything, but nothing looked like anything to him. A woman with a basket was passing between the rows of lemon trees. Up the path came a muleteer holding on to his mule by the tail. The two never set eyes on each other; at the sound of the metal-shod hoofs the woman turned around and moved toward the path but did not reach it in time. She broke into song then, but the muleteer had already rounded the bend; he listened, cracked his whip and said "Aaah!" to the mule; nothing more. Cosimo saw it all.

Now along the path passed the Abbé Fauchelefleur with his open breviary. Cosimo took something from the branch and threw it at his head. I was not sure what it was, a little spider perhaps, or a piece of bark; anyway, it did not hit him. Cosimo then began to search about with his rapier in a hole of the trunk. Out came a furious wasp. He chased it away with a wave of his hat and followed its flight with his eyes until it settled on a pumpkin plant. From the house, speedy as ever, came the Cavalier, who hurried down the steps into the gardens and vanished among the rows of vines; Cosimo climbed onto a higher branch to see where he went. There was a flutter of wings among the leaves, and out flew a blackbird. Cosimo was rather sorry it had been up there all that time without his noticing it. He looked into the sunshine for others. No, there were none.

The holm oak was near an elm: their two crests almost touched.

A branch of the elm passed a foot or so above a branch of the other tree; it was easy for my brother to pass and so reach the top of the elm, which we had never explored, as it had a high trunk with no branches reachable from the ground. From the elm, by a branch elbow-to-elbow with the next tree, he passed on to a carob, and then to a mulberry tree. So I saw Cosimo advance from one branch to another, suspended high above the garden.

Some branches of the big mulberry tree reached and overlapped the boundary wall of our property, beyond which lay the gardens of the Ondarivas. Although we were neighbors, we knew none of the Ondariva family, marquises and nobles of Ombrosa, as for a number of generations they had enjoyed certain feudal rights claimed by our father, and the two families were separated by mutual antipathy, just as our properties were separated by a high fortress-like wall put up by either our father or the Marquis, I am not sure which. To this should be added the jealous care which the Ondarivas took of their garden, full, it was said, of the rarest plants. In fact, the grandfather of the present Marquis had been a pupil of the botanist Linnaeus, and since his time all the family connections at the courts of France and England had been set in motion to send the finest botanical rarities from the colonies. For years boats had unloaded at the port of Ombrosa sacks of seeds, bundles of cuttings, potted shrubs and even entire trees with huge wrappings of sacking around the roots; until the garden—it was said—had become a mixture of the forests of India and the Americas, and even of New Holland.

All that we were able to see were some dark leaves, growing over the garden wall, of a newly imported tree from the American colonies, the *magnolia*, from whose black branches sprang a pulpy white flower. Cosimo, on our mulberry, reached the corner of the wall, balanced on it for a step or two and then, holding on by his hands, jumped down on to the other side, amid the flowers and leaves of the magnolia. Then he vanished from sight; and what I am about to tell—as also much else in this account of his life—he described to me afterwards, or I have put together from a few scattered hints and guesses.

Cosimo was on the magnolia. Although the branches were very close together, this was an easy tree to maneuver on for a boy so expert in all trees as my brother; and the branches, although they were slender and of soft wood, held his weight, and the points of his shoes tore white wounds on the black bark; he was enveloped in the fresh scent of leaves, turned this way and that by the wind in pages of contrasting greens, dull one moment and glittering the next.

But the whole garden was scented, and although Cosimo could not yet see it clearly, because of all the thick trees, he was already exploring it by smell, and trying to discern the source of the various aromas which he already knew from their being wafted over into our garden by the wind. And to us this seemed an integral part of the mystery of the place. Then he looked at the branches and saw new leaves, some big and shining as if running water were constantly flowing over them, some tiny and feathered, and tree trunks either all smooth or all scaly.

There was a great silence. A flight of little wrens went up, chirping. And now a faint voice could be heard singing: "O la-la . . . O la ba-lan-çoire . . ." Cosimo looked down. From the branch of a big tree nearby was dangling a swing, and on it was sitting a little girl about his age.

She was a blonde, with hair combed high in an odd style for a girl her age, and a light blue dress which was also too grown up; its skirt, as it rose with the swing, was swirling with lace petticoats. The girl had her eyes half closed and her nose in the air as if used to playing the lady, and she was eating an apple in little bites, bending her head down toward her hand, which had to hold the apple and balance her on the rope of the swing at the same time; and every time the swing reached the lowest point of its flight she would give herself little pushes on the ground with the end of her tiny shoes, blow out bits of apple peel and sing "O la-la-la . . . O la ba-lan-çoire . . ." as if she cared neither for the swing, nor the song, nor (though perhaps a little more) for the apple, and had other things on her mind.

Cosimo dropped from the top of the magnolia to a lower perch, and now had his feet set on each side of a fork and his elbows leaning on a branch in front as on a window sill. The flight of the swing was bringing the little girl right up under his nose.

She was not watching and did not notice. Then suddenly she saw him there, standing on the tree, in tricorn and gaiters. "Oh!" she said.

The apple fell from her hand and rolled away to the foot of the magnolia. Cosimo drew his rapier, leaned down from the lowest branch, skewered the apple and offered it to the girl, who had meanwhile made a complete turn on the swing and was up there again. "Take it, it's not dirty, only a little bruised on one side."

The fair little girl now seemed to be regretting she had shown so much surprise at the sudden appearance of this strange boy on the magnolia, and put on her disdainful air again with her nose in the air. "Are you a thief?" she said.

"A thief?" exclaimed Cosimo, offended. Then he thought it over; the idea rather pleased him. "Yes, I am," he said, pulling his tricorn down over one eye. "Any objection?"

"And what have you come to steal?"

Cosimo looked at the apple which he had skewered on the point of his rapier, and suddenly realized he was hungry, as he had scarcely touched a thing at table. "This apple," said he, and began to peel it with one side of his rapier, which, in spite of family orders, he kept very sharp.

"Then you're a fruit thief," said the girl.

My brother thought of the rabble of poor urchins from Ombrosa who scrambled over walls and hedges sacking orchards, boys he had been taught to despise and avoid; and for the first time he thought how free and enviable their life must be. Well now: he might become like them, and live as they did, from now on. "Yes," he said. He cut the apple into slices and began eating it.

The girl broke into a laugh which lasted a whole flight of the swing, up and down. "Oh, go on! The boys who steal fruit! I know them all! They're all friends of mine! And they go round barefoot, in shirt sleeves and tousled hair, not with gaiters and powder!"

My brother turned as red as the apple peel. To be laughed at not only for his powdered hair, which he didn't like at all, but also for his gaiters, which he liked a lot; to be considered inferior in appearance to a fruit thief, to boys he had despised till a moment before; and above all to find that this girl who seemed quite at home in the Ondariva gardens was a friend of all the fruit thieves but not of his, all this made him feel annoyed, jealous and ashamed.

"O la-la-la . . . In gaiters and powder!" hummed the little girl on the swing.

For a moment his pride was stung. "I'm not a thief like the boys you know!" he shouted. "I'm not a thief at all! I only said that so's not to frighten you; if you really knew who I was you'd die of fright! I'm a brigand, a terrible brigand!"

The little girl went on flying through the air under his nose, almost as if wanting to graze him with the point of her shoes. "Oh, nonsense. Where's your musket? Brigands all have muskets! And catapults! I've seen them! They stopped our coach five times on the way here from the castle!"

"But not the chief! I'm the chief! The chief of the brigands doesn't carry a musket! Only a sword!" and he held out his little rapier.

The little girl shrugged her shoulders. "The chief brigand," she said, "is a man called Gian dei Brughi, and he always brings me presents at Christmas and Easter!"

"Ah!" exclaimed Cosimo di Rondò, seized by a wave of family rancor. "Then my father's right when he says that the Marquis of Ondariva is the protector of all the brigands and smugglers around."

The girl swept down to the ground and instead of giving herself a push, braked with a quick little stamp of the foot, and jumped off. The empty swing leaped back into the air on its ropes. "Get down from there at once! How dare you come on to our land!" she exclaimed, pointing a furious finger at the boy.

"I haven't and I won't come on to it," answered Cosimo with equal warmth. "I've never set foot on your land, and I wouldn't for all the gold in the world!"

Then the girl very calmly took up a fan lying on a wicker chair, and though it was not very hot, began fanning herself and walking up and down. "Now," she said in a steady voice, "I'll call the servants and have you taken and beaten! That'll teach you to trespass on our land!" She was constantly changing tone, this girl, putting my brother out every time.

"Where I am isn't land and isn't yours!" proclaimed Cosimo, and felt tempted to add: "And I'm Duke of Ombrosa too, and lord of the whole area," but he held himself back, as he did not want to repeat things his father was always saying now that he had quarreled with him and run away from his table; he did not want to and did not think it right; also those claims to the dukedom had always seemed just obsessions to him; why should he, Cosimo, now start boasting of being a duke? But he did not want to contradict himself and so went on saying whatever came into his head. "This isn't yours," he repeated, "because it's the ground that's yours, and if I put a foot on it I would be trespassing. But up here, I can go wherever I like."

"Oh, so it's all yours, up there . . ."

"Yes! It's all mine up here"—and he waved vaguely toward the branches, the leaves against the sun, the sky. "On the branches it's all mine. Tell 'em to come and fetch me, and just see if they can!"

Now, after all that boasting, he half expected her to begin jeering at him in some way. Instead of which she seemed suddenly interested. "Ah yes? And how far does it reach, this property of yours?"

"As far as I can get on the trees, here, there, beyond the wall, in the olive groves, up the hill, the other side of the hill, the wood, the Bishop's Land . . ."

"As far as France?"

"As far as Poland and Saxony," said Cosimo, who knew nothing of geography but the names he had heard from our mother when she talked of the Wars of Succession. "But I'm not selfish like you. I invite you into my property." Now they were calling each other by the familiar "*tu*"; it was she who had begun.

"And whose is the swing, then?" said she, sitting down and opening her fan.

"The swing's yours," pronounced Cosimo, "but as it's tied to this tree, it depends on me. So, when you're touching the earth with your feet you're in your property, when you're in the air you're in mine."

She gave herself a push and flew off, her hands tight on the ropes. Cosimo jumped from the magnolia on to the thick branch which held the swing, seized the ropes from there and began pushing her himself. The swing went higher and higher.

"Are you frightened?"

"No, not me. What's your name?"

"Mine's Cosimo . . . And yours?"

"Violante but they call me Viola."

"They call me Mino, too, as Cosimo's an old man's name."

"I don't like it."

"Cosimo?"

"No, Mino."

"Ah . . . you can call me Cosimo."

"Wouldn't think of it! Listen, you, we must get things straight."

"How do you mean?" exclaimed he, who was put out by everything she said.

"What I say! I can come up into your property and be an honored guest, d'you see? I come and go as I please. You, though, are sacred and untouchable while you stay in the trees, on your property, but as soon as you set a foot on the soil of my garden you become my slave and I put you in chains."

"No, I'm not coming down into your garden or into mine either ever again. It's all enemy territory to me. You come up with me, and your friends who steal fruit, and perhaps my brother Biagio too, though he's a bit of a coward, and we'll make an army in the trees and bring the earth and the people on it to their senses."

"No, no, not at all. Just let me explain how things are. You have the lordship of the trees, all right? But if you touch the earth just once with your foot, you lose your whole kingdom and become the humblest slave. D'you understand? Even if a branch breaks under you and you fall, it's the end of you!"

"I've never fallen from a tree in my life!"

"No, of course not, but if you do fall, if you do, you change into ashes and the wind'll carry you away."

"Fairy tales. I'm not coming down to the ground because I don't want to."

"Oh, what a bore you are!"

"No, no, let's play. For instance, can I come on to the swing?"

"Yes, if you manage to sit on it without touching the ground."

Near Viola's swing was another one, hanging on the same branch, but pulled up by a knot in the ropes so it should not bump against the other. Cosimo let himself down from the branch by gripping one of the ropes—an exercise he was very good at as our mother had made him do a lot of gymnastics—reached the knot, undid it, stood up on the swing, and to give himself impetus bent down on his knees and rocked the weight of his body to and fro. So he got higher and higher. The two swings moved in opposite directions, at the same height now, and passed each other halfway.

"But if you try sitting down and giving a push with your feet you'll go higher," Viola said.

Cosimo made a face at her.

"Come down and give me a push, now, do," said she, smiling sweetly at him.

"No, I said I wouldn't come down at any cost . . ." And Cosimo began to feel put out again.

"Do, please."

"No."

"Ah, hah! You nearly fell into the trap! If you'd set a foot on the ground you'd have lost everything!" Viola got off her swing and began giving little pushes to Cosimo's. "Oh!" Suddenly she had snatched the seat of the swing on which my brother was standing and overturned it. Luckily Cosimo was holding tight to the ropes. Otherwise he would have dropped to the ground like a ripe fruit.

"Cheat!" he cried, and clambered up again on the two ropes, but going up was much more difficult than coming down, particularly with the fair-haired girl maliciously pulling the ropes as hard as she could.

Finally he reached the big branch, and got astride it. With his lace jabot he wiped the sweat off his forehead.

"Ah! Ah! You didn't get me!"

"Very nearly."

"And I thought you were a friend!"

"You thought!" and she began fanning herself again.

"Violante!" broke in a sharp female voice at that moment. "Who are you talking to?"

On the white flight of steps leading to the house had appeared a tall, thin lady, with a very wide skirt; she was looking through a lorgnette. Alarmed, Cosimo drew back into the leaves.

"With a young man, *ma tante*," said the little girl, "who was born on the top of a tree and is under a spell so he can't set foot on the ground."

Cosimo, scarlet in the face, asked himself if the little girl was talking like that to make fun of him in front of her aunt, or to make fun of the aunt in front of him, or just to continue the game, or because she did not care a rap about either him or the aunt or the game, and he saw he was being watched through the lorgnette, whose owner had approached the tree and was gazing at him as if he were some strange parrot.

"*Uh, mais c'est un des Piovasques, ce jeune homme, je crois. Viens, Violante.*"

Cosimo bridled with shame; the way the aunt recognized him so easily without even asking herself why he was there and at once called the girl away firmly though not severely, the way Viola followed her aunt's call docilely without even turning around—it all suggested that they considered him of no importance, a person who scarcely existed. And so that extraordinary afternoon of his was fading into a cloud of self-pity.

Then suddenly the girl made a sign to her aunt, the aunt lowered her head, and the child whispered in her ear. The aunt pointed her lorgnette at Cosimo again. "Well, young man," she said, "would you care to take a cup of chocolate with us? Then we too can get to know you"—and here she gave a sideways glance at Viola—"as you're already a friend of the family."

Cosimo sat there staring round-eyed at aunt and niece. His heart was beating fast. Here he was being invited by the Ondarivas of Ombrosa, the haughtiest family in the neighborhood, and the humiliation of a moment before changed to triumph: he was getting back at his father by this invitation from enemies who had always snubbed him, and Viola had interceded for him, and he was now officially accepted as a friend of hers and would play with her in that garden so different from all other gardens. All this Cosimo felt, but an opposite though confused emotion at the same time; an emotion made up of shyness, pride, loneliness and determination; and amid this contrast of feelings my brother seized the branch above him, climbed it, moved into the leafiest part, on to another tree, and vanished.

} 3 {

IT WAS endless, that afternoon. Every now and then we heard a plop, a rustle in the garden, and ran out hoping that it was him, that he had decided to come down. But no, I saw a quiver on the top of the magnolia; Cosimo appeared from the other side of the wall and climbed over.

I went up the mulberry to meet him. At seeing me he seemed put out; he was still angry with me. Sitting on a branch of the mulberry above me, he began slicing off bits of bark with his rapier, as if he did not want to speak to me.

"The mulberry is easy," I exclaimed, just for something to say. "We'd never been on it before . . ."

He went on whittling the branch with the blade, then said sourly: "Well, did you enjoy the snails?"

I held out a basket. "I've brought you some dried figs, Mino, and a slice of pie . . ."

"Did *they* send you?" he exclaimed, still distant, but his mouth watering as he looked at the basket.

"No, I had to escape from the Abbé," I said hurriedly. "They wanted to keep me doing lessons all the afternoon, so I couldn't see you, but the old man fell asleep! Mother's worried you might fall and wanted a search made for you, but since Father hasn't seen you on the holm oak for a while, he says you've come down and are hiding away brooding over your misdeeds, and we're not to worry."

"I never came down!" said my brother.

"Have you been in the Ondariva garden?"

"Yes, but always from one tree to another, without ever touching the ground!"

"Why?" I asked. It was the first time I heard him announce this rule of his, but he had said it as if it were already understood between us, almost as if he wanted to reassure me that he had not broken it; so I did not dare persist in my questions.

Instead of answering me, he said: "You know, it'd take days and days to explore that garden of the Ondarivas! If you saw the trees! From the American forests!" Then he remembered he was angry with me and so should not enjoy telling me of his finds. He finished, brusquely: "Anyway I won't take you there. You can go around here with Battista, from now on, or the Cavalier!"

"No, Mino, do take me!" I exclaimed. "You mustn't blame me about the snails, they were foul, but I couldn't bear their scolding!"

Cosimo was gulping down the tart. "I'll try you out," he said. "You've got to show me you're on my side, not on theirs."

"Ask me anything you want, then."

"Get me some ropes, long strong ones, as I'll have to tie myself to get over some places up here: then an oarlock, and hooks and nails . . . big ones . . ."

"What d'you want to make? A crane?"

"We'll need to get a lot of stuff up, we'll see later; planks, bamboo . . ."

"You want to make a hut in a tree! Where?"

"If needs be. We'll choose the place later. Meanwhile you can leave the things for me there in that hollow oak. Then I'll let down the basket by the rope and you can put whatever I need in it."

"But why? You talk as if you're going on hiding for a long time . . . Don't you think they'll forgive you?"

He turned around, red in the face. "What do I care if they forgive me or not? And I'm not hiding; I'm not afraid of anyone! What about you, are you afraid of helping me?"

Though I now realized that my brother was refusing to come down for the time being, I pretended not to understand this so as to make him declare himself and say, for instance: "Yes, I want to stay in the trees till afternoon tea, or dusk, or supper, or till it gets dark," something in fact which would show a limit, a proportion to his protest. Instead of which he said nothing of the kind, and I began to feel alarmed.

Calls came from down below. It was our father shouting, "Cosimo! Cosimo!" and then, realizing already that Cosimo would not answer him, "Biagio! Biagio!" He was calling me.

"I'll go and see what they want. Then I'll come and tell you," said I hurriedly. This eagerness to keep my brother informed also, I must admit, coincided with a hurry to get away for fear of being caught consorting with him on top of the mulberry and having to share the punishment he was certain to get. But Cosimo did not seem to see this shadow of cowardice on my face; he let me go, not without shrugging his shoulders to show how little he cared about what our father might have to say to him.

When I got back he was still there; he had found a good place to settle, on a lopped branch, and was sitting with his chin on his knees and his arms tight around his shins.

"Mino! Mino!" I called, clambering breathlessly up. "They've forgiven you! They're waiting for us! There's tea on the table, and Father and Mother already sitting down and putting out slices of cake on the plates! And there's a cream and chocolate cake, but not made by Battista, you know! She must have shut herself in her room, red with rage! They stroked my hair and said: 'Go and tell poor Mino we'll make it all up and not mention it again!' Quick, let's go!"

Cosimo was chewing a leaf. He did not move.

"Hey," said he, "try to fetch me a blanket, will you, without anyone seeing, and bring it to me. It must be cold, up here, at night."

"You're not going to spend the night in the trees!"

He did not answer. Chin on knees, he went on chewing the leaf and looking ahead. I followed his look, which went straight to the wall of the Ondariva garden, just where the white magnolia flower showed, with a kite flying beyond it.

So we got to evening. The servants came and went laying the table; in the dining room the candelabra were already lit. Cosimo must have been able to see all this from the tree, and Baron Arminio turned to the shadows outside the window and called: "If you want to stay up there, you'll starve!"

That evening we sat down to supper without Cosimo for the first time. He was astride a high branch of the holm oak, sideways, so that we could see only his dangling legs; and we could only just see those if we leaned out of the window and peered, for the room was brightly lit and it was dark outside.

Even the Cavalier felt it his duty to lean out and say something, but as usual he could not manage to express any opinion on the matter. All he said was: "Oooh . . . strong wood . . . It'll last a hundred years . . ." and then a few words in Turkish, perhaps the one for holm oak; he seemed, in fact, to be talking about the tree and not my brother.

Our sister Battista, on the other hand, showed a kind of envy for Cosimo, as if, used to keeping the family on tenterhooks with her crazy whims, she had now been outdone at her own game; and she was endlessly biting her nails (she would bite them without raising a finger to her mouth, but lowering her head and raising her elbow).

The Generalessa was reminded of some soldiers who had been on sentry duty in the trees around a camp either in Slavonia or Pomerania, and how they had sighted the enemy, and so avoided an ambush. This memory, quite suddenly, brought her out of her maternal preoccupations and back to her favorite military atmosphere, and now, as if she had finally succeeded in understanding her son's behavior, she became calmer, almost proud. No one paid any attention to her except the Abbé Fauchelefleur, who listened with grave assent to her warlike tale and the parallel she drew from it, for he would have grasped at any argument to persuade himself that what was happening was natural and so clear his mind of responsibility and worry.

After supper we went off to sleep early, not changing our schedule even that night. By now our parents had decided that they would not give Cosimo the satisfaction of taking notice of him, and would wait for exhaustion, discomfort and the cold night air to bring him down. Everyone went up to bed. Seen from the outside, the candlelight must have looked like golden eyes shining through the windows. What coziness, what memories of warmth must have seeped from that house so known and near, to my brother in the night chill. I leaned from the window of our room and made out his shadow bent over a hollow of the holm oak, between branch and trunk, wrapped in the blanket, and—I think—bound around with the rope to avoid falling.

The moon rose late and shone above the branches. In their nests slept the titmice, huddled up like him. The night, the open, the silence of the park were broken by rustling of leaves and distant sounds, and the wind sweeping through the trees. At times there was a far-off murmur—the sea. From my window I listened to the scattered whispering and tried to imagine it heard without the protection of the familiar background of the house, from which he was only a few yards. Alone with the night around him, clinging to the only friendly object: the rough bark of a tree, scored with innumerable little tunnels where the larvae slept.

I went to bed but did not blow out the candle. Perhaps that light at the window of his own room would keep him company. We shared a room, with two little cots in it. I looked at his, untouched, and at the darkness outside the window where he was, and turned over between the sheets feeling perhaps for the first time the pleasure of being naked, with bare feet, in a warm white bed, and seeming to sense at the same time the discomfort he must be in, tied up there in his rough blanket, his legs buttoned in his gaiters, without being able to turn around, with bones aching. It is something which has never left me since that night, the realization of my good fortune in having a bed, clean sheets, a soft mattress! And as that went through my mind, which had been fixed for so many hours and so completely on the person we all had on our minds, I dozed off and so fell asleep.

} 4 {

I DON'T know if it's true, the story they tell in books, that in ancient days a monkey could have left Rome and skipped from tree to tree till it reached Spain, without ever touching earth. The only place so thick with trees in my day was the whole length, from end to end, of the gulf of Ombrosa and its valley right up to the mountain crests; the area was famous everywhere for this.

Nowadays these parts are very different. It was after the arrival of the French that people began chopping down trees as if they were grass which is scythed every year and grows again. They have never grown again. At first we thought it was something to do with the war, with Napoleon, with the period. But the chopping went on. Now the hillsides are so bare that when we look at them, we who knew them before, it makes us feel bad.

Anyway, in those days wherever one went there were always leaves and branches between us and the sky. The only trees growing near the ground were the lemons, but even among them rose the twisted shapes of fig trees, arching their domes of heavy leaves over the orchards up toward the hills. There were the brown boughs of the cherry, the tender quince, peach, almond or young pear, the big plum, and sorb apples and carobs too, with an occasional mulberry or knobby walnut. Where the orchards ended, the olive groves began—silvery gray, a cloud tufted out halfway up the hillsides. In the background, crouching between the port below and the rock above, was the village; and there, too, the roofs were feathery with the tops of trees: plane trees, and oaks too, haughty and detached, branching out—an orderly riot—where the nobles had built their villas and walled in their parks.

Above the olives began the woods. At one time the pines must have dominated the whole area, for a few tufts still sprouted out here and there down the slopes as far as the beaches. The oaks then were thicker than they seem to me today, for they were the first, most valuable victims. Higher up, the pines gave way to chestnuts, which went on and on up the mountainsides as far as the eye could reach. This was the world of sap amid which we lived, we inhabitants of Ombrosa, almost without our noticing it.

The first to give any real thought to all this was Cosimo. He realized that as the trees were so thick he could move for several miles by passing from one branch to another, without ever needing to descend to earth. Sometimes a patch of bare ground forced him to make long detours, but he soon got to know all the necessary routes and came to measure distances by quite different estimates than ours, bearing always in mind the twisted trail he had to take over the branches. And where not even a jump would carry him on to the nearest branch, he began to use various tricks of his own. But all that I will describe later.

So far we have only reached that first dawn when he woke up to find himself amid fluttering starlings on top of a holm oak, soaked in cold dew, frozen stiff, with bones aching, his legs and arms tingling, and set out happily to explore the new world.

He reached the last tree of the park, a plane tree. Below him the valley swept away under a sky of wispy clouds and smoke curling up from the slate roofs of cottages hiding behind rocks like piles of stones; the figs and cherries formed another sky, of leaves; lower down thrust out the spreading branches of plums and peaches. Everything was clear and sharp, even the grass, blade by blade, all except the soil with its crawling pumpkin leaves or dotted lettuces or fuzz of crops: it was the same on both sides of the V in which the valley opened over a high funnel of sea.

Through this landscape was rippling a kind of wave, not visible, or even audible, except now and then, but what one could hear was enough to create a sense of uneasiness; a sudden sharp cry, and then the faint crash of something falling and perhaps even the crack of a breaking branch, and more cries, different ones this time, of angry voices, converging on the place where the cry had come from before. Then nothing, a sense of nothingness, as if things were happening in a completely different part of the woods; and in fact the voices and sounds now began again but seemed to be coming from one side or another of the valley, always from where the jagged little leaves of the cherry trees were moving in the wind. And so Cosimo, with a part of his mind meandering on its own—while another part seemed to know and understand it all beforehand—found the thought crossing his mind: Cherries talk.

He began moving toward the nearest cherry tree, or row, rather, of cherry trees, tall, of superb leafy green, thick with black cherries; but my brother had not yet trained his eye to distinguish at once exactly what was and what was not on branches. He paused; the sounds of before had gone. He was on the lowest boughs, and felt all the cherries above weighing down on him; he could not have explained why, but they seemed to be converging on him, as if, in fact, he were on a tree with eyes instead of cherries.

Cosimo raised his face and an overripe cherry fell on his forehead with a plop! He strained his eyes to look up against the sun (which was growing stronger), and saw that the tree he was on and the ones nearby were full of perching little boys.

When they realized that they had been seen they were no longer silent, and called to each other in sharp though muted voices something that sounded like "Just look how he's dressed!" Then, parting the leaves in front of them, each climbed down from the branch he was on to one lower, toward the boy wearing the tricorn. They were bareheaded or in ragged straw hats, and some had their heads wrapped in sacking; they wore torn shirts and breeches; those whose feet were not bare had dirty strips of rag, and one or two of them had wooden clogs hung around their necks, taken off so as to climb better; they were the great band of fruit thieves from which Cosimo and I—in obedience to parental orders—had always kept as far away as possible. That morning, though, my brother seemed to be on the lookout for them, though with no very clear idea of what he expected from the meeting.

He stood still and waited as they climbed down toward him, throwing out, in strident whispers, remarks like "What's he think he's up to, eh?" and spitting out an occasional cherry stone at him or flinging a worm-eaten, bird-pecked cherry with a little swirl as if slinging a stone.

"Unhuh!" they exclaimed all of a sudden. They had seen the rapier dangling behind him. "D'ya see what he's got?" And they burst out laughing.

Then they stopped and stifled their laughter as if something wildly funny was about to happen; two of the little urchins had very quietly moved on to a branch right above Cosimo and were lowering the top of an open sack down over his head (one of the filthy sacks that they must have used for their booty, and which when empty they arranged over their heads and shoulders like hoods). In a short time my brother would have found himself trussed into a sack without even knowing how, then tied up like a salami so they could beat him up.

Cosimo sensed the danger, or maybe he didn't sense anything. Knowing they were jeering at his rapier, he drew it as a matter of honor. As he brandished it, the blade grazed the sack and, with a twist, tore it from the hands of the two little thieves and flung it away.

It was a good move. The others gave an "Oh!" of both disappointment and surprise, and began yelling insults in dialect at the two who had let their sack be taken.

But Cosimo had no time to congratulate himself on his success. For suddenly a new commotion burst forth, this time from the earth below; barking dogs, showers of stones and yells of "You won't get away this time, you dirty little thieves!"; and up came the tops of pitchforks. The urchins on the branches yanked up legs and elbows and hugged themselves. All that noise around Cosimo had aroused the fruitgrowers, who had been on the watch.

It was an attack prepared in force. Tired of having their fruit stolen as it ripened, many of the small landowners and tenant farmers of the valley had banded together; for the only answer to the little boys' tactics of plunging into an orchard all together, sacking and stripping it, then making off in the opposite direction, was to use similar tactics themselves; that is, for all to keep watch on an orchard where the boys were bound to come sooner or later, and catch them red-handed. Now the unmuzzled dogs were baying and champing with bared teeth at the foot of the cherry trees, while hayforks were brandished in the air. Three or four of the little thieves jumped to the ground just in time to have their backs pricked by the tridents and their bottoms bitten by the dogs, and rushed off screaming and lurching down the rows of vines. No more dared go down: they stayed quivering where they were, and Cosimo too. Then the fruitgrowers began setting ladders against the trees and climbing up, preceded by points of pitchforks.

It took Cosimo some minutes to realize that there was no reason at all for him to be terrified just because the band of urchins was. And there was no reason at all for him to think that they were in the know and he wasn't. The fact that they were sitting there like idiots was proof enough; why didn't they escape on to the trees around? My brother had got there by a certain route and so could make off by the same route; he pulled his tricorn down on his head, looked around for the branch which he had used as a bridge, passed from the last cherry tree on to a carob, then dangled from the carob, dropped on to a plum tree, and so on. The others, seeing him moving on the branches as if he were at home, realized that they must follow close behind him or never find his route again, and they followed his tortuous itinerary in silence, on all fours. Meanwhile he had climbed into a fig tree, skirted a field, and swung down on a peach tree with such slender branches that the boys had to pass over it one at a time. They climbed the peach only to get a grip on the twisted trunk of an olive sprouting out of a wall; from the olive they jumped onto an oak stretching out a thick arm over the stream, and so reached the trees on the other side.

The men with pitchforks, who thought they had caught the fruit thieves at last, saw them hopping away through the air like birds. They followed, running among the barking dogs, but had to get around the thicket, then over the wall, then across the stream at a point where there was no bridge, lost time finding a ford, and saw the urchins running away in the distance.

They ran like human beings, with their feet on the ground. On the branches only my brother remained. "Where's that wagtail with the gaiters got to?" they asked each other, not seeing him ahead still. They looked up: there he was clambering about the olives. "Hey you, come down, we've shaken 'em off now!" But instead of coming down, he went leaping from bough to bough, from olive to olive, till he vanished from sight among the close-knit silvery leaves.

The band of little vagabonds, with sacks on their heads and canes in their hands, were now assaulting some cherry trees at the bottom of the valley. They were working methodically, stripping branch after branch, when, on the top of the highest tree, squatting with his legs crossed, flicking down bunches of cherries and popping them in the tricorn on his lap, who should they see but the boy with the gaiters! "Hey, how did you get here?" they asked arrogantly. But they were crestfallen because it looked as if he had flown there.

My brother was now taking the cherries one by one from his tricorn and putting them in his mouth as if they were sweets. Then he would spit out the stones with a flick of the lips, careful lest they stain his waistcoat.

"This cake-eater," said one, "what's he want from us? What's he come to bother us for? Why doesn't he go and eat the cherries in his own garden?" But they were a little abashed, because he was smarter at getting about the trees than any of them.

"Among ice-cream-eaters," said another, "a smart one does crop up now and again by mistake; take the Sinforosa for instance . . ."

At this mysterious name Cosimo pricked up his ears and, he did not know why, blushed.

"The Sinforosa betrayed us!" said another.

"But she was smart, she was, for a cake-eater herself, and this morning if she'd been there to sound her horn they wouldn't have caught us."

"Even cake-eaters can come with us, of course, if they're on our side!"

(Cosimo now understood that *cake-eater* meant an inhabitant of a villa, a noble, or at any rate someone of rank.)

"Listen, you," said one to him, "let's get this straight; if you want to come with us, you pick the stuff with us and you teach us all the tricks you know."

"And you let us into your father's orchards," said another. "They once shot at me there!"

Cosimo listened to them, half absorbed in his own thoughts. Then he said: "Tell me, who is the Sinforosa?"

Then all the ragamuffins scattered among the branches burst

into roars and roars of laughter, so that one nearly fell off the cherry tree, and one flung himself back and held on to the branch by his legs, and another let himself dangle by his hands, shrieking with laughter all the time.

Such a row did they make that their pursuers were on their heels again. In fact they must have been right underneath, the men and the dogs, for a loud barking arose and then up came the pitchforks again. Only this time, made wary by their recent setback, they first occupied the trees around and climbed up them with ladders, and from there surrounded the band with tridents and rakes. On the ground the dogs, with all their men scattered about on trees, did not know at first where to head for and wandered around barking away with muzzles in the air. So the little thieves were able to jump quickly to the ground and run away in different directions among the confused dogs, and though one or two got a bite on a calf or a blow from a stone, most of them got away safe and sound.

On the tree remained Cosimo. "Come down!" shouted the others as they made off. "What are you doing? Sleeping? Jump down while it's clear!" But he gripped the branch with his knees and drew his rapier. From nearby trees the fruitgrowers were thrusting out pitchforks tied on sticks to reach him, and Cosimo kept them off by brandishing his sword, till one got right at his chest and pinned him to the trunk.

"Stop!" called a voice. "It's the young Baron of Piovasco! What are you doing up there, sir? How on earth did you get mixed up with that rabble?"

Cosimo recognized one of our father's laborers, Giuà della Vasca.

The pitchforks withdrew. Many of the group took off their hats. My brother also raised his tricorn with two fingers, and bowed.

"Hey, you down there, tie up the dogs!" shouted they. "Let him get down! You can come down, sir, but be careful, it's a high tree! Wait a moment, we'll put up a ladder! Then I'll take you back home!"

"No, thank you, thank you," said my brother. "Don't put yourself out, I know the way, I know the way on my own!"

He vanished behind the trunk and reappeared on another branch, twirled round the trunk and reappeared on a branch higher up, vanished behind this and then only his feet were visible on an even higher branch, as there were thick leaves above; and then the feet jumped, and nothing more was seen.

"Where's he gone to?" said the men to each other, not knowing where to look, up or down.

"There he is!" He was at the top of another tree farther away, then vanished again.

"There he is!" He was at the top of still another tree, swaying as if in the wind, and jumping.

"He's fallen! No! There he is!" All that could be seen, above the waving green, was his tricorn and queue.

"What sort of master have you got?" the others asked Giuà della Vasca. "A man or a wild animal? Or is he the devil in person?"

Giuà della Vasca was gasping. He crossed himself.

A song could be heard from Cosimo, a kind of call in solfeggio: "Oh, Sin-for-ro-saaa!"

} 5 {

THE Sinforosa—gradually Cosimo came to know a lot about this personage from the chatter of the band. It was a name they had given to a little girl, from one of the villas, who went about on a small white pony, had made friends with them and protected them for a time and even, dominating as she was, commanded them. She would ride the roads and paths on her pony, tell them when she saw ripe fruit in an unguarded orchard, then follow their attack on horseback like an officer. Around her neck she wore a hunting horn, and while they were sacking the almond and pear trees she would be galloping up and down slopes from which she could see over the whole countryside, blowing her horn as soon as she noticed any suspicious movements which might mean discovery. At the sound, the urchins would jump off the trees and hide: so while the little girl was with them they had never once been caught.

What happened afterward was more difficult to understand; the Sinforosa's "betrayal" seemed to have been twofold: partly her having invited them into her own garden to eat fruit and then getting them beaten up by her servants; and then her having made a favorite of one of them, a certain Bel-Loré—who was still jeered at for it—and another, a certain Ugasso, at the same time, and set them against each other; and then it transpired that the urchins had been beaten by her servants, not when they were stealing fruit but after her dismissal of the two rivals, who had then united against her; there was also talk that she had often promised some cakes, but those she finally gave them were made with castor oil, so that they had tummy-aches for a week afterwards. One of these episodes or some episode like these or all these episodes together had caused a break between the Sinforosa and the band, and now they talked of her with a bitterness mingled with regret.

Cosimo listened eagerly to these stories, nodding as if every detail fitted into a picture he knew already, and finally decided to ask: "But which villa does she come from, the Sinforosa?"

"What, you mean you don't know her? You're neighbors! The Sinforosa from the Ondariva villa!"

Even without this confirmation Cosimo had felt sure that the friend of the urchins was Viola, the girl of the swing. It was—I think—because she had said she knew all the fruit thieves around, that he had first begun looking out for the band. And yet from then on the urge inside him, vague though it still was, grew sharper. At one moment he found himself longing to lead the band in a raid on the Ondariva orchards, then to offer her his services against them (after, perhaps, inciting them to molest her so as to be able to defend her), then to perform some feat of daring which would reach her ears indirectly. With all these ideas buzzing in his head he followed the band more and more distractedly; and when they left the trees and he was alone a veil of sadness would pass over his face, like a cloud over the sun.

Then he would suddenly jump up and, agile as a cat, scramble over branches and across orchards and gardens, humming some tense little song between his teeth, his eyes set as if seeing nothing, balancing by instinct just like a cat.

We saw him go by various times, in an absolute daze, over the branches of our garden. "There he is!" we would suddenly shout, for whatever we did he was still in the forefront of our minds, and we used to count the hours and days he had been up on the trees, and our father would say, "He's mad! He has a devil in him!" and then attack the Abbé Fauchelefleur: "The only thing is to exorcise him! What are you waiting for, you. Now I ask you, *mon abbé,* what are you doing there with your hands crossed? He's got the devil in him, my own son, you understand, *sacré nom de Dieu!*"

The word "devil" seemed to wake a precise chain of thought in the Abbé's mind; he shook himself out of his lethargy all of a sudden and launched into a most complicated theological discourse on how the presence of the devil should be properly understood, from which it was not clear if he was contradicting my father or just generalizing. He would make no pronouncement, in fact, on whether a relationship between the devil and my brother was to be considered possible or excluded a priori.

The Baron became impatient, the Abbé lost the thread, I was already bored. With our mother, on the other hand, the state of maternal anxiety, of fluid emotion, had consolidated, as every emotion tended to with her, into practical decisions and a search for concrete ways and means, as the preoccupations of a general should. She had found a field telescope, a long one, with a tripod; she would put her eye to it and so spend hours on the terrace of the villa continually regulating the lenses to keep the boy in focus among the leaves, even when we could have sworn he was out of range.

"Can you still see him?" our father would ask from the garden, where he was pacing up and down under the trees without ever succeeding in laying eyes on Cosimo, except when the boy was right above his head. The Generalessa would signal down that she could, and that we mustn't disturb her, as if she were following troops' movements from a hill. Sometimes she obviously did not see him at all, but she had got a fixed idea, I don't know how, that he must appear in a given place and not elsewhere, and there she kept her telescope trained. Every now and again she must have admitted to herself that she had made a mistake; and then she would look away from the eyepiece and begin to examine a surveyor's map which she held open on her knees, with one hand to her mouth in a thoughtful attitude and another following the hieroglyphics on the map, until she had decided on the spot which her son must have reached, plotted the angles, and pointed her telescope on some treetop in that leafy sea, slowly moving the lenses into focus; and then from the gentle little smile on her lips we would know she had seen him, that he was really there!

Next, she would take up some colored flags which she had on a stool, and wave one and then the other in decisive, rhythmic movements, like signals. (This slightly annoyed me as I did not know that our mother had those flags and knew how to manage them, and I thought how lovely it would have been if she had taught us to play at flag-signaling before, when we were both small; but our mother never played and now it was too late.)

I must say, though, that in spite of all her tools of war, she remained a mother, with her heart in her mouth, and her handkerchief screwed in her hand. One would have thought that she found acting the general a relief, or that working off her apprehensions as a general rather than a simple mother soothed her distress, for she was a fragile woman, whose sole defense was that military style inherited from her Von Kurtewitz forebears.

There she was, waving one of her flags and looking through her telescope, when suddenly her face lit up and she laughed. We realized that Cosimo had answered. How I don't know, by a wave of the hat perhaps, or by a wave of the tip of a bough. Certainly from that moment our mother changed; she lost her apprehensions, and if her destiny as a mother was different from others, with a son so strange and lost to normal affections, she came to accept this strangeness of Cosimo's before any of the rest of us, as if placated by those greetings which from then onwards he would send her unexpectedly every now and again, by this silent exchange.

The strange thing was that our mother never deluded herself that Cosimo, now he had sent her a greeting, was thinking of ending his escape and returning among us. Our father, on the other hand, lived perpetually in this hope and at the slightest news about Cosimo would repeat: "Ah yes? You've seen him? He's coming back?" But our mother, the most removed from Cosimo in a way, seemed the only one who managed to accept him as he was, perhaps because she did not try to give herself any explanation.

But let us return to that day. Peeping from behind our mother's skirts now appeared Battista, who very rarely went outside; holding up a plate with some strange pap in it and raising a spoon she cooed: "Cosimo . . . D'you want any?" But she got a slap from our father and went back indoors. Who knows what monstrous mishmash she had prepared! Our brother had vanished.

I yearned to follow him—above all, now that I knew he was taking part in the escapades of the band of little ruffians—and to me he seemed to have opened the doors of a new kingdom, one to be looked at no longer with alarm and mistrust but with shared enthusiasm. I was constantly running back and forth between the terrace and a high dormer window from which I could look over the treetops; and from there, more with the ear than the eye, I would follow the scamperings of the band through the orchards, watch the tops of the cherry trees quiver, and every now and again a hand appear plucking and picking, a tousled or hooded head, and among the voices hear Cosimo's and ask myself: "But how on earth did you get over there? You were in the park just a moment ago. Are you quicker than a squirrel?"

They were on the red plum trees above the Upper Pool, I remember, when they heard the horn. I heard it too but took no notice, not knowing what it was. But they did! My brother told me that they stood rooted to the spot, and in their astonishment at hearing the horn again seemed to forget it was a signal of alarm: they just asked each other if they'd heard aright, if it was the Sinforosa again, riding around on her pony to warn them of danger. Suddenly they scattered from the orchard, not in a rush to escape, but to look for her and reach her.

Only Cosimo remained, his face red as fire. But as soon as he saw the urchins running and realized they were running to her, he began to leap from branch to branch himself, risking his neck at every move.

Viola was on a curving slope of the lane, sitting still, one hand with the reins on the pony's crupper, the other brandishing a riding crop. As she looked down on the little boys she brought the tip of the crop to her mouth and began chewing it. Her dress was blue, the horn gilt and hanging on her neck by a chain. The boys had all stopped together and were also chewing, at plums or fingers or scabs on their hands and arms, or corners of sacking. And slowly from their chewing mouths, as if overcoming some inner disquiet and not from any real feeling, almost as if wanting to be contradicted, they began to mouth phrases under their breath, in rhythm, like a song: "What have you . . . come to do . . . Sinforosa . . . back you go . . . now you are . . . our friend no more . . . ah, ah, ah . . . ah, betrayer."

Above, the branches burst apart and there, in a high fig tree appeared the head of Cosimo, panting, surrounded by leaves. From down below, with that crop in her hand, she swept him and the others with the same look. Cosimo could not contain himself; still with his tongue out, he yelled: "D'you know I've never been down from the trees since then?"

Undertakings such as these should be kept quiet and mysterious; once declared or boasted about they are apt to seem pointless and even petty. So my brother had scarcely pronounced those words when he wished he had not said them; it did not seem to matter any more, and he even found himself wanting to come down and have done with the whole business. All the more when Viola slowly took her crop out of her mouth and said, softly: "*Haven't* you now? You clever little thing!"

From the flea-ridden urchins came rumbles of laughter, then their mouths opened and they broke into roars and screams till their bellies ached, and Cosimo went into such a paroxysm of rage on the fig tree that the brittle wood gave way, and a branch cracked under his feet. Cosimo fell like a stone.

He fell with his arms outstretched, making no effort to stop himself. That was the only time, to tell the truth, during his whole life in the trees of this world, that he had neither will nor instinct to grip hold of something. But a corner of his coat caught and impaled him on a low branch; Cosimo found himself hanging in the air with his head down, a foot or so from the ground.

The blood in his head came from the same force which was making him blush scarlet. And his first thought on looking up and seeing the screaming boys (upside down), who were now seized by a general frenzy of somersaulting in which one by one they appeared right side up as if gripping the ground above an abyss, and the little blond girl galloping up and down on her prancing pony—his one thought was that it was the first time he had ever actually spoken of being on the trees and that it would also be the last.

With a jerk he drew himself back on to the branch and got astride it. Viola had now calmed down her pony and did not seem to have noticed what had been happening. Cosimo immediately forgot his confusion. The girl brought the horn to her lips and blew the deep call of alarm. At the sound, the urchins (who—as Cosimo commented later—seemed to be sent by Viola's presence into a wild state of agitation, like hares under a full moon) went rushing off in flight. They let themselves be drawn off like that, as if by instinct, though realizing she had done it as a joke, running down the slope imitating the call of the horn with her galloping in front on her short-legged pony.

They were blundering along so blindly that every now and again they found her no longer ahead. Eventually she shook them off by galloping away from the path. Where was she going? She galloped along through the olive groves, down to the valley which sloped gradually. She looked for the tree on which Cosimo was perched at that moment, galloped right around it, and was off again. A moment later there she was at the foot of another olive, with my brother's head appearing above the leaves. And so, in lines as twisted as the branches of the olives themselves, down the valley they went together.

When the little thieves noticed them, and saw how they both were linked from branch to saddle, they all began whistling together, a spiteful whistle of derision; and whistling louder and louder, went off toward Porta Capperi, one of the gates of the town.

The girl and my brother remained alone, chasing each other among the olives, but Cosimo was disappointed to notice that when the rabble vanished Viola's enjoyment of the game seemed to fade and boredom to set in. The suspicion came to him that she was doing all this on purpose to anger the others, and at the same time the hope came that she would continue even if only to anger *him*; certainly she seemed to need the anger of others in order to make herself feel more precious. (All things scarcely more than sensed by the boy Cosimo then; in reality I imagine he was scrambling over the rough barks without any true understanding, like a fool.)

Suddenly, round a bluff they were assailed by a sharp little hail of gravel. The girl put her head down behind the pony's neck for protection and made off; my brother, in full view, up on the turn of a branch, remained under fire. But the little stones reached him too glancingly up there to hurt much, except for one or two on the forehead and ears. The little ruffians whistled and laughed, shouting: "Sin-fo-ro-sa is a bitch," as they ran away.

The fruit thieves reached Porta Capperi, with its green cascades of caper plants down the walls. From the hovels around came the shouts of mothers. But the mothers yelled at their children because they had come home to supper instead of scavenging for food somewhere else. Around Porta Capperi, in huts and thatched houses, broken-down carts and tents, were huddled the poorest folk of Ombrosa, so poor that they were kept outside the town gates and away from the fields, people who had drifted there from distant places whence they had been thrust by the famine and poverty which were on the increase in every state. It was dusk, and disheveled women with babies at their breasts were fanning smoky stoves; beggars lying in the open were bandaging their sores, and others were playing at dice, shouting raucously. The gang of urchins now added to the uproar and greasy smoke their own rioting, got slapped by their mothers and had fist fights among themselves in the dust. And already their rags had taken on the color of all the other rags, and their birdlike gaiety was muted into that dense rubbish heap of humanity. So, at the appearance of the fair girl at a gallop and Cosimo on the trees nearby, they just raised intimidated eyes, then slunk off and tried to lose themselves amid the dust and fire smoke, as if a wall had suddenly sprung up between them.

For the two of them, all this was just a moment, a glance. Then Viola left the smoke from the shacks mingling with the evening shadows and the cries of women and children behind her, to gallop among the pines on the beach.

Beyond was the sea. A faint clatter of stones. It was dark. The clatter became a hammer: the pony raced along striking sparks against the pebbles. From the low twisted branches of a pine tree my brother looked at the clear-cut shadow of the fair girl cross the beach. From the black sea rose a wave with a faint crest—it curled higher, advanced all white, broke and grazed the shadow of the horse and girl racing at full speed; Cosimo on the pine tree found his face wet with salty spray.

} 6 {

THOSE first days of Cosimo's on the trees were without aim or purpose, and were dominated entirely by the desire to know and possess his new kingdom. He would have liked to explore it to its extreme limits, to study all the possibilities it offered him, to discover it plant by plant and branch by branch. I say he would have liked to, but in fact we found him continually reappearing above our heads, with the busy quick movements of a wild animal which always seems, even when squatting and still, to be on the point of jumping away.

Why did he return to our park? Seeing him twisting about on a plane tree or an ilex within the range of our mother's telescope, one would have said that the impulse urging him, his dominating passion, was always to scare us off, make us worried or angry. (I say *us*, because I had not yet managed to understand how his mind was working; when he needed something, the alliance with me could never, it seemed, be put in doubt; at other times he went over my head as if he had not even seen me.)

But really, he was only passing us by. It was the wall by the magnolia tree which attracted him. It was there that we saw him vanish again and again, even when the fair girl could not have been up or when that host of governesses and aunts had made her go to bed. In the Ondariva gardens the branches spread out like the tentacles of extraordinary animals, and the plants on the ground opened up stars of fretted leaves like the green skins of reptiles, and waved feathery yellow bamboos with a rustle like paper. From the highest tree Cosimo, in his yearning to enjoy to the utmost the unusual greens of this exotic flora and its different lights and different silence, would let his head drop upside down, so that the garden became a forest, a forest not of this earth but a new world in itself.

Then Viola appeared. Cosimo would see her suddenly giving

herself a push on the swing, or in the saddle of the pony, or hear from the end of the garden the deep note of the hunting horn.

The Marchese and Marchesa of Ondariva had never really worried about their daughter's wanderings. When she was about on foot, she had all her aunts following behind; as soon as she mounted the pony she was free as air, for the aunts did not go out riding and could not see where she went. And her intimacy with those urchins was too inconceivable even to cross their minds. But they had immediately noticed the little Baron clambering about the branches and were on the lookout for him, though with a certain air of superior contempt.

Our father, on the other hand, linked his bitterness at Cosimo's disobedience to his aversion for the Ondarivas, almost as if wanting to blame them, as if it were they who were attracting his son into their garden, entertaining him, and encouraging him in that rebellious game of his. Suddenly he decided to organize a roundup to capture Cosimo, not on our land, but while actually in the Ondariva gardens. Almost as if to underline his aggressive intentions toward our neighbors, he decided not to lead the roundup himself (this would have meant presenting himself personally to the Ondarivas and asking them to restore his son—which, however unjustified, would have been a dignified link between noblemen), but to send a squad of servants under the command of the Cavalier Enea Silvio Carrega.

Armed with ladders and ropes they went to the gates of the Ondariva villa. The Cavalier fluttered about in robe and fez, excusing himself and asking if they could enter. At first the Ondariva servants thought that ours had come to cut some trailing branches which grew over into their garden; then, at the Cavalier's confused phrases—"We want to catch . . . to catch . . ." pacing to and fro and looking up among the branches—they asked, "But what have you lost, a parrot?"

"The son, the eldest son, the heir," said the Cavalier hurriedly, putting a ladder against an Indian chestnut and beginning to climb up it himself. Among the branches was Cosimo, dangling his legs with a carefree air. Viola, just as carefree, was bowling a hoop along the paths. The servants offered the Cavalier ropes with which to capture my brother; how, none of them exactly knew. But Cosimo, before the Cavalier had got halfway up the ladder, was already on top of another tree. The Cavalier had the ladder moved, and the same thing happened four or five times, each time with the Cavalier trampling on a flower bed and Cosimo passing in a couple of jumps on to a nearby tree. Suddenly Viola was surrounded by aunts and governesses, then led into the house and shut in, so as not to see all the commotion. Cosimo broke off a branch, brandished it in both hands and swished it in the air.

"But why can't you go into your own wide park to conduct this hunt, my dear sirs?" asked the Marchese of Ondariva, appearing solemnly on the flight of steps from the villa, in dressing gown and skullcap, which made him look strangely like the Cavalier. "I ask the whole family of Piovasco di Rondò!" And he made a wide circular gesture which embraced the young Baron on the tree, his illegitimate uncle, our servants, and everything of ours beyond the wall.

At this point Enea Silvio Carrega changed his tune. He trotted up to the Marchese and, fluttering about as if nothing was happening, began to talk to him about the fountains in the basin nearby and how he had got the idea of a much higher and more effective jet which would also serve, by changing a rosette, to water the lawns. This was a new proof of our illegitimate uncle's unpredictable and deceptive nature; he had been sent there by the Baron with a definite mandate, and with orders to treat the neighbors firmly; why, then, start a friendly chat with the Marchese as if wanting to ingratiate himself? The Cavalier only seemed to have talent as a conversationalist when it happened to suit him, and just at the very moment people were counting on his unfriendly character. The extraordinary thing was that the Marchese listened to him, began asking him questions and eventually took him off to examine all the fountains and jets. Both of them were dressed the same, both in long robes, both so much the same height that they might have been mistaken for each other. Behind them walked all our servants and theirs, some carrying ladders, which they did not know what to do with now.

Meanwhile Cosimo was climbing undisturbed on to the trees near the windows of the villa, trying to find beyond the curtains the room in which Viola had been shut. He discovered it, finally, and threw a berry against the pane.

The window opened and the face of the little blond girl appeared.

"It's all your fault I am locked in here," she said, and shut the window again, pulling the curtain.

Suddenly Cosimo felt desperate.

When my brother was taken by one of his wild moods, it really was something to worry about. We saw him running (if the word running makes any sense when referring not to the earth's surface but to a world of irregular supports at different heights, with empty air between) and any moment it seemed he might lose his footing and fall, which never happened. He jumped, moved into rapid little steps on a sloping branch, leaned over and suddenly swung on to a higher branch, and in four or five of these precarious zigzags vanished from sight.

Where did he go? That time he ran and ran, from ilex to olive to beech, till he was in the wood. There he paused, panting. Under him spread a meadow. A slight breeze was moving in a wave over the thick tufts of grass, with subtle shades of green. Over it flew the fluffy little white tufts of dandelions which had gone to seed. In the middle stood an isolated pine tree, unreachable, with oblong cones. Tree creepers, swift little birds with stippled brown wings, were perching on the thick clusters of pine needles, askew on the ends, some with their tails up and their beaks down, pecking at worms and pine nuts.

That wish to enter into an elusive element which had urged my brother into the trees, was still now working inside him unsatisfied, making him long for a more intimate link, a relationship which would bind him to each leaf and twig and feather and flutter. It was the love which the hunter has for living things, and which he can only express by aiming his gun at them; Cosimo could not yet recognize it and was trying to satisfy it by probing deeper.

The wood was thick and impenetrable. Cosimo had to open his way through by hacking with his rapier, and gradually he forgot his fixation, all taken up as he was by the practical problems to be faced one by one, and by a fear (which he did not want to recognize though it was there) of drawing too far away from familiar places. So, clearing his way on through the thick greenery, he reached a point where he saw two yellow eyes fixed on him between the leaves right ahead. Cosimo brought up his rapier, moved a branch aside and let it fall slowly back into place. Then he heaved a sigh of relief, and laughed at the fear he had felt; he had seen who those yellow eyes belonged to, a cat.

But the sight of the cat, just glimpsed in moving the branch, stuck in his mind, and a moment later Cosimo found himself trembling with fear again. For that cat, outwardly in every way the same as every other cat, was a terrible and terrifying cat, enough to make one scream just to look at it. It was difficult to say exactly what was so terrifying about it. The cat was a kind of tabby, bigger than any other tabby, but that did not mean anything; it was terrible, with its straight whiskers like hedgehogs' quills, with breath which one could almost see rather than hear, coming from between a double row of teeth sharp as claws. Its ears were sharply pointed pennants, covered with deceptively soft hair; the fur, standing on end, swelled around the neck in a yellow ring and stripes quivered over its flanks as if it were being stroked. The cat's neck was in a position so unnatural it seemed impossible to hold. All this that Cosimo had caught sight of in the second before he dropped the branch back to its proper place was in addition to what he had not had time to see but could imagine: the great tufts of hair around the paws masking the tearing strength of the claws, ready to spring at him. He could still see between the leaves the yellow irises with the rolling black pupils fixed on him. He could still hear the hoarse breathing growing heavier and hoarser. It all made him realize that he was face to face with the most savage wild cat in the woods.

All the twitter and flutter of the woods were silent. And then it leaped, the wild cat, but not at the boy, an almost vertical leap which astounded more than terrified Cosimo. The terror came afterwards, at seeing the animal on a branch right above his head. It was there, crouching, he could see the belly with its long whitish fur, the tense paws with their claws in the wood, the arched back. "Fff ... fff ..." it was hissing, ready to drop right on him. Cosimo, with a quick maneuver that was purely instinctive, moved on to a lower branch. "Fff ... fff ..." hissed the wild cat, and at each of the Fff's it jumped to one side and another, and was on a branch above Cosimo again. My brother repeated his maneuver, but found himself astride the lowest branch of the tree. The jump to the ground beneath was of some distance, but not so great that he would not have preferred to jump down rather than wait to see what the animal would do as soon as it had stopped making that torturing sound somewhere between a wheeze and a growl.

Cosimo was at the very point of jumping to the ground, but two instincts in him clashed—the natural one to save himself and the stubborn one never to leave the trees at any cost—and he tightened his legs and knees on the branch. The cat thought now, with the boy wavering, was the moment to spring; it came down at him with fur on end, claws out, and that wheeze. Cosimo could think of nothing better than to shut his eyes and bring up his rapier, a stupid move which the cat could easily evade. Then it was on him. A claw dug into Cosimo's cheek, but he, instead of falling, clinging as he was to the branch by the knees, swung out along the branch. This was quite the opposite of what the cat, who found itself thrown off balance and falling, was expecting. It tried to save itself by plunging its claws into the branch, and to do so had to twist around in the air—an instant, but enough for Cosimo, in a sudden victorious thrust, to plunge his rapier deep into its belly.

He was saved, covered with blood, the wild beast stuck on his rapier as on a spit, and a cheek torn from under his eye to his chin in a triple slash. He was screaming with pain and victory and frenziedly clinging to the branch, to the rapier, to the body of the cat, in that desperate moment that comes to one who wins for the first time and realizes the agony of victory, realizes too that now he is bound to continue on the road he has chosen and will not be granted any evasion through failure.

So I saw him arriving over the trees, covered with blood down to his waistcoat, his queue in disorder under the battered tricorn, holding by the neck that dead wild cat which now seemed just like any other cat.

I ran to the Generalessa on the terrace. "Lady Mother," I shouted, "he's wounded!"

"*Was?* Wounded? How?" She was already pointing her telescope.

"Wounded so he looks wounded!" I exclaimed, and the Generalessa seemed to understand my definition, for following him with the telescope as he came jumping on quicker than ever, she said: "*Es ist wahr.*"

At once she began to prepare lint and bandages and balsams as if for the ambulance of a battalion, and handed them all over for me to take to him, without its even occurring to her that he might decide to return home for doctoring. I ran into the park with the parcel of bandages and stood waiting under the last mulberry tree by the wall of the Ondarivas, for he had already vanished in the magnolia.

He made a triumphant appearance in the Ondariva garden with the dead animal in his hands. And what should he see in the space in front of the villa? A coach ready to leave, with servants loading bags on the luggage rack, and, amid a cluster of severe, black-robed governesses and aunts, Viola in traveling dress embracing the Marchese and Marchesa.

"Viola!" he shouted, raising the cat by its neck. "Where are you going?"

All the people around the coach raised their eyes to the

branches, and at the sight of him, lacerated, bleeding, with that mad air and that dead animal in his hands, began making gestures of disgust:"*Ici de nouveau! Et arrangé de cette façon.*" And as if swept by a sudden gust of rage all the aunts began to push the girl toward the coach.

Viola turned around, her nose in the air and an expression of contempt and boredom which might have been meant for Cosimo as well as her relations, gave a quick glance at the trees (surely in reply to his question), said: "They're sending me to school!" and turned around to get into the coach. She had not deigned to look either at him or his trophy.

The carriage door was already shut, the coachman was on the box, and Cosimo, still unable to take in this departure, was trying to attract her attention and make her understand that he had dedicated that bloodthirsty victory to her, but could only explain by shouting: "I've killed a cat!"

The whip gave a crack, the coach started off amid waving of handkerchiefs by the aunts, and from the door came: "How clever of you!" from Viola, whether of enthusiasm or denigration was not clear.

This was their farewell. And in Cosimo, tension, pain from his wounds, disappointment at not getting any glory from his victory, despair at that sudden departure, all surged up in him and he broke into violent sobs, shrieking and screaming and tearing at the twigs.

"*Hors d'ici! Hors d'ici! Polisson sauvage! Hors de notre jardin!*" shrieked the aunts, and all the Ondariva servants came running up with long sticks and threw stones to drive him away.

Still sobbing and screaming, Cosimo flung the dead cat in the faces of the people below. The servants took the animal by its neck and flung it onto a dunghill.

When I heard that our little neighbor had left, I hoped for a time that Cosimo might come down. I don't know why, but I linked with her, or with her also, my brother's decision to stay up in the trees.

But he did not even mention it. I climbed up to take him

bandages and lint, and he himself tended the scratches on his face and arms. Then he asked for a fishing rod with a hook. He used it to fish up the dead cat from an olive tree over the Ondariva's compost pile. He skinned it, cured the fur as best he could, and made a cap of it. It was the first of the fur caps which we were to see him wear his whole life through.

} *7* {

THE last attempt to capture Cosimo was made by our sister Battista. It was her initiative, of course, done without consulting anyone, in secret, as she always did things. She went out at night, with a pailful of glue and a rope ladder, and daubed a carob tree with glue from top to bottom. It was a tree on which Cosimo used to perch every morning.

In the morning, stuck to the carob tree were goldfinches beating their wings, wrens all wrapped in a sticky mess, night butterflies, leaves borne by the wind, a squirrel's tail, and also the tail torn off Cosimo's coat. Who knows if he had sat on a branch and managed to free himself, or if instead—more probably, as I had not seen him wear the jacket for some time—he put that piece of rag there on purpose to pull our legs. Anyway, the tree remained hideously covered with glue and then dried up.

All of us, even our father, began to be convinced that Cosimo would never return. Since my brother had been hopping about on trees all over Ombrosa, the Baron had not dared show himself in public, for fear the ducal dignity might be compromised. Every day he became gaunter and paler, how much due to paternal anxiety and how much to dynastic worries I do not know; but the two were now fused, for Cosimo was his eldest son, the heir to the title, and if it is difficult to imagine a baron hopping about on trees like a bird, it seems still more unsuitable for a duke, even

though a boy, and this conduct of the heir was certainly no
support for the contested title.

They were useless preoccupations, of course, for the people of
Ombrosa just laughed at our father's pomposity; and the nobles
living nearby thought him mad. By now these nobles had taken to
living in pleasantly sited villas rather than in their feudal
castles, and this already tended to make them behave more like
private citizens, avoiding unnecessary bothers. Who gave a
thought any more to the ancient Dukedom of Ombrosa? The
strange thing about Ombrosa was that it was no one's and yet
everyone's, with certain rights to the Ondarivas—lords of almost
all the land there—but a free commune for some time, tributary
of the Republic of Genoa; we did not have to worry about our
inherited lands and about others we had bought for nothing
from the commune at a moment when it was heavily in debt.
What more could anyone ask? There was a small circle of
nobles living in that area, with villas and parks down to the
sea. All of them lived a pleasant life visiting each other and
hunting. Life cost little. They had certain advantages over those
who were at court, having none of the worries, duties and ex-
penses of nobles with a royal family, capital, or politics to
beware of. But feeling himself a dethroned potentate, our father
did not enjoy this life at all. He had eventually broken off all
relations with the nobles of the neighborhood (our mother,
being a foreigner, had never had any at all, one could say). This
had its advantages, as by seeing no one, we both saved money
and hid the penury of our finances.

Not that we had better relations with the common people of
Ombrosa—you know what they are like: rather crude, thinking of
nothing but business. At that period, with the drinking of sugared
lemonade spreading among the richer classes, lemons were beginning to sell well; and they had planted lemon groves everywhere and rebuilt the port ruined by the invasions of pirates
many years before. Situated between the Republic of Genoa,
the fiefs of the King of Sardinia, the Kingdom of France and
episcopal lands, they trafficked with all and worried about none,

except for tributes owed to Genoa, which made them sweat every time they fell due and caused riots every year against the tax collectors of the Republic.

When these disturbances about taxes broke out, the Baron of Rondò always imagined that he might be approached with an offer of the ducal coronet. He would appear in the piazza, and offer himself to the people of Ombrosa as their protector, but each time he had to make a quick getaway under a hail of rotten lemons. Then he would say that a conspiracy had been formed against him; by the Jesuits, as usual. For he had got it into his head that there was a life-and-death struggle between him and the Jesuits, and that the Society thought of nothing but plotting his ruin. In fact there had been some difference of opinion between them about the ownership of an orchard which was being fought over by our family and the Society of Jesus; after some tension the Baron, being then on good terms with the Bishop, had managed to get the Father Provincial removed from the diocese. Since that time our father was certain that the Society was sending agents to make attempts on his life and rights; he on his part tried to enroll a militia of faithful to liberate the Bishop, whom he considered had fallen prisoner of the Jesuits; and he offered asylum and protection to anyone who declared himself persecuted by the Jesuits, which was why he had chosen as our spiritual father that semi-Jansenist with his head in the clouds.

There was only one person our father trusted, and that was the Cavalier. The Baron had a weakness for this illegitimate brother of his, as if he were an only son in misfortune; and I don't know if we realized it, but there must certainly have been, in our attitude toward the Cavalier Carrega, a touch of jealousy at our father being fonder of that fifty-year-old brother of his than of either of us boys. Anyway, we were not the only ones to look at him askance; the Generalessa and Battista pretended to respect him but really could not bear him; under that subdued exterior he did not care a fig for any of us, and may have hated us all, even the Baron to whom he owed so much. The Cavalier spoke so little that at certain times he might have been thought either deaf and dumb or incapable of understanding our language; I don't know how he had managed once to practice as a lawyer, and if he had been so absent-minded before his time with the Turks. Perhaps he had also been a person of intellect, if he had learned from the Turks all those calculations of hydraulics, the only job he was now capable of applying himself to, exaggeratedly praised by my father. I never knew much about his past, nor who his mother had been, nor what his relations had been in youth with our grandfather (who must surely have been fond of him too, as he had made him into a lawyer and granted him the title of Cavalier), nor how he had ended up in Turkey. It was not even certain if it was in Turkey itself that he had spent so much time, or in some Berber state such as Tunis or Algiers; anyway it was a Mohammedan country, and it was said that he had become a Mohammedan too. So many things were said of him: that he had held important appointments, been a high dignitary of the Sultan, Hydraulic Advisor to the Divan, or something of the kind, before falling into disgrace due to a palace plot or a woman's jealousy or a gambling debt, and been sold as a slave. It was known that he was found in chains rowing with the slaves in an Ottoman galley captured by the Venetians, who freed him. In Venice he had lived more or less as a beggar until he had got into some other trouble, a fight, I think (though who he could fight with, a man so timid, heaven only knows) and ended in prison again. He was ransomed by our father through the good offices of the Republic of Genoa, and returned to us, a little bald man with a black beard, very frightened, half dumb (I was a child but the scene that evening left an impression on my mind), decked out in clothes that were far too big for him. Our father imposed him on everyone as a person in authority, named him administrator, and allotted him a study, which was filled more and more with disordered papers. The Cavalier wore a long robe and a skullcap in the shape of a fez, as did many nobles and bourgeois in their studies, in those days; only he was, to tell the truth, very rarely in his study, and was seen going around dressed like that outside in the country too. Eventually he also appeared at table in those Turkish robes, and the strange thing was that our father, usually such a stickler for rules, seemed to tolerate it.

In spite of his duties as administrator, the Cavalier scarcely ever exchanged a word with bailiffs or tenants or peasants, due to his timidity and inarticulateness; and all the practical cares, giving of orders, keeping people up to scratch, in fact fell on our father. Enea Silvio Carrega kept the account books, and I do not know if our affairs were going so badly because of the way in which he kept them, or if his accounts went so badly because of our affairs. He would also make calculations and drawings of irrigation schemes, and fill a big blackboard with lines and figures, and words in Turkish writing. Every now and again our father shut himself up in the study with him for hours (they were the longest periods the Cavalier ever spent there) and after a short time the angry voice of the Baron, and the loud sounds of a quarrel, would come from behind the closed door, but the voice of the Cavalier could scarcely ever be heard. Then the door would open and the Cavalier would appear wrapped in the folds of his robe, with the skullcap stuck on the top of his head, go toward a French window with his quick little steps and out into the park and garden. "Enea Silvio! Enea Silvio!" shouted our father, running behind, but his half brother was already between the rows of vines, or among the lemon groves, and all that could be seen was the red fez moving stubbornly among the leaves. Our father would follow, calling; after a little we saw them returning, the Baron always talking and waving his arms, and the little Cavalier hobbling along beside him, his fists clenched in the pockets of his robe.

} 8 {

IN THOSE days Cosimo often challenged men on the ground to compete in aiming or skill, partly to try out his own capacities and discover just what he could manage to do up there on the treetops. The urchins he challenged to quoits. One day they were among the shacks of the vagabonds and down-and-outs near Porta Capperi, with Cosimo playing quoits with them from a dried and leafless ilex tree, when he saw a horseman approaching. It was a tall, rather bowed man, wrapped in a black cloak. He recognized his father. The rabble dispersed, while the women stood looking on from the thresholds of their shacks.

The Baron Arminio rode right up under the tree. The sunset was red. Cosimo stood among bare branches. They looked straight at each other. It was the first time since the dinner of the snails that they found themselves like that, face to face. Many days had passed, things had changed. Both of them knew that the snails did not enter into it now; nor did the obedience of sons or the authority of fathers; that all the many logical and sensible things which could be said would be out of place; yet they had to say something.

"You're making a spectacle of yourself!" began the father, bitterly. "Really worthy of a gentleman!" (He called him by the formal "voi," as he did for the most serious reprimands, but the use of the word now had a sense of distance, of detachment.)

"A gentleman, my Lord Father, is such whether he is on earth or on the treetops," replied Cosimo, and at once added: "If he behaves with decency."

"An excellent maxim," admitted the Baron gravely. "And yet only a short time ago you were stealing plums from one of our tenants."

It was true. My brother had been found out. What was he to

reply? He smiled—but not haughtily or cynically—a shy smile, and blushed.

The father smiled too, a melancholy smile, and for some reason or other blushed too.

"You're making common cause with the worst little ruffians in the area!" he said then.

"No, my Lord Father, I'm on my own, and each acts for himself," said Cosimo firmly.

"I ask you to come down to earth," said the Baron in a calm, rather faint voice, "and to take up the duties of your station!"

"I have no intention of obeying you, my Lord Father," said Cosimo. "I am very sorry."

They were ill at ease, both of them, bored. Each knew what the other would say. "And what about your studies? Your devotions as a Christian?" said the father. "Do you intend to grow up like an American savage?"

Cosimo was silent. These were thoughts he had not yet put to himself and had no wish to. Then he exclaimed: "Just because I'm a few yards higher up, does it mean that good teaching can't reach me?"

This was an able reply too, though it diminished, in a way, the range of his gesture; a sign of weakness.

His father realized this and became more pressing. "Rebellion cannot be measured by yards," said he. "Even when a journey seems no distance at all, it can have no return."

Now was the moment for my brother to produce some other noble reply, perhaps a Latin maxim, but at that instant none came into his head, though he knew so many by heart. Instead he suddenly got bored with all this solemnity, and shouted: "But from the trees I can piss farther," a phrase without much meaning, but which cut the discussion short.

As though they had heard the phrase, a shout went up from the ragamuffins around Porta Capperi. The Baron of Rondò's horse shied, the Baron pulled the reins and wrapped himself more tightly in his cloak, ready to leave. Then he turned, drew an arm out of his cloak, pointed to the sky, which had suddenly become overcast with black clouds, and exclaimed: "Be careful, son, there's Someone who can piss on us all!" and spurred his horse on.

The rain, long awaited in the countryside, began to fall in big scattered drops. Among the hovels there was a scattering and running of urchins hooded in sacks and singing in dialect: "It's raining! It's raining! No more complaining." Cosimo vanished through leaves drooping with water, which poured showers on his head at a touch.

As soon as I realized it was raining, I began to worry about him. I imagined him soaking wet, cowering against a tree trunk without ever managing to avoid the oblique rain. And I knew that a storm would not make him return. So I hurried off to our mother. "It's raining! What will Cosimo do, Lady Mother?"

The Generalessa shook the curtain and looked out at the rain. She was calm. "The worst nuisance from heavy rain is the mud. Up there he's away from that."

"But will he find enough shelter in the trees?"

"He'll withdraw to his tents."

"Which, Lady Mother?"

"He'll have had the foresight to prepare them in time."

"But don't you think I'd better go find him and give him an umbrella?"

As if the word "umbrella" had suddenly torn her from her observation post and flung her back into maternal preoccupations, the Generalessa began saying: *"Ja, ganz gewiss!* And a bottle of apple syrup, well heated, wrapped in a woolen sock! And some oilcloth, to stretch over the branches and stop the wet coming through . . . But where'll he be now, poor boy! . . . Let's hope you manage to find him . . ."

Loaded with parcels I went out into the rain, under an enormous green umbrella, holding under my arm another umbrella, shut, for Cosimo.

I gave our particular whistle, but the only answer was the

endless patter of the rain on the trees. It was dark; once outside
the garden precincts I did not know my way and put my feet
haphazardly on slippery stones, spongy grass, puddles, whistling
all the time and tipping the umbrella back to send the whistle
upwards, so that the rain lashed my face and washed the whistle
from my lips. My idea was to go toward some public lands full of
tall trees where I thought he might possibly have taken refuge,
but in that darkness I got lost and stood there clutching the
umbrellas and packages, with only the bottle of syrup, wrapped
in its woolen sock, to give me a little warmth.

Then, among the trees, high in the darkness above, I saw a
light which could not be coming from either moon or stars.
And at my whistle I seemed to hear his in reply.

"Cosimooo!"

"Biagiooo!" came a voice through the rain from the treetops.

"Where are you?"

"Here . . . I'm coming toward you, but hurry up as I'm getting
wet!"

We found each other. Wrapped in a blanket, he came down
onto the low fork of a willow to show me how to climb up,
through complicated interlacing branches, as far as a beech tree
with a high trunk, from which came that light. I gave him the
umbrella and some of the parcels at once, and we tried to
struggle up with the umbrellas open, but it was impossible and
we got wet all the same. Finally I reached the place he was
leading me to; but I saw nothing except for a faint light that
seemed to be coming from the flaps of a tent.

Cosimo raised one of those flaps and let me in. By the light
of a lantern I saw I was in a kind of little room, covered and
enclosed on every side by curtains and carpets, crossed by the
trunks of the beech tree, with a floor of stakes, all propped on
thick branches. At that moment it seemed a palace to me, but
soon I began to realize how unstable it was, for the fact that
there were two of us inside was upsetting the balance and Cosimo
at once had to get down to the business of repairing leaks. He
also opened and put out the two umbrellas I had brought to

cover two yawning holes in the roof; but the water was pouring in from various other points and we were both soaked and as cold as if we'd stayed outside. However, such a quantity of blankets was amassed there that we were able to bury ourselves under them, leaving only our heads outside. The lantern sent out an uncertain sputtering light, and the branches and leaves threw intricate shadows on the roof and walls of that strange construction. Cosimo drank the apple syrup in great gulps, gasping, "Puah! Puah!"

"It's a nice house," said I.

"Oh, it's only provisional," replied Cosimo hurriedly. "I've got to think it out better."

"Did you build it all yourself?"

"Of course, who d'you think? It's secret."

"Can I come here?"

"No, or you'll show someone else the way."

"Father said he's giving up the search for you."

"This must be a secret all the same."

"Because of those boys who steal? But aren't they your friends?"

"Sometimes they are and sometimes they aren't."

"And the girl on the pony?"

"What's that to do with you?"

"I meant she's your friend, isn't she, and you play together, don't you?"

"Sometimes we do and sometimes we don't."

"Why only sometimes?"

"Because I may not want to or she may not want to."

"And her, would you let her up here?"

Cosimo, frowning, was trying to spread a straw mat over a branch. "Yes. If she came, I'd let her up," he said gravely.

"Doesn't she want to?"

Cosimo flung himself down. "She's left."

"Say," I whispered, "are you engaged?"

"No," answered my brother and wrapped himself in a long silence.

Next day the weather was fine, and it was decided that Cosimo would begin taking lessons again with Abbé Fauchelefleur. How, was not said. Simply and rather brusquely, the Baron asked the Abbé (". . . instead of just standing there looking at the flies, *mon Abbé* . . .") to go and find my brother wherever he might be and get him to translate a little Virgil. Then, fearing he had put the Abbé in too embarrassing a position, he tried to ease his task, and said to me: "Go and tell your brother to be in the garden in half an hour for his Latin lesson." This he said in as natural a tone as he could, the tone which he intended to keep from then on; even with Cosimo in the trees everything must continue as before.

So the lesson took place. They sat, my brother astride an oak branch, his legs dangling, and the Abbé on the grass beneath, on a stool, intoning hexameters in chorus. I played around there and then wandered off for a short time. When I got back, the Abbé was in the tree. With his long thin legs in their black stockings he was trying to hitch himself onto a fork and Cosimo was helping him by an elbow. They found a comfortable position for the old man, and together deciphered a difficult passage, bending over the book. My brother seemed to be showing great diligence.

Then I don't know what happened, why the pupil made off; perhaps because the Abbé's mind had wandered and he had begun staring into the void as usual; the fact is that suddenly only the black figure of the old priest was left crouched in the branches, his book on his knees, looking at a white butterfly flying by and following it with mouth agape. When the butterfly vanished, the Abbé suddenly realized he was there alone on the tree and felt frightened. He clutched the trunk and began shouting: "*Au secours! Au secours!*" until people came with a ladder and little by little he calmed down and descended.

} 9 {

IN FACT, Cosimo, despite that escape of his, which had upset us all so much, lived almost as closely with us as he had before. He was a solitary who did not avoid people. In a way, indeed, he seemed to like them more than anything else. He would squat above places where peasants were digging, turning manure, or scything the fields, and call out polite greetings. They would raise their heads in surprise and he at once tried to show them where he was, for he had got over the pastime we had so often indulged in when we had been together on the trees *before*, of thumbing his nose and making faces at passers-by. At first the peasants were rather confused at seeing him covering such distances all on branches, and did not know whether to greet him by doffing their hats as they did with the gentry or to shout at him as they did with urchins. Then they got into the habit of chatting with him about their work or the weather, and seemed to find the game he was playing up there no better and no worse than so many other games they had seen the gentry play.

He would sit for whole half-hours at a time, watching their work from the trees and asking questions about seeds and manure, which it had never occurred to him to do when he'd been on the ground, prevented then by shyness from ever addressing a word to villagers or servants. Sometimes, he would point out if the furrow they were digging was going straight or crooked; or if the tomatoes in a neighbor's field were already ripe; sometimes he would offer himself for little assignments, such as going to tell the wife of a scyther to bring a whetstone, or warning someone to turn off the water in an orchard. And if, when he was moving around with these messages for the peasants, he happened to see a flight of sparrows settling on a field of corn, he would shout and wave his cap to scare them away.

In his solitary turns around the woods, encounters with humans were memorable though rare, for they were with folk whom people like us never used to meet. In those times a variety of wanderers used to camp in the forests: colliers, tinkers, glass cutters, families driven far from their homes by hunger, to earn their bread by these unstable jobs. They would set up their workshops in the open, and erect shacks, made of branches, to sleep in. At first they were rather alarmed by the boy dressed in fur passing over their heads, particularly the women, who took him for a hobgoblin; then he became friends with them, and spent hours watching them work, and in the evening when they sat around the fire he would settle on a branch nearby, to hear the tales they told.

In a glade covered with beaten cinders the colliers were the most numerous. They would shout *"Hura! Hota!"* as they were from Bergamo and their speech was impossible to understand. They were the strongest and most self-contained, a corporate body ranging throughout the woods, with links of blood and friendship and enmity. Cosimo would sometimes act as messenger between one group and another, pass on news, and he was asked to go on various errands for them.

"The men under the Red Oak have told me to tell you *Hanfa la Hapa Hota'l Hoc!*"

"Answer 'em *Hegn Hobet Ho de Hot!*"

He would remember the mysterious aspirated syllables, and try to mimic them, as he tried to mimic the twitter of the birds which woke him in the morning.

By now the news had spread that a son of the Baron of Rondò had been up in the trees for months; yet our father tried to keep it secret from strangers. There came to visit us, for instance, the Count and Countess of Estomac, on their way to France, where they had estates in the bay of Toulouse. I do not know what self-interest lay behind this visit; claims to certain rights, or the confirmation of a diocese to their son, who was a bishop, for which they needed the agreement of the Baron of Rondò; and our father, as can be imagined, built on this alliance a castle of projects for his dynastic pretensions on Ombrosa.

There was an agonizingly boring dinner, with endless ceremonial, and bowing and scraping all around. The guests had with them a young son, a bewigged little prig. The Baron presented his sons, that is me alone, and added: "My daughter Battista, poor girl, lives such a retired life, is so very pious, that I don't know if you'll be able to see her," and at that moment she showed up, that idiot, in a nun's wimple covered all over with ribbons and frills, a powdered face, and mittens. It should be emphasized that since that business of the young Marchese della Mela she had never once set eyes on a young man, apart from pages and village lads. The young Count of Estomac bowed; she broke into hysterical laughter. The Baron, who had already given up his daughter as a lost cause, now began to mill over new possibilities in his mind.

But the old Count made a show of indifference. He asked: "Didn't you have another son, Monsieur Arminio?"

"Yes, the eldest," said our father, "but, as luck would have it, he's out shooting."

He had not lied, as at that period Cosimo was always in the woods with his gun, after hares and thrushes. The gun was one I had got for him, it was the light one Battista had used against the mice and which for some time she—having given up that particular sport—had abandoned on a nail.

The Count began to ask about the game thereabouts. The Baron in his replies kept to generalities, as, taking no interest in the world around him, he did not know how to shoot. I now interrupted the conversation, though I had been forbidden to say a word when grownups were talking.

"And what does anyone as young as you know about it?" asked the Count.

"I go and fetch the game my brother brings down, and take them up the . . ." I was just saying when our father interrupted me.

"Who asked you to say anything? Go and play."

We were in the garden. It was evening and still light, since it was summer. And now over the plane trees and oaks Cosimo came calmly along, with his cap of cat's fur on his head, his gun slung on one shoulder, a spear on the other, and his legs in gaiters.

"Hey, hey!" exclaimed the Count, getting up and moving his head to see better, much amused. "Who's that? Who's that on the trees?"

"What? What? I really don't know . . ." began our father, and instead of looking in the direction where the other was pointing, looked in the Count's eyes as if to assure himself he could see well.

Cosimo meanwhile had reached a point right above them, and was standing on a fork with legs spread apart.

"Ah, it's my son, yes, Cosimo. Just a boy, you see. To give us a surprise he's climbed up there . . ."

"Is he your eldest son?"

"Yes, yes, of the two boys he's the eldest, but only by a little, you know. They're still children, playing . . ."

"But he must be a bright lad to go over branches like that. And with that arsenal on him . . ."

"Eh, just playing," and with a terrible effort at lying which made him go red all over he called: "What are you doing up there? Eh? Will you come down? Come and greet our Lord Count here!"

Cosimo took off his cat's-fur cap, and bowed. "My respects, Lord Count."

"Ah, ah, ah!" laughed the Count. "Fine, fine! Let him stay up there, let him stay up there, Monsieur Arminio! A very clever boy at getting about trees!" and he laughed.

And even that little dolt of a count kept on repeating: *"C'est original, ça c'est très original!"*

Cosimo sat down there on the fork, our father changed the subject and talked on and on in the hope of diverting the Count's attention. But every now and again the Count raised his eyes and there my brother always was, up that tree or another, cleaning his gun, or greasing his gaiters or, as night was coming on, donning his flannel shirt.

"Oh, but look! He can do everything up there, that boy can! What fun! Ah, I'll tell them about it at Court, the very first time I go there! I'll tell my son the Bishop! I'll tell my aunt the Princess!"

My father could scarcely control himself any longer. And he had another worry on his mind; he could not see his daughter around, and the young Count had vanished too.

Cosimo had gone off on one of his tours of exploration, and now came panting back. "She's given him the hiccups! She's given him the hiccups!"

The Count looked worried. "Oh, that's unfortunate. My son suffers a lot from hiccups. Do go, like a good boy, and see what's happening. Tell 'em to come back."

Cosimo went jumping off, and came back panting more than ever. "They're chasing each other. She wants to put a live lizard under his shirt to get rid of his hiccups! He doesn't want her to!" And off he skipped for another look.

So we spent that evening at home, not so very different in truth from others, with Cosimo sneaking around the edges of our lives from up on the trees; but that time we had guests, and as a result the news of my brother's behavior spread over the courts of Europe, to the great shame of our father. Quite a baseless shame, for the Count of Estomac went away with a favorable impression of our family, and as a result our sister Battista became engaged to the little Count.

} 10 {

THE olives, because of their tortuous shapes, were comfortable and easy passages for Cosimo, patient trees with rough, friendly bark on which he could pass or pause, in spite of the scarcity of thick branches and the monotony of movement which resulted from their shapes. On a fig tree, though, as long as he saw to it that a branch could bear his weight, he could move about forever; Cosimo would stand under the pavilion of leaves, watching the sun appear through the network of twigs and branches, the gradual swell of the green fruit, smelling the scent of flowers budding in the stalks. The fig tree seemed to absorb him, permeate him with its gummy texture and the buzz of hornets; after a little Cosimo would begin to feel he was becoming a fig himself, and move away, uneasy. On the hard sorb apple or the mulberry he was all right; a pity they were so rare. Or the nut . . . sometimes seeing my brother lose himself in the endless spread of an old nut tree, like some palace of many floors and innumerable rooms, I found a longing coming over me to imitate him and go and live up there too; such is the strength and certainty that this tree had in being a tree, its determination to be hard and heavy expressed even in its leaves.

Cosimo would spend happy hours, too, amid the undulating leaves of the ilex (or holm oak, as I have called them when describing the ones in our park, perhaps influenced by our father's stilted language) and he loved its peeling bark from which, when preoccupied, he would pick off a piece with his fingers, not from any desire to do harm, but to help the tree in its long travail of rebirth. Or he would peel away the white bark of a plane tree, uncovering layers of old yellow mildew. He also loved the knobby trunks like the elm, with the tender shoots and clusters of little jagged leaves and twigs growing out of the whorls; but it wasn't an easy tree to move about on as the branches grew upwards, slender and thickly covered, leaving little foothold. In the woods he preferred beeches and oaks; the pines had very close-knit branches, brittle and thick with cones, leaving him no space or support; and the chestnut, with its prickly leaves, husks and bark, and its high branches, seemed a good tree to avoid.

These sympathies and antipathies Cosimo came to recognize in time—or to recognize consciously, but already in those first days they had begun to be an instinctive part of him. Now it was a whole different world, made up of narrow curved bridges in the emptiness, of knots or peel or scores roughening the trunks, of lights varying their green according to the veils of thicker or scarcer leaves, trembling at the first quiver of the air on the shoots or moving like sails with the bend of the tree in the wind. While down below our world lay flattened, and our bodies looked quite disproportionate and we certainly understood nothing of what he knew up there—he who spent his nights listening to the sap running through its cells; the circles marking the years inside the trunks; the patches of mold growing ever larger helped by the north wind; the birds sleeping and quivering in their nests, then resettling their heads in the softest down of their wings; and the caterpillar waking, and the chrysalis opening. There is the moment when the silence of the countryside gathers in the ear and breaks into a myriad of sounds: a croaking and squeaking, a swift rustle in the grass, a plop in the water, a pattering on earth and pebbles, and high above all, the call of the cicada. The sounds follow one another, and the ear eventually discerns more and more of them—just as fingers unwinding a ball of wool feel each fiber interwoven with progressively thinner and less palpable threads. The frogs continue croaking in the background without changing the flow of sounds, just as light does not vary from the continuous winking of stars. But at every rise or fall of the wind every sound changes and is renewed. All that remains in the inner recess of the ear is a vague murmur: the sea.

Winter came. Cosimo made himself a fur jacket. He sewed it from the fur of various animals he had hunted: hares, foxes, martens and ferrets. On his head he still wore that cap of wildcat's fur. He also made himself some goatskin breeches with leather knees. As for shoes, he eventually realized that the best footgear for the trees was slippers, and he made himself a pair of some skin or other—perhaps badger.

So he defended himself against the cold. It should be said that in those days the winters in our parts were mild, and never had the freezing cold of nowadays which they say was loosed from its lair in Russia by Napoleon and followed him all the way here. But even so, spending the winter nights out in the open could not have been easy.

At night Cosimo eventually found a fur sleeping bag best; no more tents or shacks; a sleeping bag with fur inside, hung on a branch. He got inside, the outside world vanished and he slept tucked up like a child. If there was an unusual sound in the night, from the mouth of the bag emerged the fur cap, the barrel of the gun, then his round eyes. (They said that his eyes had become luminous in the dark like a cat's or owl's; but I never noticed it myself.)

In the morning, on the other hand, when the jackdaw croaked, from the bag would come a pair of clenched fists; the fists rose in the air and were followed by two arms slowly widening and stretching, and in the movement drawing out his yawning mouth, his shoulders with a gun slung over one and a powder horn over another, and his slightly bandy legs (they were beginning to lose their straightness from his habit of always moving on all fours or in a crouch). Out jumped these legs. They stretched too, and so, with a shake of the back and a scratch under his fur jacket, Cosimo, wakeful and fresh as a rose, was ready to begin his day.

He went to the fountain, for he had a hanging fountain of his own, invented by himself, or rather made with the help of nature. There was a stream which at a certain place dropped sheer in a cascade, and nearby grew an oak, with very high branches. Cosimo, with a piece of scooped-out poplar a couple of yards long, had made a kind of gutter which brought the water from the cascade to the branches of the oak tree, where he could drink and wash. That he did wash is sure, for I have seen him doing so a number of times; not much and not even every day, but he did wash; he also had soap. With the soap, when he happened to feel like it, he would also wash his linen; he had taken a tub into the oak tree for this purpose. Then he would hang the things to dry on ropes from one branch to another.

In fact he did everything in the trees. He had also found a
way to roast the game he caught, on a spit, without ever coming
down. This is what he did; he would light a pine cone with a
flint and throw it to the ground on a spot already arranged for
a fire (I had set this up, with some smooth stones); then he
would drop twigs and dried branches on it, regulating the flame
with a poker tied on a long stick in such a way that it reached the
spit, which was hanging from two branches. All this called for
great care, as it is easy to start a fire in the woods. And the
fireplace was set on purpose under the oak tree, near the cascade
from which he could draw all the water he wanted in case of
danger.

Thus, partly by eating what he shot, partly by bartering with
the peasants for fruit and vegetables, he managed very well,
and we no longer needed to send any food out to him from the
house. One day we heard that he was drinking fresh milk every
morning; he had made friends with a goat, which would climb up
the fork of an olive tree a foot or two from the ground; but it
did not really climb up, it just put its two rear hoofs up, so that
he could come down onto the fork with a pail and milk it. He
had a similar arrangement with a chicken, a red Paduan, a very
good layer. He had made it a secret nest in the hole of a trunk,
and on alternate days he would find an egg, which he drank after
making two holes in it with a pin.

Another problem: doing his daily duties. At the beginning he
did them wherever he happened to be, here or there it didn't
matter, the world was big. Then he realized this was not very
nice. So he found, on the banks of a stream called the Merdanzo,
an alder tree leaning over a most suitable and secluded part of
the water, with a fork on which he could seat himself comfortably. The Merdanzo was a dark torrent, hidden among the
bamboos, with a quick flow, and the villages nearby threw their
slops into it. So the young Piovasco di Rondò lived a civilized life,
respecting the decencies of his neighbor and himself.

But he lacked a necessary complement to his huntsman's life—
a dog. There was I, flinging myself among the thorns and bushes,

searching for a thrush, a snipe or a quail, which had fallen after being shot in mid air, or even looking out for foxes when, after a night on the prowl, one of them would stop with its long tail extended just outside the bushes. But only rarely could I escape to join him in the woods; lessons with the Abbé, study, serving Mass, meals with my parents kept me back; the hundred and one duties of family life I submitted to, because, after all, the phrase which was always being repeated around me—"One rebel in a family is enough"—made sense and left a mark on me all my life.

So Cosimo almost always went hunting alone, and to recover the game (except in rare cases such as when a golden oriole's wings would catch on a branch as it fell) he used a kind of fishing tackle; rods with string and hooks, but he did not always succeed in reaching it, and sometimes a snipe ended black with ants in the bottom of a gully.

I have spoken up to now only of retrievers. For Cosimo then did only the kind of shooting which meant spending mornings and nights crouched on his branch, waiting for a thrush to pause on some exposed twig, or a hare to appear in the open space of a field. If not, he wandered about at random, following the song of the birds, or guessing the most probable tracks of the animals. And when he heard the baying of hounds behind a hare or a fox, he knew he must avoid them, for these were not animals for him, a solitary casual hunter. Respectful of the rules as he was, when from his observation post he noticed or could aim at some game chased by the hounds of others, he would never raise his gun. He would wait for the huntsman to arrive panting along the path, with ears cocked and eyes bleared, and point out to him the direction the animal had taken.

One day he saw a fox on the run: a red streak in the middle of the green grass, whiskers erect, snorting fearfully; it crossed the field and vanished into the undergrowth. And behind: *"Oohowowah!"*—the hounds.

They arrived at a gallop, their noses to the ground, twice found themselves without the smell of fox in their nostrils and then turned away at a right angle.

They were already some way off when, with a howl of *"Oohee,*

Oohee!" cleaving through the grass with leaps that were more like a fish's than a dog's, came a kind of dolphin; he was swimming along and sniffing, with a nose sharper and ears droopier than a bloodhound's. His rear end was just like that of a fish propelled by fins, or web feet, legless and very long. He came out into the open; a dachshund.

He must have tagged after the hounds and been left behind, young as he was, almost a puppy. The sound of the hounds was now a "*Boohahf*" of annoyance, because they had lost the scent, and the running pack became scattered all around an open field, too anxious to find the lost scent again and to make a real search for it, and losing their impetus, so that already one or two of them were taking the opportunity of raising their legs against a rock.

The dachshund, panting hard, trotting along with his nose in the air in unjustified triumph, finally reached the hounds. He was still triumphant and gave a cunning howl: "*Ooheeyah! Ooheeyah!*"

The hounds snarled at once"—*Owrrrch*"—and quit their search for the fox's scent a minute and went toward the dachshund, their mouths open ready to bite—"*Ghrrrr!*" Then they quickly lost interest again, and ran off.

Cosimo followed the dachshund, which was now moving about haphazardly, and the dog, wavering with a distracted nose, saw the boy on the tree and wagged his tail. Cosimo felt sure that the fox was still hidden nearby. The hounds were scattered a long way off. They could be heard every now and again from the opposite slope barking in a broken and aimless way, urged on by the muted voices of the hunters. Cosimo said to the dachshund: "Go on! Go on! Look for it!"

The puppy flung himself about sniffing hard, and every now and again turned his face up to look at the boy.

"Go on! Go on!" Cosimo urged him.

Now Cosimo could not see the dog any more. He heard a crashing among the bushes, then, suddenly: "*Owowowah! Eeayee! Eeayeeah!*" the dachshund had raised the fox!

Cosimo saw the animal run out into the field. But could he fire at a fox raised by someone else's dog? Cosimo let it pass and did not shoot. The dachshund lifted his snout toward the boy, with the look of dogs when they do not understand and are not sure whether they should understand, and flung his nose down again, behind the fox.

"*Eeayee, eeayee, eeayee!*" The fox made a complete round. There, it was coming back. Could he fire or couldn't he? He didn't. The dachshund turned a sad eye up at him. He was not barking any more, his tongue was drooping more than his ears. He was exhausted, but he still went on running.

The dachshund's raising of the fox had baffled both hounds and hunters. Along the path was running an old man with a heavy arquebus. "Hey," called Cosimo, "is that dachshund yours?"

"A plague on you and all your family!" shouted the old man, who must have been a bit cracked. "Do we look like people who hunt with a dachshund?"

"Then whatever he puts up, I can shoot," insisted Cosimo, who really wanted to do the right thing.

"Shoot at your guardian angel for all I care!" replied the other, as he hurried off.

The dachshund chased the fox back again to Cosimo's tree. Cosimo shot at it and hit it. The dachshund was his dog; he called him Ottimo Massimo.

Ottimo Massimo was no one's dog, he had joined the pack of hounds from youthful enthusiasm. But where did he come from? To discover this, Cosimo let him lead him.

The dachshund, his belly grazing the ground, crossed hedges and ditches; then he turned to see if the boy up there was managing to follow his tracks. So unusual was his route that Cosimo did not realize at once where they had got to. When he understood, his heart gave a leap; it was the garden of the Ondarivas.

The villa was shut, the shutters pulled to; only one, on an attic window, was banging in the wind. More than ever the garden had the look of a forest from another world. And along the alleys now overgrown with weeds and the bush-laden flower beds, Ottimo Massimo moved happily, as if at home, chasing butterflies.

He vanished into a thicket and came back with a ribbon. Cosimo's heart gave another leap. "What is it, Ottimo Massimo? Eh? Whose is it? Tell me?"

Ottimo Massimo wagged its tail.

"Bring it here, Ottimo Massimo!"

Cosimo came down on to a low branch and took from the dog's mouth a faded piece of ribbon which must have been a hair ribbon of Viola's, just as that dog was certainly Viola's dog, forgotten there in the last move of the family. In fact, Cosimo now seemed to remember him from the summer before, as still a puppy, peeping out of a basket in the arms of the fair-haired girl; perhaps they had just that moment brought him to her as a present.

"Search, Ottimo Massimo!" The dachshund threw himself among the bamboos; and came back with other mementos of her, a skipping rope, a piece of an old kite, a fan.

At the top of the trunk of the highest tree in the garden, my brother carved with the point of his rapier the names *Viola and Cosimo* and then, lower down, certain that it would give her pleasure even if he called him by another name, *Ottimo Massimo, Dachshund.*"

From that time on, whenever we saw the boy on the trees we could be sure he was looking for the dachshund. Ottimo would trot along belly to ground. Cosimo had taught him how to search, stop, and bring back game, the jobs every hunting dog does, and there was no woodland creature that they did not hunt together. To bring him the game, Ottimo Massimo would clamber with two paws as high up the trunk as he could; Cosimo would lean down, take the hare or the partridge from his mouth and pat him on the head. These were all their intimacies, their celebrations. But between the two on the ground and branches ran a continual dialogue, an understanding, of monosyllabic baying and tongue-clicking and finger-snapping. That necessary presence which man is for a dog and a dog for man, never betrayed either; and though they were different from all other men and dogs in the world, they could still call themselves happy, as man and dog.

} 11 {

FOR a long time—one whole period of his adolescence—hunting was Cosimo's world. And fishing too, for he would wait for eels and trout with a line in the ponds and streams. Sometimes he seemed almost to have developed instincts and senses different from ours, as if those skins he had made into clothes corresponded to a total change in his nature. Certainly the continual contact with the barks of trees, his eyes trained to the movement of a feather, a hair, a scale, to the range of colors of his world, and then the various greens circulating through the veins of leaves like blood from another world; all those forms of life so far removed from the human as the stem of a plant, the beak of a thrush, the gill of a fish, those borders of the wild into which he was so deeply urged—all might have molded his mind, made him lose every semblance of man. But, no matter how many new qualities he acquired from his closeness with plants and his struggles with animals, his place—it always seemed to me—was clearly with us.

But even without meaning to, he found certain habits becoming rarer—and finally abandoned them altogether—such as following High Mass in Ombrosa. For the first months he tried to do so. Every Sunday, as we came out of the house—the whole family dressed up ceremonially—we would find him on the branches, he too rigged in an attempt at ceremonial dress, such

as his old tunic, or his tricorn instead of the fur cap. We would
set off, and he would follow us over the branches. So we reached
the entrance to the church, with all the people of Ombrosa
looking at us (soon even my father became used to it and his
embarrassment decreased)—we were all walking with great
dignity, he jumping in the air. A strange sight, particularly in
winter, with the trees bare.

We would enter the cathedral and sit at our family pew, while
he stayed outside, kneeling on an ilex beside one of the naves,
just at the height of a big window. From our pew we would see,
through the windows, the shadows of the branches and, in the
middle, Cosimo's with hat on chest and head bowed. By agreement between my father and one of the sacristans, that window
was kept half open every Sunday, so that my brother could attend Mass from his tree. But as time went by we saw him there
no more. The window was closed as it made a draught.

Many things which would have been important to him before
were now no longer. In the spring our sister got engaged. Who
would have thought it only a year before? That Count and
Countess of Estomac came with the young Count and there were
great celebrations. Every room in our house was lit up, all the
local nobility were invited, and there was dancing. Why should
we think of Cosimo, then? Well, we did think of him, all of
us. Every now and then I looked out the window to see if he
was coming. Our father was sad, and at that family celebration
he must have been thinking of him who had excluded himself
from it. The Generalessa, who was ordering the whole party about
as if she were on a parade ground, was only doing so as an outlet
for her feelings about her absent son. Perhaps even Battista,
pirouetting around, unrecognizable now that she was out of her
nunnish clothes—wearing a wig which looked like marzipan, and
a *grand panier* decorated with corals, made up for her by some
dressmaker or other—even she was thinking of him I could have
sworn.

And he was there, unseen—I heard about it afterwards—in the

shadows, on the top of a plane tree, in the cold, watching the brightly lit windows, the rooms he knew so well festooned for the party, the bewigged dancers. What thoughts could have crossed his mind? Did he regret our life a little? Was he thinking how brief was the step which separated him from a return to our world, how brief and how easy? I have no idea what he thought, what he wanted, up there. I only know that he stayed for the whole of the party, and even beyond it, until one by one the chandeliers were put out and not a lit window remained.

So Cosimo's relations with the family, either good or bad, continued. In fact, they became closer with one member of it—whom he only really now got to know—the Cavalier Enea Silvio Carrega. This vague, elusive little man (nobody ever knew where he was and what he was doing), Cosimo discovered to be the only one of the whole family who had a great number of pursuits and none of them useless.

He would go out, sometimes in the hottest hour of the afternoon, with his fez stuck on the top of his head, shambling along, his long robe trailing on the ground, and vanish almost as if he had been swallowed up by a crevice in the earth or hedges, or the stones in the walls. Cosimo, too, who passed his time always on the watch (or rather it was not a pastime now, it was his natural state, as if his eye had to embrace a horizon wide enough to understand all), would suddenly lose sight of him. Sometimes he used to start running from branch to branch toward the place where the old man vanished, without ever succeeding in finding where he had gone. But one sign always appeared in the area where he was last seen: flying bees. Eventually Cosimo was convinced that the presence of the Cavalier was linked with the bees, and that in order to find him he would have to follow their flight. But how could he? Around each flowering plant was a scattered buzz of bees; he must not let himself be distracted into isolated and secondary routes, but follow the invisible airy way in which the coming and going of bees was growing thicker and thicker, until he reached a dense cloud rising like smoke from behind a bush. There behind were the beehives, one by one or in rows on a table, and busy about them, with bees buzzing all around him, was the Cavalier.

Beekeeping was in fact one of our uncle's secret activities; secret to a point only, for he himself every now and again would bring to the table a gleaming honeycomb fresh from the hive; but this activity of his took place outside the boundaries of our property, in places which he evidently did not want us to know about. It must have been a precaution on his part, to prevent the profits of this personal industry of his from passing through the family accounts; or—since the man was certainly not a miser, and anyway could not expect much of a profit from such small quantities of honey and wax—in order to have something in which the Baron, his brother, could not poke his nose, or pretend to be guiding him; or again in order not to mingle the few things which he loved, such as beekeeping, with the many which he did not love, such as administration.

Anyway, the fact remained that our father had never allowed him to keep bees near the house, as the Baron had an unreasonable fear of being stung; when by chance he happened to come across a bee or a wasp in the garden he would run along the alleys, looking ridiculous, thrusting his hands into his wig as if to protect himself from the pecks of an eagle. Once, as he was doing this, his wig slipped, the bee, disturbed by his sudden movement, turned against him and plunged its sting into his bald pate. For three days he tended his head with compresses soaked in vinegar, for he was that kind of man, very proud and strong in serious matters, but frenzied by a slight scratch or pimple.

And so Enea Silvio Carrega had scattered his beehives all over the valley of Ombrosa; various landowners had given him permission to keep a beehive or two on a strip of their land in return for a little honey, and he was always going the rounds from one to the other, working at the beehives busily moving his hands, which, in order not to be stung, he had thrust into long black mitts. On his face, beneath his fez, he wore a black veil which clung to him or blew out at every breath. He used to wave about an instrument that scattered smoke, so as to chase the insects away while he was searching in the beehive. The whole scene, the buzz of bees, the veils and clouds of smoke, all seemed to Cosimo a spell which the old man was trying to cast so as to vanish, be obliterated, flown off, and then be reborn elsewhere, in another time or another place. But he was not much of a magician as he always reappeared just the same, though sometimes sucking a bitten thumb.

It was spring. One morning Cosimo saw the air vibrating with a sound he had never heard, a buzz growing at times almost into a roar, and a curtain of what looked like hail, which instead of falling was moving in a horizontal direction and turning and twisting slowly around, but following a kind of denser column. It was a great mass of bees; and around was greenery and flowers and sun; and Cosimo, he did not understand why, felt himself gripped by a wild and savage excitement. "The bees are escaping! Cavalier! The bees are escaping!" he shouted, running along the trees searching for Carrega.

"They're not escaping, they're swarming," said the voice of the Cavalier, and Cosimo saw he had sprung up like a mushroom below him and was making signs for him to be quiet. Then suddenly the old man ran off and vanished. Where had he gone to?

It was swarming time. A group of bees was following a queen bee outside the old hives. Cosimo looked around. Now the Cavalier reappeared from the kitchen door with a saucepan and ladle in his hand. He banged the ladle against the saucepan and raised a very loud dong-dong which resounded in the eardrums and died away in a long vibration so disturbing that it made Cosimo want to stop up his ears. The Cavalier was following the swarm of bees, hitting these copper instruments at every three steps. At each bang the swarm seemed seized by shock, made a rapid dip and turn, and its buzz lowered, its line of flight got more uncertain. Cosimo could not see well, but it seemed to him that the whole swarm was now converging toward a point in

the wood and not going beyond it. And Carrega went on banging his pots.

"What's happening, Cavalier? What are you doing?" my
brother asked him, coming up closer.

"Quick!" hissed the other. "Go to the tree where the swarm
has stopped, but be careful not to move it till I arrive!"

The bees were making for a pomegranate tree. Cosimo reached
it and at first saw nothing, then suddenly realized that what
looked like a big pine cone hanging from a branch, was in fact
bees clinging to each other, with more and more coming along to
make the cone bigger.

Cosimo stood at the top of the pomegranate, holding his
breath. Beneath him was the cluster of bees, and the bigger it became the lighter it seemed, as if it were hanging by a thread, or
even less, by the claws of an old queen bee; it was all thin tissue,
with rustling wings spreading diaphanous grays over the black
and yellow stripes on bellies.

The Cavalier came leaping up, holding a beehive in his hand.
He held it upside down under the cluster of bees. "Hey," he
whispered to Cosimo. "Give the branch a little shake, will you?"

Cosimo made the pomegranate just quiver. The swarm of
thousands of bees broke off like a leaf and fell into the hive, over
which the Cavalier put a plank. "There we are."

So between Cosimo and the Cavalier there arose an understanding, a collaboration which could almost have been called
friendship, if friendship did not seem too excessive a term for
two people who were both so unsociable.

My brother and Enea Silvio also got together, eventually,
on the subject of hydraulics. That may seem odd, for one living
on the trees must find it rather difficult to have anything to do
with wells and canals, but I have mentioned the kind of hanging
fountain Cosimo had made from a length of scooped-out poplar
to bring water from a fall to an oak. Now the Cavalier, though
apparently so vague, noticed everything that had to do with

moving water over the whole countryside. From above the cascade, hidden behind a privet hedge, he had watched Cosimo pull out this wooden pipe from between the branches of the oak (where he kept it when he did not use it, following the habit of wild animals, which had immediately become his, of hiding everything), prop it on a fork of the tree on one side and on some stones on the other, and drink.

At this sight something seems to have taken wing in the Cavalier's head; he was swept by a rare moment of euphoria. He jumped out of the bush, clapped his hands, gave two or three skips as if on a rope, splashed the water, and nearly jumped into the cascade and flew down the precipice. And he began to explain to the boy the idea he had had. The idea was confused and the explanation very confused. The Cavalier normally spoke in dialect—from modesty rather than ignorance of the language —but in these sudden moments of excitement he would pass from dialect to Turkish without noticing it, and not another word of his could be understood.

To make a long story short: his idea was a hanging aqueduct, with a conducting pipe held up by branches of trees, which would reach the bare slope of the valley opposite it and irrigate it. Cosimo supported the project at once, and suggested a refine-ment: using pierced tree trunks at certain points for the water to sprinkle over the crops like rain; this sent the Cavalier almost into ecstasy.

He rushed back to his study, and filled pages and pages with plans. Cosimo took to working on this idea too, for everything that could be done on trees pleased him, and gave, he felt, a new importance and authority to his position up there; and in Enea Silvio Carrega he seemed to have found an unexpected companion. They made appointments on certain low trees; the Cavalier would climb up with a triangular ladder, his arms full of rolls of drawings; and they would discuss for hours the ever more complicated developments of their aqueduct.

But it never reached a practical stage. Enea Silvio grew tired, his discussions with Cosimo became rarer, and after a week he probably forgot all about it. Cosimo did not regret it; he had soon realized it would become just a tiresome complication in his life and nothing else.

It was clear our uncle could have achieved much in the field of hydraulics. He had a bent for it—a particular turn of mind necessary to that branch of study—but he was incapable of putting his projects into practice; he would waste more and more time, until every plan ended in nothing, like badly channeled water which after whirling around a little is sucked up into the porous earth. The reason perhaps was this, that while he could dedicate himself to beekeeping, on his own, almost in secret, without having to deal with anyone, producing every now and again just a present of a honeycomb which no one had asked him for, this work of irrigation, on the other hand, meant considering the interests of this man or that, following the opinions and the orders of the Baron or of whoever else commissioned the work. Timid and irresolute as he was, he would never oppose the will of others, but would soon dissociate himself from the work and leave it.

He could be seen at all hours in the middle of a field among men armed with stakes and spades, he with a slide rule and the rolled sheet of a map, giving orders to dig for a canal and pacing the ground out by greatly exaggerating his normal stride. He would get the men to begin digging in one place, then in another, then call a halt, then start taking measurements again. Night fell and the work was suspended. Next day he would rarely resume work where they'd left off. And then for a week he was nowhere to be found. His passion for hydraulics consisted of aspirations, impulses, yearnings. It was a memory he had in his heart of the lovely, well-irrigated lands of the Sultan, of orchards and gardens in which he must have been happy, the only really happy time of his life; and to those gardens of Barbary or Turkey he would be continually comparing our countryside at Ombrosa, and so felt an urge to correct it, to try to identify it with the landscape in his memory, and being a specialist in hydraulics, he concentrated in that his desire for change, continually came up against a different reality, and was disappointed.

He also practiced water divining, not openly, though, for those were still times when that strange art could be considered witchcraft. Once Cosimo found him in a field twirling and holding a forked stick. That must have been just an experiment too, as nothing came of it.

Understanding the character of Enea Silvio Carrega was a help to Cosimo; it made him understand a lot about loneliness, which was to be of use to him later in life. I should say that he always carried with him the strange image of the Cavalier, as a warning of what can happen to a man who separates his own fate from others, and he managed never to be like him.

} 12 {

SOMETIMES Cosimo used to be awakened in the night by cries of "Help! Brigands! Quick!"

Off he would hurry through the trees toward the direction from which the cries were coming. This might turn out to be some peasant cottage, with a half-naked family outside tearing their hair.

"Help, help, Gian dei Brughi has just come and taken our whole earnings from the crop!"

People crowded together.

"Gian dei Brughi? Was it him? Did you see him?"

"Yes, it was! It was! He had a mask on his face and a long pistol, and he had two masked men behind him and was ordering 'em about! It was Gian dei Brughi!"

"And where is he? Where did he go?"

"Oh, catch Gian dei Brughi? He might be anywhere, by now!"

Or the shouts might be coming from a passer-by left in the middle of the road robbed of everything—horse, purse, cloak and baggage. "Help! Thief! Gian dei Brughi!"

"Which way did he go? Tell me!"

"He jumped out of there! Black, bearded, musket at the ready, I'm lucky to be alive!"

"Quick! Let's follow him! Which way did he go?"

"That way! No, perhaps this! He was running like the wind!"

Cosimo was determined to see Gian dei Brughi. He would go through the length and breadth of the wood behind hares or birds, urging on the dachshund: "Go on, to it, Ottimo Massimo!" What he longed for was to track down the bandit in person, not to do or say anything to him, but just to look someone so renowned in the face. But he never succeeded in meeting him, even by prowling all night. "That means he hasn't been out tonight," Cosimo would say to himself; but in the morning, on one side or other of the valley, he would find groups of people standing on their doorsteps or at a turn of the road and commenting on the new robbery. Cosimo would hurry up and listen with bated breath to their stories.

"But you're always on the trees in the woods," someone said to him. "Surely you must have seen Gian dei Brughi?"

Cosimo felt very ashamed. "But . . . I don't think so . . ."

"How could he have seen him?" asked another. "Gian dei Brughi has hiding places no one can find, and uses paths not a soul knows about!"

"With that reward on his head, whoever gets him can spend the rest of their lives in comfort!"

"Yes, indeed! But those who do know where he is have as many accounts with justice as he has, and if they say a word they'll go straight to the gibbet themselves!"

"Gian dei Brughi! Gian dei Brughi! But d'you think he really commits all these crimes himself?"

"Of course, he's got so much to account for that even if he managed to be cleared of ten thefts, he'd still be hanged for the eleventh!"

"He's been a brigand in all the woods along the coast!"

"He's even killed a leader of his, in his youth!"

"He's been banished by the bandits themselves!"

"That's why he's taken refuge in our area."

Cosimo would go and talk over every new incident with the colliers. Among the people camped in the wood, beside the colliers, tinkers and glass cutters, there were men who covered chairs in straw, rag-and-bone merchants, people who went around houses and planned in the morning the theft they would commit that night. In the woods they hid their loot in a secret refuge which was also their workshop.

"D'you know, Gian dei Brughi attacked a coach last night!"

"Ah yes? Well, maybe . . ."

"He stopped the galloping horses by grasping their bits!"

"Well, either it wasn't him or those horses were grass-hoppers . . ."

"What's that you're saying? Don't you believe it was Gian dei Brughi?"

"Ha, ha, ha!"

When he heard them talk of Gian dei Brughi like that, Cosimo did not know if he was on his head or his heels. He moved about the wood and went and asked another encampment of tramps.

"Tell me, d'you think that job on the carriage last night was Gian dei Brughi's?"

"Every job is Gian dei Brughi's, when it succeeds. Didn't you know?"

"Why, when it succeeds?"

"Because when it doesn't, it means it really *is* Gian dei Brughi's!"

"Ha, ha! That bungler!"

Cosimo could not understand at all. "D'you mean Gian dei Brughi's a bungler?"

The others then hurriedly changed their tone. "No, no, of course not, he's a brigand who frightens everyone!"

"Have you seen him yourself?"

"Us? Has anyone ever seen him?"

"But are you sure he exists?"

"What a thing to say! Sure he exists? Why, even if he didn't exist . . ."

"If he didn't exist?"

". . . it wouldn't make any difference. Ha, ha, ha!"

"But everyone says . . ."

"Sure, what should they say; that it's Gian dei Brughi who steals and robs everywhere, that terrible brigand! We'd just like to see anyone doubting that!"

"And you, boy, you don't doubt it, do you?"

Cosimo began to realize that Gian dei Brughi was more feared down in the valley, and that the farther one got into the woods, the more the attitude changed into one of doubt and even open derision.

So his longing to meet the brigand passed as he realized that the real experts did not bother about Gian dei Brughi at all. And it was just then that he did happen to come across him.

Cosimo was on a nut tree, one afternoon, reading. He had recently begun to pick up a few books again. Spending the whole day with a gun watching for a chaffinch gets boring in the long run.

Well, there he was reading Lesage's *Gil Blas*, holding his book in one hand and his gun in the other. Ottimo Massimo, who did not like seeing his master read, was wandering around in circles looking for excuses to disturb him; by barking, for instance, at a butterfly, to see if that would make Cosimo point his gun at it.

And then down the path from the mountain came running and panting a bearded, shabby, unarmed man, with two constables brandishing sabres and shouting behind him: "Stop him! Stop him! It's Gian dei Brughi! We've caught him, at last!"

Now the brigand had gained a little on the constables, but he was moving rather awkwardly as if afraid of mistaking the way or falling into a trap, and so having them soon on his heels again.

Cosimo's nut tree did not offer much chance for anyone to climb up it, but on his branch he had a rope which he always took about with him for difficult parts. He flung one end on to the ground and tied the other to the branch. The brigand saw this rope falling almost on his nose, faltered a moment, and then quickly clambered up, thus showing himself to be one of those impulsive waverers or wavering impulsives who always seem to be incapable of catching the right moment for doing anything and yet hit it every time.

The constables reached the spot. The rope had already been pulled up and Gian dei Brughi was sitting by Cosimo among the leaves of the nut tree. There was a fork in the path ahead. The constables took one each, then met again, and did not know where to go next. And then they bumped into Ottimo Massimo, who was sniffing around there.

"Hey," said one of the constables to the other, "doesn't that dog belong to the Baron's son, the one who's always up trees? If the boy is around anywhere here, he might be able to tell us something."

"I'm up here!" Cosimo called out. But he did it not from the nut tree where he had been before and where he had hidden the brigand, but from a chestnut opposite, to which he had quickly moved, so that the constables raised their heads at once in that direction without beginning to look at the trees around.

"Good day, your Lordship," said they. "You haven't by chance seen the brigand Gian dei Brughi?"

"I don't know who he is," replied Cosimo, "but if you're looking for a little man, running, he took the road over there by the stream . . ."

"A little man? He's a great big man who frightens everyone . . ."

"Well, from up here everyone seems quite small . . ."

"Thank you, your Lordship!" and they moved off toward the stream.

Cosimo went back into the nut tree and began to read *Gil Blas* again. Gian dei Brughi was still clinging to the branch, his face pale in the midst of red hair, his beard disheveled, stuck all over with dried leaves, chestnuts and pine needles. He was looking at Cosimo with a pair of green, round, stunned eyes; how ugly he was!

"Have they gone?" he decided to ask.

"Yes, yes," said Cosimo affably. "Are you the brigand Gian dei Brughi?"

"How d'you know me?"

"Oh, just by reputation."

"Are you the one who never comes down from the trees?"

"Yes. How do you know that?"

"Well, I hear of reputations too."

They looked at each other politely, like two respectable folk meeting by chance, who are pleased to find they are not unknown to each other.

Cosimo did not know what else to say, and began reading again.

"What are you reading?"

"Lesage's *Gil Blas*."

"Is it good?"

"Oh yes."

"Have you a lot more to read?"

"Why? Well, twenty pages or so."

"Because when you've finished it, I'd like to ask if I can borrow it." He smiled rather confusedly. "You know, I spend my days hiding, and never know what to do with myself. If I only had a book every now and then, I say. Once I stopped a carriage, very little in it, except for a book, and I took that. I brought it up with me, hidden under my jacket. I'd have given all the rest of the booty to keep that book. In the evening, lighting my lantern, I went to read it . . . it was in Latin! I couldn't understand a word . . ." He shook his head. "You see, I don't know Latin . . ."

"Oh well, Latin. That's difficult," said Cosimo, feeling that in spite of himself he was taking a protective attitude "This one is in French . . ."

"French, Tuscan, Provençal, Spanish—I can understand them all," said Gian dei Brughi, "and even a bit of Catalán; *bon dia! Bona nit! Está la mar molt alborotada!*"

In half an hour Cosimo finished the book and lent it to Gian dei Brughi.

And so began the friendship between my brother and the brigand. As soon as Gian dei Brughi had finished a book, he would quickly return it to Cosimo, take another out on loan, hurry off to hide in his secret refuge, and plunge into reading.

Before, I used to get Cosimo books from the library of our house, and when he had read them he would give them back to me. Now, he began to keep them longer, as after he had read them he would pass them to Gian dei Brughi, and they often came back with their covers stained, with marks of damp, streaks of snails, from the places where the brigand had kept them.

Cosimo and Gian dei Brughi would arrange meetings on stated days on a certain tree, exchange books and go off, as the woods were always being searched by police. This simple operation was very dangerous for both of them; for my brother, too, who would certainly not have been able to justify his friendship with that criminal! But Gian dei Brughi was taken with such a longing to read that he would devour novel after novel, and, as he spent the whole day long reading, he would devour in one day certain tomes which my brother had spent a week over, and then he had to have another at once, and if it was not the day for their meeting he would rush all over the countryside searching for Cosimo, terrifying families in all the cottages and setting the whole police force of Ombrosa on the move.

Now, Cosimo, being always pressed by the bandit's demands, began to find that the books I got him were not enough, and he had to go and find other supplies. He knew a Jewish book-dealer named Orbecche, who also got him works in a number of volumes. Cosimo would go and knock at his window from the branches of a carob tree, bringing him hares, thrushes, and partridges he had shot, which he would exchange for books.

But Gian dei Brughi had his own special tastes; one could not give him just any book, or he would return it to Cosimo the next day to have it exchanged. My brother was at the age at which people begin to enjoy more serious reading, but he was forced to go slowly, as Gian dei Brughi had brought him back the *Adventures of Telemachus*, warning him that if he gave him such a dull book another time, he would saw the tree down from under him.

At this point Cosimo would have liked to separate the books which he wanted to read leisurely by himself, from those which he got only to lend the bandit. But this was impossible, for he had to read these over too, as Gian dei Brughi became more exacting and distrustful, and before taking a book he wanted Cosimo to tell him something about the plot, and made a great fuss if he caught him out. My brother tried to pass him some light novels; and the brigand came back furiously asking if he'd taken him for a woman. Cosimo never could succeed in guessing what he would like.

In fact, with Gian dei Brughi always at him, reading, instead of just being Cosimo's pastime for half an hour, became his chief occupation, the aim of his entire day. And what with handling the books, judging and acquiring them and getting to know of new ones, what with his reading for Gian dei Brughi and his own increasing need to read as well, Cosimo acquired such a passion for reading and for all human knowledge, that the hours from dawn to dusk were not enough for what he would have liked to read, and he, too, would go on by the light of a lantern.

Finally, he discovered the novels of Richardson. Gian dei Brughi liked these. Having finished one, he immediately wanted another. Orbecche got Cosimo a whole pile of volumes. The brigand now had enough to read for a whole month. Cosimo, having found peace again, plunged into the *Lives* of Plutarch.

Gian dei Brughi, meanwhile, lying in his hiding place, his coarse red hair full of dried leaves and hanging down his wrinkled forehead, his green eyes growing red in the effort to see, was reading and reading, moving his jaws in a frenzied spelling motion, holding up a finger damp with saliva ready to turn the page. This reading of Richardson seemed to bring out a disposition long latent in him; a yearning for the cozy habits of family life, for relations, for sentiments known in the past, a sense of virtue and of dislike for the wicked and vicious. Nothing around him interested him any more, or it filled him with disgust. He never came out of his nest now, except to run to Cosimo to exchange a volume, particularly if it was a novel in many volumes and he had got to the middle of the story. And so he lived in isolation, without realizing the storm of resentment gathering around his head, even among the inhabitants of the wood who had once been his confidants and accomplices, but were tired now of an inactive brigand who still had the whole of the local police force after him.

In the past, around him had gathered all the locals who had fallen foul of the police, even in small ways: petty thieves such as the vagabonds, and tinkers, or real criminals, such as his bandit comrades. These people not only made use of his authority and experience for each of their thefts or raids, but also used his name as a cover, for it would go by word of mouth, and leave them unknown. And even those who did not take part in these operations drew advantage from their success, for the wood would fill with stolen goods and contraband of every kind which had to be disposed of or resold, and all those who trafficked round there did good business. And then anyone who did a job of thieving on his own account, unknown to Gian dei Brughi, would use that terrible name to frighten his victims and get more out of them; people lived in terror, thinking they saw Gian dei Brughi or one of his band in every evildoer they came across, and so loosen the strings of their purses.

These good times had lasted a long while; then gradually Gian dei Brughi found he could live on unearned income and draw apart more and more. It would all go on like this forever, he thought, instead of which things changed, and his name no longer inspired the reverence it had before.

What use was he, Gian dei Brughi, now? With him tucked away somewhere, bleary-eyed, reading novels, never doing a job, never getting any stuff, people couldn't go about their business quietly any longer, what with the police always around looking for him and arresting anyone at the slightest suspicion. Add the temptation of the price on Gian dei Brughi's head, and it is obvious the poor bandit's days were numbered.

Two other brigands, youths who had been taught by him and could not resign themselves to losing such a fine leader, decided to give him a chance to rehabilitate himself. They were named Ugasso and Bel-Lorè, and, as boys, had been in the band of fruit stealers. Now, as youths, they had become apprentice brigands.

So they went to see Gian dei Brughi in his cave. There he was, lying on the straw. "Yes, who is it?" he muttered, without raising his eyes from the page.

"We've an idea to discuss, Gian dei Brughi."

"Mmmmm . . . what idea?" and he went on reading.

"Do you know where Costanzo the exciseman's house is?"

"Yes, yes . . . eh? Who? What exciseman?"

Bel-Lorè and Ugasso exchanged an irritated look. If the brigand didn't take that accursed book from under his eyes, he wouldn't understand a single word they said. "Do shut that book a moment, Gian dei Brughi, and listen to us."

Gian dei Brughi seized the book with both hands, got up on his knees and made as if to hold it against his chest while keeping it open at the mark. Then the urge to go on reading was too much and, still holding it tight against him, he raised it enough to plunge his nose in again.

Bel-Lorè had an idea. He saw a cobweb with a big spider on it. Bel-Lorè raised the cobweb with the spider on top and threw it at Gian dei Brughi, between his book and his nose. And poor Gian dei Brughi had gone so soft he was even frightened of a spider. He felt the spider's legs tickling and the web sticking to his nose, and without even understanding what it was, gave a little yelp of disgust, dropped the book and began fanning his hands in front of his face, with starting eyes and dribbling mouth.

Ugasso swooped down and managed to seize the book before Gian dei Brughi could put a foot on it.

"Give me back that book!" said Gian dei Brughi, trying to free himself from spider and web with one hand, and tear the book from Ugasso's hand with the other.

"No, listen to us first!" said Ugasso, hiding the book behind his back.

"I was just reading *Clarissa*. Do give it back! I'd just reached a bit . . ."

"Listen to us. Tonight we're to take a load of wood to the exciseman's house. In the sack, instead of wood, there'll be you. When it's dark, you come out of the sack . . ."

"But I want to finish *Clarissa!*" He had managed to free his hands from the last remains of the cobweb and was struggling with the two youths.

"Listen to us . . . when it's dark, you come out of the sack, armed with pistols, get the exciseman to give you all the week's take, which he keeps in the coffer at the head of the bed . . ."

"Do just let me finish the chapter . . . pl-e-ease."

The two youths thought of the times when Gian dei Brughi used to plant a pair of pistols in the belly of anyone who dared contradict him. It gave them a twinge of nostalgia. "Well, you take the bags of money, d'you understand?" They went on sadly. "Bring 'em back to us, and we'll give you your book back, so's you can read to your heart's content. All right? You going?"

"No. It's not all right. I'm not going!"

"Ah, not going, aren't you . . . so you're not going . . . Well, we'll just see!" And Ugasso took a page toward the end of the book ("No!" screamed Gian dei Brughi), tore it out ("No, stop!"), crumpled it up and threw it in the fire.

"Ah! Swine! You can't do that! I shan't know how it ends!" And he ran after Ugasso to snatch the book.

"Are you going to the exciseman's then?"

"No, I'm not!"

Ugasso tore out another two pages.

"Stop! I haven't reached that yet! You can't burn them!"

Ugasso had already flung them in the fire.

"Swine! *Clarissa!* No!"

"Well, are you going?"

"I . . ."

Ugasso tore out another three pages and flung them in the flames.

Gian dei Brughi threw himself down with his head in his hands. "I'll go," he said. "But promise you'll wait with the book outside the exciseman's."

So the brigand was thrown in a sack with branches covering his head. Bel-Lorè carried the sack on his shoulders. Behind came Ugasso with the book. Every now and again, when Gian dei Brughi by a jerk or groan inside the sack seemed to be regretting his bargain, Ugasso let him hear the sound of a page being torn out, and Gian dei Brughi would calm down at once.

By this method they took him as far as the exciseman's, dressed up as colliers, and left him there. Then they went and hid a short way off, behind an olive tree, waiting for him to perform the robbery.

But Gian dei Brughi was in too much of a hurry, and came out of the sack before dark, when the place was still full of people.

"Up with your hands!" he called. But he wasn't the same man as before; he seemed to be seeing himself from the outside, and felt a little ridiculous. "Up with your hands, I said. Get against the wall, all of you . . ."

Oh dear, he didn't believe it himself. He was just acting. "Is this the lot?" He hadn't noticed that a child had escaped.

Well, there wasn't a minute to be lost on a job of that kind. But he dragged it out, the exciseman pretended to be stupid and not able to find the keys. Gian dei Brughi realized they were no longer taking him seriously and felt rather pleased at this deep down.

Finally, he came out, his arms loaded with bags of coins, and ran almost blindly toward the olive tree fixed as the meeting place.

"Here's the lot! Now give me back *Clarissa!*"

Four—seven—ten arms flung themselves around him, gripped him from shoulder to ankle. He was raised up bodily and tied like a sausage. "You'll see Clarissa behind bars!" and they took him off to prison.

The prison was a small tower beside the sea. A pine copse grew nearby. From the top of one of these pine trees, Cosimo could get quite near Gian dei Brughi's cell and see his face through the grate.

The brigand did not worry about his interrogation or trial. Whatever happened, his only worry was those empty days in prison without being able to read, with that novel left half finished. Cosimo managed to lay hands on another copy of *Clarissa* and took it up on the pine tree.

"What part did you get to?"

"The part where Clarissa is escaping from the brothel!" Cosimo turned over a few pages. "Ah, yes, here we are. Well . . ." and facing the grate, on which he could see Gian dei Brughi's gripping hands, he began reading out loud.

The prosecution took a long time preparing its case. The bandit resisted the rack; it took days to make him confess each one of his innumerable crimes. So before and after the interrogations every day he would listen to Cosimo reading. When *Clarissa* was finished, Cosimo saw that Gian dei Brughi was rather sad, and it struck him that Richardson might be a little depressing to one shut up like that, so he decided to start on a novel by Fielding whose plot and movement might give him back a sense of his lost liberty. That was during the trial, and Gian dei Brughi could think of nothing but the adventures of Jonathan Wilde.

The day of execution came before the novel was finished. Gian dei Brughi made his last journey in the land of the living on a cart with a friar. Hangings at Ombrosa were from a high oak in the middle of the square. The whole population was standing around in a circle.

When his head was in the noose, Gian dei Brughi heard a whistle between the branches. He raised his face. There was Cosimo with a shut book.

"Tell me how it ends," said the condemned man.

"I'm sorry to tell you, Gian," answered Cosimo, "that Jonathan ends hanged by the neck."

"Thank you. Like me! Good-by!" And he himself kicked away the ladder and was strangled.

When the body ceased to twitch, the crowd went away. Cosimo remained till nightfall, astride the branch from which the hanged man was dangling. Every time a crow came near to peck at the corpse's eyes or nose, Cosimo chased it away with a wave of his cap.

} 13 {

FROM this time spent in the brigand's company Cosimo had acquired a passion for reading and study which remained with him for the rest of his life. The attitude in which we now usually found him was astride a comfortable branch with a book open in his hand, or leaning over the fork of a tree as if he were on a school bench, with a sheet of paper on a plank and an inkstand in a hole in the tree, writing with a long quill pen.

Now it was he who would go and look for the Abbé Fauchele-fleur to give him lessons, to explain Tacitus or Ovid and the celestial bodies and the laws of chemistry. But the old priest, apart from a bit of grammar and bit of theology, was floundering in a sea of doubts and lack of knowledge, and at his pupil's questions he would open his arms and raise his eyes to the sky.

"*Mon Abbé*, how many wives can one have in Persia?" "*Mon Abbé*, who is the Savoyard Vicar?" "*Mon Abbé*, can you explain the system of Linnaeus?"

"*Alors* . . . *Maintenant* . . . *Voyons* . . ." the Abbé would begin, then hesitate and go no further.

But Cosimo, who was devouring books of every kind, and spending half his time in reading and half in hunting, in order to pay the bookseller's bills, always had some new story to tell him. Of Rousseau botanizing on his walks through the forests of Switzerland, or Benjamin Franklin trying to capture lightning with a kite, of the Baron de la Hontan living happily among the Indians of America.

Old Fauchelefleur seemed to listen to all this with surprised attention, whether from real interest or only from relief at not having to teach himself, I don't know; and he would nod and interject a "*Non! Dites-moi!*" when Cosimo turned to him and asked "Do you know how it is that . . . ?" or with a "*Tiens! C'est bien épatant!*" when Cosimo gave him a reply; and sometimes a "*Mon Dieu!*" which could be either from exaltation at this new revelation of the greatness of God, or from regret at the omnipresence of Evil still rampant in the world under so many guises.

I was too much of a boy and Cosimo's only friends were illiterate—hence his need to comment on the discoveries he kept on making in books found an outlet in this spate of questions and rejoinders to the old tutor. The Abbé, of course, had the gentle accommodating outlook that comes from a higher understanding of the vanity of all; and Cosimo profited by it. Thus the relationship of pupil and teacher between the two was reversed. It was Cosimo who became the teacher and Fauchelefleur the pupil. And my brother was acquiring such authority that he even managed to drag the trembling old man behind him up into the trees. He made him spend an entire afternoon with his thin legs dangling from a chestnut tree, in the Ondariva gardens, contemplating the rare plants and the sunset reflected in the basins of the fountains and discussing monarchies and republics, the right and truth in various religions, Chinese rituals, the Lisbon earthquake, the Leyden jar, and Condillac's philosophy called sensationism.

I was supposed to have my Greek lesson with him and could not find the tutor. The whole family was alerted, the countryside was searched and even the fishing pond dragged for him, lest in a careless moment he had fallen in and got drowned. But back he came that evening, complaining of lumbago after all the hours he had spent sitting so uncomfortably.

It must not be forgotten, though, that this state of general passive acceptance by the old Jansenist alternated with momentary returns of his old passion for spiritual rigor. And if while in a careless and yielding mood he accepted without resistance any new or libertarian idea, such as the equality of all men before the law, or the honesty of primitive people, or the bad influence of superstitions, he would be assailed a quarter of an hour later by an excess of austerity and absolutism, and attack with all his need for coherence and moral severity the ideas he had accepted so lightly just before. On his lips, then, the duties of free and equal citizens or the virtues of natural religion became hard and fast dogmatic rules, articles of fanatical faith, beyond which he could only see a black picture of corruption; to him, then, all the new philosophers were far too bland and superficial in their denunciation of evil, for the way of perfection was arduous and left no room for compromises or halfway measures.

To these sudden about-faces of the Abbé, Cosimo did not dare say a word, for fear of being criticized for incoherence and lack of rigor, and the prolific world which he tried to create would die as if in some marble cemetery. Luckily, the Abbé would soon tire of this sustained mental effort and would sit there looking exhausted, as if this whittling away of every concept to its pure essence left him the prey of impalpable shadows; he would blink, give a sigh, turn the sigh to a yawn, and go back into his nirvana.

But between one and another of these habits of mind, he was now spending his entire days following the studies being pursued by Cosimo, shuttlecocking between the trees where Cosimo was perched and Orbecche's shop, ordering books from Amsterdam or Paris, and taking out those newly arrived. And thus he prepared the way for his own downfall. For the rumor reached the Ecclesiastical Tribunal that there was a priest at Ombrosa who read all the most forbidden books in Europe. One afternoon the police appeared at our house with orders to inspect the Abbé's cell. Among his brevaries they found the works of Bayle, still uncut, but this was enough for them to take him away.

It was a sad little scene, on that misty afternoon; I remember the dismay with which I watched it from the window of my room, and stopped studying the conjugation of Greek verbs, as there would be no more lessons. Old Abbé Fauchelefleur went off down the alley between the two armed ruffians, raising his eyes toward the trees; and at a certain point he staggered as if he wanted to run to an elm tree and climb up it, but had not the strength. Cosimo was hunting in the woods that day and knew nothing of it all; so they did not even say good-by.

We could do nothing to help him. Our father shut himself up in his room and refused all food for fear of being poisoned by the Jesuits. The Abbé spent the rest of his days going back and forth between prison and monastery in continual acts of abjuration, until he died, after an entire life dedicated to the faith, without ever knowing what he believed in, but trying to believe firmly until the last.

Anyway, the Abbé's arrest had no effect on the progress of Cosimo's education. And from that period dates his correspondence with the major philosophers and scientists of Europe, to whom he wrote in the hope that they might resolve his queries and objections, or perhaps just for the pleasure of discussion with superior minds and also the practice of foreign languages. It was a pity that all his papers, which he kept in a hollow tree trunk known only to himself, have never been found and must certainly by now be moldy or nibbled away by squirrels; there would be letters among them in the handwriting of the best known scholars of the century.

To keep his books Cosimo constructed a kind of hanging bookcase, sheltered as best he could from rain and nibbling mouths. But he would continuously change them around, according to his studies and tastes of the moment, for he considered books as rather like birds and it saddened him to see them caged or still.

On the strongest of these bookcases were ranged the tomes of Diderot and D'Alembert's *Encyclopaedia* as they reached him from a bookseller at Leghorn. And though recently all his living with books had put his head rather in the clouds and made him less and less interested in the world around him, now on the other hand reading the *Encyclopaedia*, and beautiful words like *Abeille, Arbre, Bois, Jardin*, made him rediscover everything around him as if seeing it for the first time. Among the books he sent for there began also to figure practical handbooks—for example, one on tree culture—and he found himself longing for the moment when he could experiment with his new knowledge.

Human labor had always interested Cosimo but, just like a bird, up till now his life in the trees, his constant movements and his hunting had been enough to satisfy his sporadic, incongruous urges. Now, on the other hand, he found coming over him a need to do something useful for his neighbor. And this too, if one analyzes it, was something he had learned from his friendship with the brigand—the pleasure of making himself useful, of performing some service necessary to other people.

He learned the art of pruning trees, and offered his help to the fruitgrowers, in winter, when the trees stuck out an irregular maze of twigs and seemed to long for a change to more ordered forms so as to cover themselves with flowers and leaves and fruit. Cosimo was good at pruning and charged little; so every owner or tenant of an orchard around would ask for his help, and he could be seen, in the crystalline air of those early mornings, standing with legs apart on low bare branches, his neck wrapped in a

scarf to his ears, raising his shears and, *clip! clip!* off flew secondary branches and twigs under his sure touch. He did the same in
gardens with trees planted for shade or ornament, which he
would attack with a short saw, and in the woods, where instead
of the woodsman's ax, whose only use was chopping down some
ancient trunk completely, he would lop away with his swift
hatchet only on the tops and upper branches.

In fact, his love for this arboreal element made him, as all
real loves do, become merciless even to the point of hurting,
wounding and amputating so as to help growth and give shape.
Certainly he was always careful when pruning and lopping to
serve not only the interests of the owner but also his own, as a
traveler with a need to make his own routes more practicable;
thus he would see that the branches which he used as a bridge
between one tree and another were always saved, and reinforced
by the suppression of others. And so, these trees of Ombrosa
which he had already found so welcoming, now, with his newly
acquired skill, he made more directly helpful, thus being at
the same time a friend to his neighbor, to nature and to himself.
The advantages of this wise work of his he was to appreciate
above all at a much later period, when the shape of the trees
made up more and more for his loss of strength. Then, with the
advent of more careless generations, of improvident greed, of
people who loved nothing, not even themselves, all was to
change, and no Cosimo will ever walk the trees again.

} 14 {

IF THE number of Cosimo's friends grew, so did the number of
his enemies. The vagabonds of the wood, in fact, after Gian dei
Brughi's conversion to a love of literature and subsequent fall,
had gone against him. One night my brother was sleeping in

his leather bag hung on an ash tree in the wood, when he was awakened by the barking of the dachshund. He opened his eyes and saw a light. It came from down below. There was a fire right at the bottom of the tree and the flames were already licking the trunk.

A fire in the wood! Who could have set it going? Cosimo was quite certain he had never struck his flint that night. So it must have been those ruffians! They wanted to set the wood alight in order to get firewood and at the same time to put the blame on Cosimo and burn him alive.

At the moment Cosimo did not think of the danger which was threatening him so closely. His only thought was that the vast kingdom of paths and retreats which were his alone might be destroyed, and that was his only terror. Ottimo Massimo was already rushing away to avoid being burnt, turning around every now and again to give a desperate yelp. The fire was spreading in the undergrowth.

Cosimo did not lose heart. He had taken a variety of objects up in the ash tree which was then his refuge, and among these was a bottle full of barley water, to quench his summer thirst. He climbed to the bottle. Alarmed squirrels and bats were fleeing up the branches of the ash tree, and birds were flying away from their nests. He seized the bottle and was about to unscrew the cork and pour it over the trunk of the ash tree to save it from the flames, when he realized that the fire was already spreading to the grass, the dried leaves and bushes of the undergrowth, and would soon burn all the trees around. He decided to take a risk: "Let the ash burn! If I manage to wet the earth all around where the flames have not got to yet, I'll stop the fire!" And opening the top of the bottle he poured it down with a twisting, circular movement on to the farthest tips of fire, putting them out. And so the fire in the undergrowth found itself in the midst of a circle of damp grass and leaves, and could not spread any more.

From the top of the ash tree, Cosimo jumped down onto a beech nearby. He was only just in time. The trunk eaten away by fire at the base crashed down in a great funeral pyre amid the vain squeaks of squirrels.

Would the fire be limited to that point? Already hundreds of sparks and little flames were flying around; certainly the slippery barrier of wet leaves would not prevent its spreading! "Fire! Fire!" Cosimo began to shout at the top of his voice. "Fire!"

"Who's there? Who's shouting?" replied voices. Not far from the spot was a colliers' site, and a group of men from Bergamo—friends of his—were sleeping in a shack nearby.

"Fire! Fire!"

Soon the whole mountainside was resounding with the cry. The colliers scattered over the woods shouted it to each other in their incomprehensible dialect. They came running along from all directions. And the fire was subdued.

This first attempt at arson and the attack on his life should have warned Cosimo to keep clear of the wood. Instead of that he began going into the whole matter of controlling fires. It was the summer of a hot, dry year. In the coastal woods toward Provence, a huge fire had been burning for a week. At night its gleam reflected on the mountainside like the last of a sunset. The air was dry, trees and bushes like tinder in the drought. The wind seemed to be urging the flames in our direction, where occasional fires, either by chance or on purpose, would break out, joining the rest in a single belt of flame along the whole coast. Ombrosa was stunned by the danger, as if it were a fortress with a straw roof attacked by enemy incendiaries. The sky itself was charged with fire; every night shooting stars would fly all over the firmament and we would wait for them to fall right on us.

In those days of general dismay, Cosimo bought up a lot of barrels, filled them with water, and hoisted them up to the tops of the highest trees in strategic places. "One never knows, but this sort of thing's been useful once." Not content with this, he studied the courses of the streams crossing the woods, half dried up as they were, and found that their springs sent out only a trickle of water. Then he went to consult the Cavalier.

"Oh, yes," exclaimed Enea Silvio Carrega, clapping a hand to his forehead. "Reservoirs! Dykes! We must make plans!" and he broke out into little cries and jumps of enthusiasm with the myriad ideas crowding in his mind.

Cosimo set him to work at calculations and drawings, and meanwhile approached the owners of the private woods, the tenants of the public woods, the woodcutters, the colliers. All together, headed by the Cavalier (though the Cavalier did not come up to their heads, and was forced to direct them and not let his thoughts wander), with Cosimo superintending the work from above, they accumulated reserves of water in such a way that they could get pumps to every point where a fire might break out.

But this was not enough; squads of men had to be organized to put the fires out, groups who in case of alarm knew how to organize themselves at once into chains to pass buckets of water from hand to hand and halt the fire before it spread. So there appeared a kind of militia which took turns at guard and night inspection. The men were recruited by Cosimo among the peasants and artisans of Ombrosa. And at once, as happens in every association, there grew up a corporate spirit, a sense of competition between the groups. All felt capable of great things. Cosimo, too, felt a new strength and content. He had discovered his ability to bring people together and to put himself at their head—an aptitude which, luckily for himself, he was never called on to abuse, and which he used only a very few times in his life, always when there were important results to be carried out, and always with great success.

This he understood: that association renders men stronger and brings out each person's best gifts, and gives a joy which is rarely to be had by keeping to oneself, the joy of realizing how many honest decent capable people there are for whom it is worth giving one's best (while living just for oneself very often the opposite happens, of seeing people's other side, the side which makes one keep one's hand always on the hilt of one's sword).

So that was a good summer, the summer of the fires; there was a common problem which everyone, at heart, wanted to resolve, and each put it above every other personal interest, and all were repaid by the pleasure of finding themselves in agreement and mutual esteem with so many others.

Later Cosimo came to realize that when a problem in common no longer exists, associations are not as good as they were before, and it is better then to be a man alone and not a leader. But being a leader, meanwhile, he spent the nights all alone in the woods on sentry duty, up on a tree as he had always lived.

He had arranged a bell on the top of a tree which could be heard from a distance and give the alarm at the first glimmer of an incipient fire. By this system they managed to catch three or four fires in time, when they first broke out, and save the woods. The fires were attempts at arson, and the culprits were the two brigands Ugasso and Bel-Lorè, who were banished from the territory of the Commune. Rain set in at the end of August; the danger of fires had passed.

At that time one heard nothing but good said of my brother at Ombrosa. These favorable voices also reached our home—"How nice he is!" "He really does know about *some* things"—in the tone of people wanting to make an objective judgment on someone of a different religion or another political party, and trying to show themselves so open-minded that they can even appreciate ideas far removed from their own.

The reactions of the Generalessa to this news were brusque and summary. "Are they armed?" she would ask, when they talked of the squads of guards against fires formed by Cosimo. "Do they go on maneuvers?" For she was already thinking of the formation of an armed militia which could, in case of war, take part in military operations.

Our father, on the other hand, would listen in silence, shaking his head, so that it was difficult to understand if all these items of news about his son were painful to him or bored him, or flattered him in some way as if his one longing was a chance to hope in him again. This last must have been the right explanation, as a few days later he mounted his horse and went to look for him.

It was an open place, where they met, with a row of saplings around. The Baron rode up and down the row two or three times without looking at his son, though he had seen him. Jump by jump the boy moved down from the last tree until he got nearer and nearer. When he was facing Father he took off his straw hat (which took the place in summer of that cap of wild-cat fur) and said: "Good day, my Lord Father."

"Good day, son."

"Are you in good health?"

"Considering my years and sorrows."

"I am pleased to see you so well."

"That is what I want to say to you, Cosimo. I hear that you are busying yourself for the common good."

"I hold dear the forest in which I live, Lord Father."

"Do you know that a part of the wood is our property, inherited from your poor grandmother, the late Lady Elizabeth?"

"Yes, my Lord Father. In the Belrio area there are thirty chestnuts, twenty-two ashes, eight pines, and a maple. I have copies of all the surveyors' maps, and it was as a member of a family owning woods that I tried to collect together all those with a common interest in preserving them."

"Ah yes," said the Baron, receiving this answer favorably. "But," he added, "they tell me that it is an association of bakers, market-gardeners and blacksmiths."

"Them too, Lord Father. Of all professions that are honest."

"Do you realize that you could lead noble vassals with the title of Duke?"

"I realize that when I have more ideas than others, I give those others my ideas, if they want to accept them; and that, to me, is leading."

"And to lead, nowadays, d'you need to be on a tree?" was on the tip of the Baron's tongue to say. But what was the use of bringing that up again? He sighed, absorbed in his thoughts, then loosened the belt on which his sword was hanging. "You are now eighteen years of age . . . It is time you considered yourself an adult . . . I no longer have long to live . . ." and he held out the sword flat on his two hands. "Do you remember you are the Baron of Rondò?"

"Yes, Lord Father, I remember my name."

"Do you wish to be worthy of the name and title you bear?"

"I will try to be as worthy as I can of the name of man, and also of his every attribute."

"Take this sword—my sword." The Baron raised himself in his stirrups. Cosimo stooped down on the branch and the Baron managed to strap the belt around his waist.

"Thank you, Lord Father . . . I promise I will make good use of it."

"Farewell, my son." The Baron turned his horse, gave a slight tug at the reins, and rode slowly away.

Cosimo stood there a moment wondering whether he ought not to salute him with the sword, then reflected that his father had given it to him as a defense not as an instrument of ceremony, and he kept it sheathed.

} 15 {

IT WAS at this time, when he began seeing a lot of the Cavalier, that Cosimo noticed something odd in his behavior, or rather something different from usual, whether odder or less odd. It was as if that abstracted air of his no longer came from a wandering mind, but from a fixed and dominating thought. He would often, now, have talkative moments; and though before, unsociable as he was, he never set foot in the town, now, on the other hand, he was always down at the port, mingling with groups or sitting on the pavements with old sailors and boatmen, commenting on the arrival and departure of ships and the misdeeds of the pirates.

Off our coasts there still cruised the feluccas of the Barbary pirates, molesting our traffic. Nowadays it was petty piratage, no longer as in the days when an attack by pirates meant one's ending as a slave at Tunis or Algiers, or losing nose and ears. Now when the Mohammedans managed to overtake a tartan from Ombrosa, they took only the cargo: barrels of dried fish, rounds of Dutch cheese, bails of cotton and the like. Sometimes our people were faster and would escape, firing a round of grapeshot at the felucca's rigging; and the Barbary sailors would reply by spitting, making lewd gestures and shouting insults.

In fact, it was just petty piracy, and went on because the pashas of those countries claimed certain credits from our merchants and shipowners, which they exhorted, as according to them they had not been properly treated, or even cheated, in some business deal or other. And so they tried to settle their accounts piecemeal by robbery while at the same time continuing their commercial transactions, with constant bickering and bargaining. So it was to neither side's interest to come to a definite break; and navigation hereabouts went on full of hazards and risks, without ever degenerating to tragedy.

The story I am about to tell was narrated to me by Cosimo in a number of different versions; I am keeping to the one which had the most details and was also the most logical. My brother when describing his adventures certainly added many out of his own head, but I always try to give a faithful report of what he told me, as he is the only source.

Well, one night Cosimo, who since that watching for fires had got into the habit of waking up at all hours, saw a light coming down into the valley. He followed it silently over the branches with his cat's tread, and saw Enea Silvio Carrega walking along very quietly, in his fez and robe, holding a lantern.

What was the Cavalier, who usually retired to bed with the chickens, doing up at that hour? Cosimo followed some distance behind. He was careful not to make any noise, even knowing too that his uncle, when walking along so concentratedly, was as good as deaf and saw only a few inches in front of his nose.

By mule paths and short cuts the Cavalier reached the edge of the sea, on a stretch of pebbly beach, and began to wave his lantern. There was no moon and nothing could be seen on the sea, except moving foam on the nearest waves. Cosimo was on a pine tree a little way from the shore, as at that level the vegetation petered out and it was not so easy to get about on branches. Anyway, he could see quite clearly the old man in his high fez on the deserted beach, waving his lantern toward the dark sea; and then suddenly from that darkness another lantern replied, very near, as if it had been lit that minute, and there emerged, moving very fast, a little boat with a dark square sail and oars—a different boat from the ones of these parts—coming toward the shore.

By the quavering light of the lantern, Cosimo saw men with turbans on their heads; some remained on the boat and kept it to the beach with little strokes of the oars; others landed, and they had wide swelling red pantaloons, and gleaming scimitars tied to their waists. Cosimo was all eyes and ears. His uncle and the Berbers talked among themselves, in a language which he could not understand but which he felt he almost could grasp, and must surely be the famous Lingua Franca. Every now and again Cosimo understood a word or two in our language, which Enea Silvio would emphasize, mingling these with other incomprehensible words, and the words in Italian were the names of ships, well-known sloops and brigantines belonging to the shipowners of Ombrosa, plying between our port and others nearby.

It didn't require much imagination to realize what the Cavalier must have been saying! He was informing the pirates about the times of arrival and departure of the Ombrosa boats, and about the cargoes they were carrying, their routes, and the weapons they had on board. And now the old man must have told them everything he knew, for he turned around and hurried away, while the pirates climbed back onto their boat and vanished into the dark sea. From the speed at which they talked he realized that they must have done this often before. Who knows how long those Berbers' attacks had taken place because of the information supplied by our uncle!

Cosimo stayed on the pine tree, incapable of tearing himself away from there, from the deserted shore. A wind was blowing, waves were gnawing at the beach. The tree groaned in all its joints and his teeth chattered, not from the cold air, but from the cold of his sad discovery.

So that timid and mysterious old man whom we, as boys, had always judged to be false and whom Cosimo had thought he had gradually learned to appreciate and understand was now revealed as a miserable traitor, an ungrateful wretch willing to harm his own country, which had taken him in when he was but driftwood after a life of errors. Had he been swept to such a point of nostalgia for countries and people where he must have found himself, for once in his life, happy? Or did he nurture a deep rancor against the home in which every mouthful he ate must have been one of humiliation? Cosimo was divided between the impulse to rush off and denounce him as a spy and so save our merchants' cargoes, and the thought of the pain it would cause our father, because of the affection which linked him so inexplicably to his half brother. Cosimo could already imagine the scene: the Cavalier manacled amid police, between two rows of Ombrosans cursing him, and so being led to the square, having the noose put over his head, being hanged . . . After that night of watching over the dead body of Gian dei Brughi, Cosimo had sworn to himself that he would never again be present at an execution; and now he had to be the judge of whether to condemn to death one of his own relations!

This thought tortured him the whole night long and all of the next day too, as he moved endlessly from one branch to another, slipping, saving himself with his arms, letting himself slither on the bark, as he always did when preoccupied. Finally he made his decision; a compromise: to terrify both the pirates and his uncle, and put a stop to their criminal dealings without the intervention of the law. He would perch on that pine tree at night, with three or four loaded guns (by now he had collected an entire arsenal for his various hunting needs). When the Cavalier met the pirates he would begin firing one musket after another, making the bullets whistle over their heads. On hearing that firing, pirates and uncle would each make his own escape. And the Cavalier, who was certainly not brave, at the chance of being recognized and the certainty that his meetings on the beach were now watched, would be sure to break off relations with the Berber crew.

So Cosimo waited on the pine tree for a couple of nights, his muskets at the ready. And nothing happened. The third night, down came the old man in his fez, trotting along the pebbles of the beach, waving his lantern, and again a boat approached, with sailors in turbans.

Cosimo had his finger ready on the trigger, but did not fire, for this time everything was different. After a short colloquy, two of the pirates landed and signaled toward the boat and the others began unloading cargo: barrels, bales, sacks, demijohns, cases full of cheeses. There was not just one boat, but a number of them, all heavily loaded; and a row of porters in turbans began winding along the beach, preceded by our uncle, leading them with his hesitant steps to a cave among the rocks. There the Moors set down all those goods, certainly fruit of their latest piracies.

Why were they bringing this on shore? Later it was easy to reconstruct the circumstances. As the Berber felucca had to anchor in one of our ports (for some legitimate business, as was always going on between them and us in the middle of all their piracy) and therefore had to undergo a search by our customs, they had to hide their stolen goods in a safe place, so as to retrieve them on their return. In this way the men of the felucca would prove they had nothing to do with the latest robberies on the high seas, and strengthen their normal commercial relations with Ombrosa too.

All this was clear afterwards. At that moment Cosimo did not stop to ask himself questions. There was a pirate treasure hidden in a cave, the pirates were re-embarking and leaving it there; it must be moved as soon as possible. The first idea that crossed my brother's mind was to go and wake the merchants of Ombrosa, who were presumably the legitimate owners of the stuff. But then he remembered his collier friends starving in the woods with their families. He did not hesitate, but hurried off over the branches straight to where, around patches of gray beaten earth, the Bergamese were sleeping in rough shacks.

"Quick! Come on, all of you! I've found the pirates' treasure!"

From under the tents and branches of the shacks came puffing, shuffling, cursing, and finally exclamations of surprise, and questions. "Gold? Silver?"

"I haven't seen properly . . ." said Cosimo. "From the smell, I'd say that there was a lot of stockfish and goat's cheese."

At these words all the men of the woods sprang to their feet. Those of them who had muskets snatched them up, others took hatchets, spits, spades, or stakes, but they all took some receptacle or other to put the stuff into, even broken coal hods and blackened sacks. A long procession started. "Hura! Hota!" Even the women went down with empty baskets on their heads, and the boys all hooded in sacks, holding torches. Cosimo went ahead from land pine to olive, from olive to sea pine.

They were just about to reach the other side of the rock, with the cave opening beyond, when on top of a twisted fig tree appeared the white shadow of a pirate, who raised his scimitar and shouted the alarm. A few leaps and Cosimo was on a branch above him. He pointed his sword at the man's back, till he jumped over the cliff.

In the cave a meeting of the pirate chiefs was taking place. (Cosimo, in all that coming and going of unloading, had not realized they had stayed behind.) Hearing the sentinel's cry they came out and found themselves surrounded by a hoard of men and women black with charcoal, hooded in sacks and armed with stakes. Baring their scimitars the Moors rushed forward to cut a way through. "Hura! Hota!" "Inshiallah!" The battle began.

The colliers were superior in number, but the pirates better armed. It's well known, though, that for fighting scimitars there's nothing better than stakes. Cling! Cling! And the Damascene blades withdrew all jagged at the edges. Their muskets, on the other hand, thundered and smoked, but to no purpose. Some of the pirates (officers, as could be seen) had lovely muskets, entirely embossed; but the tinder had got damp in the cave and wouldn't spark. Now some of the colliers began stunning the pirate officers by hitting them over the head with stakes, to get their muskets away from them. But with those turbans, every blow on the Berbers' heads was muffled as if by cushions; it was better to kick them in the stomach, as their midriffs were bare.

Seeing that the one weapon in good supply was stones, the colliers began flinging them in handfuls. The Moors, then, began throwing stones back. With this stone throwing, the battle eventually took on a more orderly aspect, but as the colliers were trying to enter the cave, attracted more and more by the smell of stockfish coming out of it, and the Berbers were trying to escape toward their tender still on the beach, there was no great reason to fight.

Then the Bergamese launched an assault to break into the cave. The Mohammedans were still resisting under hails of stones when they saw the way to the sea was free. Why go on resisting, then? Better hoist sails and be off.

On reaching the boat, three pirates, all nobles and officers, unfurled the sails. With a leap from a pine tree on the beach, Cosimo flung himself onto the mast, gripped the crossbar at the top, and from up there, hanging on by the knees, unsheathed his sword. The three pirates raised their scimitars. My brother, with slashes to right and slashes to left, kept all three at bay. The boat was still beached and wobbling now from side to side. At that moment the moon came out and glinted on the sword given by the Baron to his son, and on the Mohammedan blades. My brother slipped down the mast and plunged his sword into the breast of a pirate who was dropping overboard. Up he went again, swift as a lizard, defending himself with two parries from the others' slashes, slid down once more and thrust the sword through a second pirate, went up, had a short skirmish with the third, slid down and transfixed him too.

The three Mohammedan officers were lying half in the sea, their beards full of seaweed. The other pirates at the cave mouth were stunned with stones and blows from stakes. Cosimo was looking triumphantly around from the top of the mast, when from the cave, like a cat with its tail afire, leaped the Cavalier Carrega, who had been hidden there till now. He ran up the beach with head down, gave the boat one shove, which floated it away from the beach, jumped in, seized the oars and began rowing as hard as he could out to sea.

"Cavalier! What are you doing! Are you mad?" said Cosimo, gripping the mast. "Go back to shore! Where are we going?"

No answer. It was clear that Enea Silvio Carrega wanted to reach the pirate ship to save himself. Now his felony had been discovered once and for all, and if he stayed on shore he would certainly end on the gibbet. So he rowed and rowed, and Cosimo, though he still had his bared sword in his hand and the old man was disarmed and weak, was at a loss what to do next. At bottom he didn't want to do his uncle any harm at all, and, another thing, to reach him he would have to come right down the mast and this descent onto a boat was equivalent to descending to earth, and the question whether he had not already deviated from his unspoken inner laws by jumping from a tree with roots to the mast of a boat was too complicated to think out at that moment. So he did nothing and settled on top of the mast, his legs astraddle, moving off on the waves, while a slight wind swelled the sail, and the old man never stopped rowing.

He heard a bark. And started with pleasure. The dog, Ottimo Massimo, whom he had lost sight of during the battle, was crouching there at the bottom of the boat, and wagging his tail as if nothing unusual was happening. Oh, well, reflected Cosimo, there was not so very much to worry about; it was a family reunion, what with his uncle and his dog; and he was going on a boating trip, which after so many years of arboreal life, was a pleasant diversion.

The moon shone on the sea. Now the old man was tiring. He was rowing with difficulty, sobbing and saying again and again: "Ah, Zaira . . . ah, Allah, Allah, Zaira . . . *Inshiallah* . . . !" then he'd relapse into Turkish, repeating over and over again amid tears this woman's name which Cosimo had never heard.

"What are you saying, Cavalier? What's the matter with you? Where are we going?" he asked.

"Zaira . . . Ah, Zaira . . . Allah, Allah . . ." exclaimed the old man.

"Who is Zaira, Cavalier? Do you think you are going to Zaira this way?" and Enea Silvio Carrega nodded his head, and spoke in Turkish in between sobs, and called that name out to the moon.

Cosimo at once began to mull over suppositions about this Zaira. Perhaps the deepest mystery of that reserved and mysterious man was about to reveal itself. If the Cavalier, going toward the pirate ship, hoped to join this Zaira, she must then be a woman out there, in those Ottoman lands. Perhaps the whole of his life had been dominated by nostalgia for that woman, perhaps she was the image of the lost happiness which he had expressed by raising bees and tracing irrigation channels. Perhaps she was a mistress, a wife whom he had left over there, in the gardens of those lands beyond the seas, or perhaps she was really his daughter, a daughter whom he had not seen since she was a child, to find whom he had tried for years to establish contact with one of the Turkish or Moorish ships that came to our parts, until finally he had got news of her. Perhaps he had learned that she was a slave, and as a ransom they had suggested his informing on the movements of the Ombrosan tartans. Or perhaps it was a price he had to pay in order to be readmitted among them and embark for the country of Zaira.

Now, his intrigue discovered, he was forced to flee from Ombrosa, and now the Berbers could not refuse to take him with them and carry him back to her. In his panting snatches of talk were mixed accents of hope, of invocation, and also of fear; fear that this might still not be the right opportunity, or that some mischance might still separate him from the creature for whom he yearned.

He was just getting to the end of his rope in rowing when a shadow drew near—another Berber boat. Perhaps from the ship they had heard the sounds of battle on the shore, and were sending out scouts.

Cosimo slipped halfway down the mast, so as to hide behind the sail, but the old man began to shout in Lingua Franca for them to fetch him and take him to the ship, stretching out imploring arms. His petition was granted; two janissaries in turbans, as soon as they were within reach, took him up by the shoulders, light as he was, and pulled him onto their boat. The boat Cosimo was on got pushed away, the wind caught the sail, and so my brother, who had really felt he was done for this time, escaped discovery.

As the wind bore him away from the pirate boat, Cosimo heard voices raised as if in argument. A word said by the Moors, which sounded like "Marrano!" and the old man's voice repeating faintly, "Ah, Zaira!" left no doubts as to the Cavalier's reception. Certainly they held him responsible for the ambush at the cave, for the loss of their booty and the deaths of their men, and were accusing him of treachery. . . . A last shout, a plop, then silence. And to Cosimo came as clearly as if he heard it, the sound of his father's voice shouting, "Enea Silvio! Enea Silvio!" as he followed his half brother over the countryside; and Cosimo hid his face in the sail.

He climbed the yard again, to see where the boat was going. Something was floating in the midst of the sea as if carried by a current, an object, a kind of buoy, but a buoy with a tail . . . A ray of moonlight fell on it, and he saw that it was not an object but a head, a head stuck in a fez with a tassel, and he recognized the upturned face of the Cavalier looking up with his usual abstracted air and his mouth open; but below the beard the rest of him was in the water and could not be seen, and Cosimo shouted: "Cavalier! What are you doing? What are you doing? Why don't you get in? Catch hold of the boat! I'll help you in, Cavalier!"

But his uncle did not answer; he was floating, floating, looking up with that dismayed air as if he could see nothing. And Cosimo said: "Hey! Ottimo Massimo! Throw yourself in the water! Take the Cavalier by the nape of the neck! Save him! Save him!"

The obedient dog plunged in, tried to get his teeth into the old man's nape, did not succeed, and took him by the beard.

"By the nape, I said, Ottimo Massimo!" insisted Cosimo, but the dog raised the head by the beard and pushed it to the edge of the boat, and then it could be seen that there was no nape of neck any more; no body or anything, just a head; the head of Enea Silvio Carrega struck off by the stroke of a scimitar.

} 16 {

THE first version of the Cavalier's end, as given by Cosimo, was very different. When the wind brought the boat to the shore, with him clinging to the crossbar and Ottimo Massimo dragging the truncated head, he told the people who came hurrying to his call a very simple story (meanwhile he quickly moved into a tree with the help of a rope); that the Cavalier had been kidnapped by the pirates and then killed. Perhaps it was a version prompted by the thought of his father, who would be so struck down with sorrow at the news of his half brother's death and the sight of that pathetic relic that Cosimo lacked the heart to load him with the revelation of the Cavalier's felony too. In fact, afterwards, when he heard of the deep gloom into which the Baron had fallen, he tried to make up an imaginary glory for our natural uncle, inventing a secret and astute intrigue against the pirates to which the Cavalier had dedicated himself for some time and whose discovery had brought him to his death. But this account was contradictory and full of holes, also because there was something else that Cosimo wanted to hide, which was the unloading of the stolen goods by the pirates in the cave and the intervention of the colliers. For, if the whole story had been known, the entire population of Ombrosa would have gone into the woods to take their merchandise back from the Bergamese, and would have treated them as robbers.

After a week or so, when he was certain that the colliers had disposed of the goods, he told of the assault on the cave, and anyone who went up to try and recover their property came back with empty hands. The colliers had divided it all up into equal parts: the stockfish fillet by fillet, and with the sausages and cheeses, and all the rest they had made a great banquet which lasted all day.

Our father had aged very much, and sorrow over the loss of Enea Silvio had strange effects on his behavior. He was taken by a mania to prevent any of his brother's work being lost, so he insisted on looking after the beehives himself, and set to work with great ceremony, though he had never before seen a beehive close up. For advice he turned to Cosimo, who had learned something about them; not that he would ask him direct questions, but just draw the conversation on to apiculture, listen to what Cosimo said, and then repeat it as orders to the peasants in an irascible self-sufficient tone, as if it were all quite obvious. To the hives themselves he tried not to get too close for fear of being stung, but he was determined to conquer this phobia, and must have gone through agonies because of it. He also gave orders for certain watercourses to be dug, in order to carry out a project initiated by poor Enea Silvio; and had he succeeded it would have been an excellent thing, as his poor dear brother had never completed a single one.

This belated passion of the Baron for practical affairs lasted only a short time, alas. One day he was busying himself nervously among the beehives and watercourses when, at some brusque movement of his, a swarm of bees made for him. He took fright, began to wave his hands about, overturned a beehive, and rushed off with a cloud of bees behind him. He ran blindly, fell into the channel which they were trying to fill with water, and was pulled out soaking wet.

He was put to bed. What with a fever from the stings, and another from the wetting, he was in bed a week. Then he was more or less cured, but he went into such a decline that he never pulled up again.

He had lost the will to live and would stay in bed all day long. Nothing in his life had turned out as he hoped. No one mentioned the dukedom any more. His eldest son spent his whole life on trees even now that he was grown up; his half brother had been murdered; his daughter was far away and married into a family even more unpleasant than herself; I was too young to be anything of a companion; his wife too impulsive and hectoring. He began getting hallucinations that the Jesuits had taken over his house and would not allow him to leave his room, and so, bitter and bizarre as he had lived, he came to death.

Cosimo followed the funeral too, from one tree to another, but he could not enter the cemetery, as the branches of cypresses are too close together to climb. He watched the burial from beyond the cemetery wall and when we all flung a handful of earth on the coffin he threw down a small branch of leaves. We had all, I thought, been as far removed from my father as Cosimo was in the trees.

So now Cosimo was Baron of Rondò. There was no change in his life. He looked after the family interests, it is true, but always rather haphazardly. When the bailiffs and tenants wanted to find him they did not know where to look; and just when they least wanted him to see them, there he would be on a branch.

Partly in connection with estate matters, Cosimo was now more often seen in the town, perched on the big nut tree in the square or on the ilexes by the quays. The people treated him with great respect, called him "Lord Baron," and he came to take on certain attitudes of an older man, as young men sometimes do, and would sit there telling stories to groups of Ombrosians, clustered around the foot of the tree.

He would often describe our uncle's end, though never twice in the same way, and bit by bit he began to disclose the Cavalier's complicity with the pirates. But in order to prevent the immediate upsurge of indignation from all below, he at once added the story of Zaira, almost as if Carrega had confided it to him before dying; and eventually he even moved them to sympathy over the old man's sad end.

From complete invention, Cosimo, I believe, had arrived, by successive approximations, at an almost entirely truthful account of the facts. He told this two or three times; then finding his audience never tired of listening to the story and new listeners always coming and asking for details, he found himself making new additions, amplifying, exaggerating, and introducing new characters and episodes, so that the tale got quite distorted and became even more of an invention than it had been at first.

Cosimo now had a following which would listen open-mouthed to everything he said. He began to enjoy telling stories about his life on the trees, and his hunting, and the brigand Gian dei Brughi, and the dog Ottimo Massimo. They all became material for tales that went on and on and on. (Many episodes in this account of his life are taken from what he would narrate at the request of his rustic audience, and I mention this to excuse myself if not all I write seems likely or conforming to a harmonious view of humanity and fact.)

For example, one of the idlers would ask: "But is it true you have never once set foot off the trees, Lord Baron?"

And that would start Cosimo off. "Yes, once, but by mistake. I climbed the horns of a stag. I thought I was passing on to a maple tree, and it was a stag escaped from the royal game preserve, standing still at that particular spot. The stag felt my weight on its horns and ran off into the wood. You can imagine the state I was in. Up there I felt things sticking into me all over; what with the sharp points of the horns, the thorns, the branches hitting my face . . . The stag backed, trying to rid itself of me. I held on tight . . ."

There he would pause, and wait till the others asked: "And how did you get out of that, sir?"

And every time he would bring out a different ending. "The

stag raced on and on, reached the herd, most of which scattered at seeing it with a man on its horns, while some came up from curiosity. I aimed the gun I still had slung over my shoulder and brought down every stag I saw. I killed fifty of 'em . . ."

"Have there ever been fifty stags round these parts?" asked one of those loiterers.

"It's extinct now, that breed. For those fifty were all does, d'you see? Every time my stag tried to get close to a doe, I fired and the animal fell dead. The stag simply did not know what to do next. Then . . . then it suddenly decided to kill itself, rushed on to a high rock and flung itself down. But I managed to cling on to a jutting pine tree, and here I am!"

Or he would tell how a fight had started between two of the stags with horns and at every clash he jumped from the horns of one to the horns of the other, till at a particular sharp butt he found himself tipped on to an oak tree . . .

In fact he was carried away by that mania of the storyteller, who never knows which stories are more beautiful—the ones that really happened and the evocation of which recalls a whole flow of hours past, of petty emotions, boredom, happiness, insecurity, vanity, and self-disgust, or those which are invented, and in which he cuts out a main pattern, and everything seems easy, then begins to vary it as he realizes more and more that he is describing again things that had happened or been understood in lived reality.

Cosimo was still at the age when the desire to tell stories makes one want to live more, thinking one has not done enough living to recount, and so off he would go hunting, and be away weeks, then return to the trees in the square, dangling by their tails polecats, badgers and foxes, and tell the folk of Ombrosa new stories, which originally true, became, as he told them, invented, and from invented, true.

But behind all this restlessness of his there was a deeper dissatisfaction, and in this need for listeners, a different lack. Cosimo did not yet know love, and what is any experience without that?

What point is there in risking life, when the real flavor of life is as yet unknown?

Peasant girls and fishmongers used to pass through the square of Ombrosa, and young ladies in coaches, and Cosimo would look them sharply over from the trees, unable to understand why something that he was looking for was there in all of them, and not there completely in any one of them. At night, when the lights went on in the houses, and Cosimo was alone on the branches with the yellow eyes of the owls, he would begin dreaming of love. The couples who met behind bushes or amidst vines filled him with admiration and envy, and he would follow them with his eyes as they went off into the dark, but if they lay down at the foot of his particular tree, he would rush off in embarrassment.

Then, to overcome his shyness, he would stop and watch the love-making of animals. In the spring the world on the trees was a world of nuptials; the squirrels made love with squeals and movements that were almost human, the birds coupled with flapping wings; even the lizards slid off united, with their tails tight in knots; and the porcupines seemed to soften their quills to sweeten their embraces. Ottimo Massimo, in no way put off by the fact that he was the only dachshund in Ombrosa, would court big shepherd bitches, or police dogs, with brazen ardor, trusting to the natural sympathy this inspired. Sometimes he would return bitten all over; but a successful love affair was enough to repay for all defeats.

Cosimo, like Ottimo Massimo, was the only example of a species. In his daydreams, he would see himself courting girls of exquisite beauty; but how could he fall in love up in the trees? In his fantasies, he managed to avoid specifying where it would happen; on earth, or up in the element where he lived now: a place without a place, he would imagine; a world reached by going up, not down. Yes, that was it. Perhaps there was a tree so high that by climbing it, he would touch another world—the moon.

Meanwhile, as this habit of chattering in the square grew, he began to feel less and less satisfied with himself. And then, one market day, a man who came from the nearby town of Olivabassa exclaimed: "Ah, so you've got your Spaniard too, I see!" When asked what he meant, he replied: "At Olivabassa there's a whole tribe of Spaniards living on the trees!" Cosimo could not rest till he made the journey through the woods to Olivabassa.

} 17 {

OLIVABASSA was a town in the interior. Cosimo reached it after two days' journey and many a dangerous passage over the less wooded parts of the route. Whenever he passed near any houses, people who had never seen him before gave cries of surprise, and one or two of them even threw stones at him, so that he tried to move as inconspicuously as possible. But as he neared Olivabassa, he noticed that any woodman or ploughman or olive picker who saw him showed no surprise at all, in fact the men even greeted him by doffing their hats as if they knew him, and said words which were certainly not in the local dialect and sounded strange in their mouths, such as "*Señor! Buenos días, Señor!*"

It was winter; some of the trees were bare. In Olivabassa a double row of elms and plane trees crossed the town. And my brother, as he came nearer, saw that there were people up on the bare branches, one, two, or even three to each tree, sitting or standing in grave attitudes. In a few jumps he reached them.

There were men in noble garb, plumed tricorns, big cloaks; and noble-looking women too, with veils on their heads, sitting on the branches in twos and threes, some embroidering, and looking down on to the road now and then with a little sideways jerk of the bosom and a stretch of their arms along the branch, as if at a window sill.

The men bade him greetings that seemed full of rueful understanding: "*Buenos días, Señor.*" And Cosimo bowed and doffed
his hat.

One who seemed the most authoritative, a heavily built man
wedged in the fork of a plane tree from which he appeared unable to extricate himself, with a liverish complexion through
which his shaved chin and upper lip showed black shadows in
spite of his advanced years, turned to his neighbor, a pale gaunt
man dressed in black and also with cheeks blackish in spite of
shaving, and seemed to be asking who was this unknown man
coming toward them across the trees.

Cosimo thought the moment had come to introduce himself.
He moved on to the stout gentleman's plane tree, bowed and
said: "The Baron Cosimo Piovasco di Rondò, at your service."

"*Rondos?*" exclaimed the fat man, "*Rondos? Aragonés? Gali-
ciano?*"

"No, sir."

"*Catalán?*"

"No, sir. I am from these parts."

"*Desterrado también?*"

The gaunt gentleman now felt it his duty to intervene and act
as interpreter, very bombastically, with: "His Highness Federico
Alonso Sánchez y Tobasco asks if your lordship is also an exile,
as we see you climbing about on branches."

"No, sir. Or, at least, not exile by anyone else's decree."

"*Viaja usted sobre los árboles por gusto?*"

And the interpreter: "His Highness Federico Alonso is gracious
enough to ask if it is for pleasure that your lordship uses this
mode of travel."

Cosimo thought a little, then replied: "I do it because I think
it suits me, not because I'm forced to."

"*Felíz usted!*" exclaimed Federico Alonso Sánchez, sighing.
"*Ay de mi, ay de mi!*"

And the man in black began explaining, more bombastically
than ever: "His Highness deigns to say that your lordship is to
be held fortunate in enjoying such a liberty, which we cannot

but compare to our own restriction, endured, however, with resignation to the will of God," and he crossed himself.

And so, from Prince Sánchez' laconic exclamations and a detailed account by the gentleman in black, Cosimo succeeded in reconstructing the story of this colony living on plane trees. They were Spanish nobles who had rebelled against King Charles III about certain contested feudal privileges, and been exiled with their families as a result. On reaching Olivabassa they had been forbidden to continue their journey. Those parts, in fact, on account of an ancient treaty with His Catholic Majesty, could neither give hospitality nor even allow passage to persons exiled from Spain. The situation of those noble families was a very difficult one to cope with, but the magistrates of Olivabassa, who wanted to avoid any trouble with foreign chancelleries, but also had no aversion to these rich foreigners, came to an understanding with them. The letter of their treaty laid down that no exiles were to "touch the soil" of their territory; they only had to be up on trees, and all was in order. So the exiles had climbed up onto the elms and plane trees, on ladders supplied by the commune, which were then taken away. They had been roosting up there for some months, putting their trust in the mild climate, the hoped-for arrival of a decree of amnesty from Charles III, and Divine Providence. They were well supplied with Spanish doubloons and bought many supplies, thus giving trade to the town. To draw up the dishes they had installed a system of pulleys. And on other trees they had set up canopies under which they slept. In fact they had settled themselves very comfortably, or rather, the people of Olivabassa had settled them well, as it was to their advantage. The exiles, for their part, never moved a finger the whole day long.

It was the first time Cosimo had ever met other human beings living on trees, and he began to ask practical questions.

"And when it rains, what do you do?"

"*Sacramos todo el tiempo, Señor.*"

Then the interpreter, who was Father Sulpicio de Guadalete, of the Society of Jesus, an exile since his Order had been banned in Spain, explained: "Protected by our canopies, we turn our thoughts to Our Lord, thanking Him for the little that suffices us . . ."

"Do you ever go hunting?"

"*Con el visco, Señor, alguna vez.*"

"Sometimes one of us daubs a branch with glue, for amusement!"

Cosimo was never tired of finding out how they had resolved problems that he had had to deal with too.

"And washing, what d'you do about that?"

"*Por lavar? Hay lavanedras!*" said Don Federico, with a shrug of the shoulders.

"We give our linen to the washerwomen of the village," translated Don Sulpicio. "Every Monday, to be exact, we drop the dirty clothes basket."

"No, I meant washing your faces and bodies."

Don Federico grunted and shrugged his shoulders, as if this problem had never presented itself to him.

Don Sulpicio thought it his duty to interpret this: "According to His Highness's opinion, these are matters private to each one of us."

"And, I beg your pardon, but where d'you do your daily duties?"

"*Ollas, Señor.*"

And Don Sulpicio, in his modest tone, said: "We use certain jars, in truth."

Taking his leave of Don Federico, Cosimo, with Father Sulpicio as guide, went on a round of visits to the other members of the colony, in their respective residential trees. All these *hidalgos* and ladies preserved, even in circumstances that were still of some discomfort, their usual manners and air of composure. Some of the men used horses' saddles to straddle the branches, and this appealed very much to Cosimo, who in all these years had never thought of such a system (stirrups—he noted at once—did away with the discomfort of having to keep the feet dangling, which brought on pins and needles after a bit). Others were pointing naval telescopes (one of them had the rank of admiral) which they probably only used to look at each other from one tree to another, in idleness and gossip. The ladies, old and young, all sat on cushions embroidered by themselves, sewing (they were the only ones doing anything at all) or stroking big cats. On those trees there were a great number of cats, as well as birds, in cages—perhaps they were victims of the glue—except for some free pigeons which came and perched on the hand of some girl, and were stroked longingly.

In this arboreal drawing room Cosimo was received with grave hospitality. They offered him coffee, then at once began talking of the palaces they had left behind in Sevilla, or Granada, and of their possessions and granaries and stables, and invited him to visit them when they were reinstated. Of the king who had banished them they spoke in a tone that was both of fanatical aversion and devoted reverence, sometimes being able to separate clearly the person with whom they had a family feud and the royal title from whose authority their own stemmed. Sometimes, on the other hand, they combined these two viewpoints in a single outburst; and Cosimo, every time the conversation fell on their sovereign, did not know where to look.

Over all the gestures and conversation of the exiles there hung an aura of mourning and gloom, which corresponded in part to their natures, in part to conscious determination—as sometimes happens to those struggling for a cause with a rather vague conviction, which they try to eke out by an imposing bearing.

In the girls—who at first glance all seemed to Cosimo a little hairy and sallow—there rippled a note of gaiety that was always bridled in time. Two of these were playing at shuttlecock from one tree to another. *Tic tac, tic tac,* then a little scream; the shuttlecock had fallen into the road. A beggar from Olivabassa gathered it up and threw it back for a fee of two *pesetas*.

On the last tree, an elm, was an old man, called *El Conde,* without a wig, and poorly dressed. Father Sulpicio, as he drew near, lowered his voice, and Cosimo found himself doing the same. *El Conde* was moving aside a branch with an arm every now and then and looking down over at the slope of the hill and a plain of bare green and gold merging into the distance.

Sulpicio murmured to Cosimo a story about one of his sons held in King Charles' prisons and tortured. Cosimo realized that while all those *hidalgos* were in a way acting the exile, and every now and again having to recall and repeat to themselves why they were there, this old man was the only one really suffering. This gesture of moving the branch as if waiting for another land to appear, this plunging of his gaze deeper and deeper into the undulating distance as if hoping never to see the horizon, but to succeed, perhaps, in making out some place, alas, far too far away —this was the first real sign of exile that Cosimo saw. And he understood, too, how much those other *hidalgos* must depend on *El Conde's* presence, as being the only thing that held them together, gave them a purpose. It was he, perhaps the poorest of them and certainly the least important of them back home, who told them what they should be suffering and hoping.

On his way back from these visits, Cosimo saw on an alder tree a girl whom he had not seen before. In a couple of leaps he joined her.

She was a girl with lovely eyes the color of periwinkles, and sweet-smelling skin. She was holding a bucket.

"How is it that when I saw everyone I never saw you?"

"I was drawing water at the well," and she smiled. From the bucket, which was a little askew, was dripping some water. He helped her to set it straight.

"So you get down from the trees?"

"No, there's a twisted old cherry tree whose branches hang over a courtyard wall. We drop our buckets from there. Come."

They went along a branch, and climbed the wall. She went first, as a guide over the cherry tree. Beneath was the well.

"Do you see, Baron?"

"How d'you know I'm a baron?"

"I know everything." She smiled. "My sisters told me of your visit at once."

"Those girls playing shuttlecock?"

"Irena and Raimunda, yes."

"The daughters of Don Federico?"

"Yes."

"And what's your name?"

"Ursula."

"You're much better at getting about trees than anyone else here."

"I've been on 'em since I was a child; at Granada we had huge trees in the *patio*."

"Can you pick that rose?" At the top of a tree was flowering a rambling rose.

"A pity, no."

"All right, I'll pick it for you." He went off and came back with the rose.

Ursula smiled and held out her hands.

"I want to pin it on myself. Tell me where."

"On my head, thank you." And she guided his hands.

"Now tell me," Cosimo asked, "d'you know how to reach that walnut tree?"

"Can one?" She laughed. "I'm not a bird."

"Wait." Cosimo threw her the end of a rope. "If you tie yourself to that rope, I'll swing you over."

"No . . . I'm afraid . . ." But she was laughing.

"It's my system. I've been traveling like this for years, doing it all by myself."

"*Madre mía!*"

He ferried her over. Then he came himself. It was a young walnut tree, not big at all. They were very close. Ursula was still panting and red from her flight.

"Frightened?"

"No." But her heart was beating fast.

"You haven't lost the rose." And he touched it to set it straight.

So, close together in the tree, their arms were around each other at every move.

"Uh!" said she; and then, he first, they kissed.

So began their love, the boy happy and amazed, she happy

and not surprised at all (nothing happens by chance to girls). It was the love so long awaited by Cosimo which had now inexplicably arrived, and so lovely that he could not imagine how he had even thought it lovely before. And the thing most new to him was that it was so simple, and the boy at that moment thought it must be like that always.

} 18 {

THE peach and almond and cherry trees were in blossom. Cosimo and Ursula spent their days together on the trees. The spring even colored with gaiety the funereal proximity of her relatives.

My brother soon made himself useful among the colony of exiles, teaching them various ways of moving from one tree to another, and encouraging the grandees to abandon, for a moment, their habitual composure and practice a little movement. He also threw across some rope bridges, which allowed the older exiles to pay each other visits. And so, during the year, almost, that he spent with the Spaniards, he gave the colony many devices invented by himself: water tanks, ovens, bags of fur to sleep in. It was his joy in new inventions that made him help those *hidalgos* in their habits, even though they in no way agreed with the opinions of his favorite authors; thus, seeing the desire of those pious persons to go regularly to confession, he scooped out a confessional from a tree trunk, in which the lanky Don Sulpicio could insert himself and through a little curtained grating listen to their sins.

The pure passion for technical innovation, in fact, was not enough to save him from paying homage to accepted forms; ideas were needed. Cosimo wrote to Orbecche, the bookseller, to send him by the post from Ombrosa to Olivabassa some volumes that had arrived meanwhile. So he was able to read out loud to Ursula *Paul et Virginie* and *La Nouvelle Heloïse*.

The exiles would often hold meetings on a big oak tree, parliaments in which they drafted letters to their sovereign. At first these letters must always have had a tone of indignation, protest and threat, almost of ultimatum; but gradually one or another of them proposed formulas that were blander and more respectful, and eventually they drafted a petition in which they prostrated themselves humbly at His Gracious Majesty's feet and implored his forgiveness.

Then *El Conde* rose. All were silent. *El Conde*, looking up, began speaking in a low vibrant voice, and said everything that he had in his heart. When he sat down again, the others were serious and mute. No one mentioned the petition any more.

Cosimo had by now become one of the community and took part in the discussions. And there, with ingenious youthful fervor, he would explain the ideas of philosophers and the wrongdoings of sovereigns, and how states could be governed by justice and reason. But the only ones among them who listened at all were *El Conde*, who though old, was always searching for new ways of understanding and acting; Ursula, who had read a few books; and a couple of girls who were rather more wide awake than the others. The rest of the colony had heads like leather soles, fit only to drive nails into.

In fact, *El Conde* now began to want to read books instead of spending his time brooding over the landscape. Rousseau he found a little crude, but he liked Montesquieu; it was a first step. The other *hidalgos* read nothing, though one or two of them secretly asked Father Sulpicio to get Cosimo to lend them *La Pucelle* so they could go off and read the more risqué passages. So, with *El Conde* chewing over his new ideas, the meetings on the oak tree took on a new turn; there was even talk of going off to Spain and starting a revolution.

At first, Father Sulpicio did not sense the danger. He was not a man of great subtlety himself, and being cut off from all the hierarchy of his superiors he was no longer in touch with the way people's minds were being poisoned these days. But as soon as he was able to reorder his ideas (or as soon, said others, as he received certain letters with the bishop's seal) he began to say that the devil had insinuated itself into that community of theirs and that they would bring a hail of lightning down on themselves which would burn up the trees with everyone on them.

One night Cosimo was awakened by a groan. He hurried toward it with a lantern and on *El Conde's* oak tree saw the old man bound to the trunk with the Jesuit tightening the knots.

"Stop, Father! What are you doing?"

"The arm of the Holy Inquisition, son! Now it is for this wretched old man to confess his heresy and spit out the devil. Then it will be your turn."

Cosimo drew his sword and cut the ropes. "*En garde,* Father! There are other arms which serve reason and justice!"

The Jesuit drew a naked sword from his cloak. "Baron of Rondò, for some time your family has had accounts to settle with my Order!"

"He was right, my poor old father," exclaimed Cosimo, as the steel crossed. "The Society does not forgive!"

They fought, swaying about on the trees. Don Sulpicio was an excellent fencer, and my brother very often found himself in difficulties. They were at the third round when *El Conde* pulled himself together and began to call out. The other exiles woke, hurried to the spot, and intervened. Sulpicio put his sword away at once, and, as if nothing had happened, at once began calling for calm.

An event so serious would have been impossible to silence in any other community, but not in that, considering their wish to reduce all thought in their heads to a minimum. So Don Federico offered his good offices, and a kind of reconciliation was arranged between Don Sulpicio and *El Conde,* which left everything as it had been before.

Certainly Cosimo had to be careful, and when he went about the trees with Ursula he was in constant fear of being spied on by the Jesuit. He knew that their relationship was worrying Don Federico, for the girl was no longer allowed out with him. Those noble families, in truth, were accustomed to a very strict moral code; but they were on the trees there, in exile, and did not worry so much any longer about such things. Cosimo seemed to them a fine young man, with a title too, and one who knew how to make himself useful, and who stayed there with them of his own free will; and if there did happen to be a tenderness between him and Ursula and they often saw them going off among the trees looking for fruit and flowers, they shut an eye so as not to find anything to criticize.

Now, however, with Don Sulpicio putting pressure on him, Don Federico could no longer pretend to know nothing. He called Cosimo to an audience on his plane tree. At his side was the long black figure of Sulpicio.

"*Baron*, you are often seen about with my *niña*, they tell me."

"She is teaching me to speak *vuestra idioma*, Your Highness."

"How old are you?"

"Almost *diez y nueve*."

"*Joven!* Too young! My daughter is of marrying age. Why do you go about with her?"

"Ursula is seventeen."

"Are you thinking already of *casarte?*"

"Of what?"

"My daughter teaches you Spanish badly, *hombre*. I mean if you are thinking of choosing yourself a *novia*, of setting up a home."

Sulpicio and Cosimo both moved their hands forward. The conversation was taking a turn desired neither by the Jesuit nor, even less, by my brother.

"My home . . ." said Cosimo, waving a hand toward the highest branches and the clouds, "my home is everywhere, everywhere I can climb to, upwards . . ."

"*No es esto*," and Prince Federico Alonso shook his head. "*Baron*, if you care to visit Granada when we return, you will see the richest fief in the Sierra. *Mejor que aquí.*"

Don Sulpicio could contain himself no longer. "But, Highness, this young man is a follower of Voltaire . . . He must not go about in your daughter's company . . ."

"Oh, *es jovèn*, he's young, ideas come and go, *que se case*, let him marry and they'll change, now come to Granada, do."

"*Muchas gracias a usted* . . . I'll think it over . . ." And Cosimo, twiddling his cap of cat's fur in his hands, withdrew with many a bow.

When he saw Ursula again he was very preoccupied. "You know, Ursula, your father talked to me about you . . . He broached certain subjects . . ."

Ursula looked alarmed. "You mean he doesn't want us to see each other any more?"

"No, not that . . . When you are no longer exiled, he wants me to come with you to Granada . . ."

"Ah, yes! How nice!"

"But, you see, though I love you, I've always lived on the trees, and I want to stay on them . . ."

"Oh, Cosimo, we've got lovely trees too . . ."

"Yes, but meanwhile I'd have to come down to earth for the journey, and once down . . ."

"Don't worry now, Cosimo. We're exiles, anyway, for the moment and may so remain for the rest of our lives."

And my brother ceased to think about it.

But Ursula had guessed wrong. Shortly afterwards, a letter with the royal seal on it reached Don Federico. By gracious clemency of His Catholic Majesty, the ban was revoked. The noble exiles could return to their own homes and their own fiefs. At once there was a great coming and going among the plane trees. "We're returning! We're returning! Madrid! Cádiz! Cádiz!"

The news soon spread to the town. The inhabitants of Olivabassa arrived with ladders. Some of the exiles descended amid acclamations, others stayed to collect their luggage.

"But it's not over!" *El Conde* kept on saying. "The *cortes* will hear of it! And the Crown!" but as none of his companions in exile showed any desire to agree with him at that moment, and already the ladies were thinking only of their dresses which were now out of fashion and of their wardrobes to be renewed,

he began to make speeches to the population of Olivabassa.
"Now we're going to Spain and then you'll see! We'll settle our
accounts there. I and this young man here will get justice!" and
he pointed to Cosimo. Cosimo, confused, made signs of disagreement.

Don Federico, carried by many hands, had descended to earth.
"*Baja, joven bizarro!*" he shouted to Cosimo. "Come down, you
gallant young man! Come with us to Granada!"

Cosimo was crouching on a branch, reluctant to move.

And the Prince went on: "Why not? You'll be like a son to me!"

"The exile is over," said *El Conde*. "Finally we can put into
operation what we have brooded on for so long! Why stay up
there on the trees, Baron? There's no reason now."

Cosimo stretched out his arms. "I came up here before you, my
lords, and here I will stay afterwards too!"

"You want to withdraw!" cried *El Conde*.

"No, to resist," replied the Baron.

Ursula, who had been among the first to go down, and with
her sisters was busy filling a coach full of luggage, rushed toward
the tree. "Then I'll stay with you! I'll stay with you!" and she
began running up the ladder.

Four or five of the others stopped her, tore her away, took the
ladders from the trees.

"*Adiós, Ursula*, be happy!" said Cosimo as they carried her
forcibly to the coach, which then set off.

There was a gay barking. The dachshund, Ottimo Massimo,
who had snarled with discontent all the time his master had been
at Olivabassa, seemed finally happy again. He began to chase, just
as a joke, the little cats left behind and forgotten on the trees,
and they bristled their fur and hissed at him.

The exiles departed, some on horseback, some by coach. The
road cleared. No one remained on the trees of Olivabassa but
my brother. Stuck on the branches here and there was some
feather or ribbon or scrap of lace fluttering in the wind, and a
glove, a fringed parasol, a fan, a spurred boot.

} 19 {

IT WAS a summer—all full moons, croaking frogs, twittering chaffinches—when the Baron was seen at Ombrosa once again. He seemed restless as a bird too, hopping from branch to branch, frowning, inquisitive, indecisive.

Soon there began to circulate rumors that a certain Cecchina, on the other side of the valley, was his mistress. This girl certainly lived in an isolated house, with a deaf aunt, and an olive branch did pass near her window. The idlers in the square discussed whether she was or not.

"I saw them, she at the window sill, he on the branch. He was fluttering his arms, like a bat, and she was doubled up with laughter!"

"Later on he jumps in!"

"Nonsense; he's sworn never to leave the trees for his whole life . . ."

"Well, he's set the rule, he can also allow the exceptions . . ."

"Eh, if we're talking about exceptions . . ."

"No, no; it's she who jumps out of the window onto the olive!"

"How do they set about it then? They must be very uncomfortable . . ."

"I say, they've never touched each other. Yes, he courts her, or maybe it's her who's leading him on. But he'll never come down from up there . . ."

Yes, no, he, she, sill, jump, branch . . . the discussions seemed endless. Betrothed youths and husbands, now, reacted at once if their girls or wives as much as raised eyes toward a tree. The women, on their side, would chatter away as soon as they met; what were they talking about? Him.

Whether it was Cecchina or anyone else, my brother had his love affairs without ever leaving the trees. Once I met him running over the branches with a mattress slung over his shoulder, as easily as he slung guns, ropes, hatchets, water flasks or powder horns.

A certain Dorothea, a courtesan, admitted to me that she had met him, on her own initiative, and not for money, but just to get an idea.

"And what idea did you get?"

"Eh! I'm quite satisfied . . ."

Another, a certain Zobeide, told me she had dreamed of the "man on the trees" (as they called him) and this dream was so detailed, so remarkably well informed, that I think she must have lived it in reality.

Well, I don't know how those stories got about, but Cosimo must certainly have had a fascination for women. Since he had been with the Spaniards he had begun to take more care of his appearance, and had stopped going around muffled in furs like a bear. He wore stockings and a tapered coat and a tall hat in the English fashion, shaved his beard and combed his wig. In fact, one could tell for sure now, from his dress, whether he was going off on a hunting expedition or to a rendezvous.

The story goes that a mature and noble lady whose name I will not give, as she was from Ombrosa (her sons and grandsons still live here and might be offended, but at that time it was a well-known story), always used to go about in a coach, alone, with an old coachman on the box, and had herself driven over a part of the main road which passed through the wood. At a certain point she would say to the coachman: "Giovita, the wood is simply chockful of mushrooms. Get down, will you. Fill this and then come back," and she would hand him a big basket. The poor man, racked with rheumatism, got down from the box, loaded the basket on his shoulders, went off the road and began searching among the ferns in the dew, and got deeper and deeper into the beechwood, bowing down under every leaf to find a parasol mushroom or a puffball. Meanwhile, the noble lady would vanish from the coach, as if swept up to heaven, into the thick boughs overhanging the road. No more is known, except that often people passing by would find the coach standing there empty in the wood. Then, as mysteriously as she had vanished, there was the noble lady sitting in the coach again, looking languid. Giovita would return, soaking, with a few mushrooms at the bottom of the basket, and they would set off again.

Many of these stories were told at the house of five Genoese ladies who gave parties for rich young men (I frequented them myself when I was a bachelor), and that's how these ladies were suddenly taken with the whim to visit the Baron. A certain oak tree, in fact, is still called the Oak of the Five Sparrows, and we old men know what that means. The tale comes from a certain Gè, a raisin merchant, a man whom one can believe. It was a fine sunny day, this Gè was out shooting in the wood, he reached the oak tree, and what did he see? Cosimo had taken all five of them up on to the branches, and there they were, one here and one there, enjoying the warm afternoon, quite naked, with their little umbrellas open so as not to catch the sun, and the Baron in the midst of them reading Latin verses, Gè could not make out whether by Ovid or Lucretius.

So many stories were told of him, and what truth there was in them I don't know. At that time he was rather reserved and coy about these things; but, as an old man, he would tell many stories, almost too many—most of them, though, so fantastic that he could not thread his way through them himself. The fact was that people got into the habit, when a girl was pregnant and no one knew who was responsible, of finding it easiest to blame him. Once a girl described how as she was going picking olives she felt herself raised up by two long arms like a monkey's . . . Shortly afterwards she had twins. Ombrosa became filled with bastards of the Baron, real or false. Now they are all grown up and some, it is true, do resemble him; but this could also have been due to the power of suggestion, as when pregnant women saw Cosimo suddenly jumping from one branch to another, they were apt to get a turn.

Myself, I don't believe most of these stories told to explain certain births. Nor do I know if he had relations with as many women as they say, but what is sure is that those who had known him preferred to be silent about him.

And then, if he did have so many women after him, how can one explain the moonlight nights when he wandered like a cat on the fig trees, plums and quinces around the village, in the orchards overlooking the outer circle of the houses of Ombrosa; and there he would lament, with sighs, or yawns, or groans, which, however much he tried to control and render into normal sounds, usually came out of his throat as wails or growls. And the people of Ombrosa, who knew his habits, were not even alarmed when they heard all this in their sleep; they would just turn in bed and say, "There's the Baron out for a woman. Let's hope he finds one and we can sleep."

Sometimes an old man, one of those who suffer from insomnia and are quite ready to go to the window if they hear a noise, would look out into the orchard and see Cosimo's shadow among the branches of the fig trees, thrown on the ground by the moon. "Can't you get to sleep tonight, your Lordship?"

"No, the more I toss and turn, the more awake I feel," Cosimo would say, as if talking from his bed, with his face deep in the pillows, longing to feel his eyelids droop, while in fact he was hanging suspended there like an acrobat. "I don't know what it is tonight, the heat, nerves; perhaps the weather is going to change, don't you feel it too?"

"Oh, I feel it, I feel it . . . but I'm old, your Lordship. You, on the other hand, have a pull at your blood . . ."

"Yes, it does pull . . ."

"Well, try and get it to pull a little farther away, Lord Baron, as there's nothing here to give you any relief; only poor folk who have to wake at dawn and want to sleep now . . ."

Cosimo did not answer. He just rustled off into the orchard. He always knew how to keep within decent limits, and on their side the people of Ombrosa always knew how to tolerate these vagaries of his; partly because he was always the Baron and partly because he was a different Baron from others.

Sometimes those animal calls of his reached other windows,

ears more curious to hear; the lighting of a candle, the sound of muffled laughter, of feminine murmurs in the shadows were certainly meant as jokes on him, or mimicking him. And yet it was already something serious, almost a love call to this human derelict jumping about branches like a werewolf.

And now one of the more shameless girls would come to the window as if to see what was outside, still warm from her bed, her breasts showing, her hair loose, a white smile between her strong lips. Then a conversation would ensue.

"Who is it? A cat?"

And he: "It's a man, a man."

"A man meowing?"

"No, sighing."

"Why? What's up?"

"Something's up . . ."

"What?"

"Come here and I'll tell you . . ."

But he never got insults from the men, nor were there any vendettas—signs, it seems to me, that he was never as dangerous as all that. Only once, mysteriously, was he wounded. The news spread one morning. The Ombrosa doctor had to clamber up on to the nut tree where he was moaning away. He had a leg full of grapeshot, the little ones used to shoot sparrows with; they had to be taken out one by one with pincers. This hurt, but he soon recovered. It was never quite known how this had happened; he said that he had been hit by mistake while climbing a branch.

Convalescent, immobilized in the nut tree, he plunged into serious study. At that time he began to write a *Project for the Constitution of an Ideal State in the Trees*, in which he described the imaginary Republic of Arborea, inhabited by just men. He began it as a treatise on laws and governments; but as he wrote, his impulse to invent complicated stories intervened and out poured a rough sketch of adventures, duels and erotic tales, the latter inserted in a chapter on matrimonial rights. The epilogue of the book should have been this: the Author, having founded the perfect state in the treetops and convinced the whole of humanity to establish itself there and live there happily, came down to inhabit the earth, which was now deserted. This is what it should have been, but the work remained incomplete. He sent a précis to Diderot, signing it simply: "Cosimo Rondò, Reader of the *Encyclopaedia.*" Diderot thanked him with a short note.

}   20   {

I CANNOT say much of that period, because it was the time of my first journey into Europe. I was a young man and could make whatever use I liked of the family patrimony, as my brother needed very little. The same was true of my mother, who had been getting very much older recently, poor dear. My brother had asked to sign a power of attorney in my favor over all our possessions, on the condition that I give him a monthly allowance, pay his taxes, and keep his affairs in order. All I had to do was to take over direction of the estate and choose myself a wife, and already I saw ahead of me that regulated and pacific life which, in spite of all the great upheavals at the turn of the century, I have succeeded, in fact, in living.

But before starting this, I allowed myself a period of travel. I also went to Paris, just in time to see the triumphant reception of Voltaire on his return there after many years, for the staging of one of his plays. But these are not the memoirs of my life, which would not be worth writing; I only mention this journey, because everywhere I went I was struck by the fame of the tree-climbing man of Ombrosa, in foreign countries too. Once in an almanac I saw a figure with the words beneath: *"L'homme sauvage d'Ombreuse (Rep. Génoise). Vit seulement sur les arbres."*

They had represented him all covered in leaves, with a long beard and a long tail, eating a locust. This figure was in the Chapter of Monsters, between the Hermaphrodite and the Siren.

When faced with this kind of fantasy I was usually careful not to reveal that the man was my brother. But I proclaimed it very loud when I was invited to a reception in honor of Voltaire in Paris. The old philosopher was in his armchair, surrounded by a court of ladies, gay as a cricket and prickly as a porcupine. When he heard I came from Ombrosa he addressed me thus: "Is it near you, *mon cher Chevalier*, that there is that famous philosopher who lives on the trees *comme un singe?*"

And I, flattered, could not prevent myself replying: "He's my brother, *Monsieur, le Baron de Rondeau.*"

Voltaire was very surprised, perhaps partly at finding the brother of such a phenomenon apparently so normal, and began asking me questions, such as: "But is it to be nearer the sky that your brother stays up there?"

"My brother considers," answered I, "that anyone who wants to see the earth properly must keep himself at a necessary distance from it," and Voltaire seemed to appreciate this reply.

"Once it was only Nature which produced living phenomena," he concluded. "Now 'tis Reason." And the old sage plunged back into the chatter of his theistic adorers.

Soon I had to interrupt my journey and return to Ombrosa, recalled by an urgent dispatch. Our mother's asthma had suddenly got worse and the poor woman could no longer leave her bed.

When I crossed the threshold and raised my eyes toward our house I was sure I would see him there. Cosimo was crouching on a high branch of a mulberry tree just outside the sill of our mother's bedroom. "Cosimo," I called, but in a muffled voice. He made me a sign which meant both that our mother was rather better but still in bed, and that I should come up quietly.

The room was in shadow. My mother lay in bed with a pile of pillows propping up her shoulders, and she seemed larger than I had ever seen her. Around her were a few women of the house. Battista had not yet arrived, as the Count her husband, who was to accompany her, had been held back for the vintage. In the shadow of the room glowed the open window in which Cosimo was framed on the branch of a tree.

I bent down to kiss our mother's hand. She recognized me at once and put her hand on my head. "Ah, so you have arrived, Biagio . . ." She spoke in a faint voice when the asthma did not grip her throat too much, but clearly and with great feeling. What struck me, though, was hearing her addressing both of us, Cosimo and myself, as if he were at her bedside too. And Cosimo answered her from the tree.

"Is it long since I took my medicine, Cosimo?"

"No, only just a few minutes, Mother. Wait before you take more, as it won't do you any good just now."

At a certain point she said, "Cosimo, give me a sliver of orange," and I felt surprised. But I was even more surprised when I saw Cosimo stretching into the room through the window a kind of ship's harpoon and with it pick up a sliver of orange which was put into our mother's hand.

I noticed that for all these little services she preferred to turn to him.

"Cosimo, give me my shawls."

And he with his harpoon would search among the things thrown on an armchair, take up the shawls and hand them to her. "Here they are, Mother."

"Thank you, Cosimo, my son." She always spoke as if he were only a yard or two away, but I noticed that she never asked him services which he could not do from the tree. In such cases she always asked either me or the women.

At night our mother could not sleep; Cosimo remained watching over her from the tree with a little lantern hanging on the branch so that she could see him also in the dark.

The morning was the worst time for her asthma. The only remedy was to try and distract her, and Cosimo played little tunes on a flute or imitated the song of the birds, or caught butterflies and then made them fly into the room, or made festoons of wisteria.

It was a day of sunshine. Cosimo with a reed began to blow

soap bubbles from the tree and puff them through the window toward the sick woman's bed. Our mother saw those iridescent colors flying and filling the room and said: "Oh, what games you are playing." This made me think of when we were little children and she always disapproved of our games as being too futile and infantile, but now, perhaps for the first time, she was enjoying our games. The soap bubbles even reached her face, and she would burst them with a puff and a smile. A bubble even reached her lips and stayed there intact. We bent down over her. Cosimo let the reed fall. She was dead.

Mourning is followed sooner or later by happy events; it is the law of life. A year after our mother's death I became engaged to a girl from the local nobility. It was very difficult to bring my fiancée around to the idea of coming to live at Ombrosa; she was afraid of my brother. The thought that there was a man moving among the leaves who was watching every move through the windows, who would appear when least expected, filled her with terror. Then too, she had never seen Cosimo and imagined him as some kind of Indian. To get this fear out of her head I arranged a luncheon in the open, under the trees, to which Cosimo was also invited. Cosimo ate above us on an ilex tree, with his dishes on a little tray, and I must say that although he was rather out of practice for social dining, he behaved very well. My fiancée was somewhat calmed, and realized that apart from his being on the trees he was a man just like all the others; but she was still left with an unconquerable feeling of distrust.

Even when, after we had married, we settled down together in the villa at Ombrosa, she avoided as much as possible not only any converse, but even the sight of her brother-in-law, although he, poor man, every now and again would bring her bunches of flowers and rare furs. When children began to be born and grow up, she got it into her head that their uncle's proximity would have a bad influence on their education. She was not happy until we put in order the old castle on our estate at Rondò which had been uninhabited for a long time; and we began staying up there much more than at Ombrosa, so that the children should be away from bad influences.

Cosimo too began to notice the passing of time: a sign of this was the aging of the dachshund Ottimo Massimo, who had lost his desire to join the bitches of the pack to go after the foxes, nor would he try any more absurd love affairs with local mongrels. He was always lying down because his stomach was so near the ground when he was standing that it was not worth while for him to keep upright. And lying there stretched out from muzzle to tail at the foot of the tree on which Cosimo was, he would raise a tired look toward his master and scarcely wag his tail. Cosimo was becoming discontented; the sense of the passing of time made him feel a kind of dissatisfaction with his life, spent forever wandering up and down the same old trees. And nothing any longer gave him full contentment, neither hunting, fleeting affairs nor books. He himself did not know what he wanted; taken by one of these moods, he would clamber quickly over the tenderest and most fragile boughs as if searching for other trees growing still higher, so as to climb those too.

One day Ottimo Massimo was restless. There seemed to be a spring wind. The dog raised his muzzle, sniffed and then flung himself down again. Two or three times he got up, moved around and lay down again. Suddenly he began to run. He trotted along slowly, every now and again stopping to take breath. Cosimo followed on the branches.

Ottimo Massimo made toward the woods. He seemed to have a very precise direction in mind, because even when he stopped every now and again to lift a leg, he would stand there with tongue out looking at his master, then scratch himself and begin moving once more with certainty. He was moving into parts little frequented by Cosimo, in fact almost unknown to him, toward the shooting reserves of the Duke Tolemaico. The Duke Tolemaico was a broken-down old rake and certainly had not been out shooting for a very long time, but no poacher could set foot in his reserve as the gamekeepers were numerous and vigilant, and Cosimo, who had had dealings with them, preferred to keep away. Now Ottimo Massimo and Cosimo were plunging deeper and deeper into the Duke's game reserves, but neither one nor the other thought of chasing the precious game; the dog trotted along following some secret call of his own, and the Baron was gripped by an impatient curiosity to discover where on earth the dog was going.

So the dachshund reached a point in which the forest ended and there was an open field. Two stone lions crouched on pillars were holding up a coat-of-arms. Beyond them should have begun a park, a garden, a more private part of the Tolemaico estate; but there was nothing except for those two stone lions with the field beyond, an immense field of short green grass, whose boundaries faded away in the distance against a background of black oak trees. The sky was filmy with clouds. No bird sang.

This field, for Cosimo, was a sight which filled him with discomfort. Having always lived in the thickness of the vegetation at Ombrosa, certain of being able to reach any place by his own routes, the Baron only had to see in front of him an empty and impassable space, bare under the sky, to feel dizzy.

Ottimo Massimo rushed into the field, and began running along at full tilt as if he had become young again. From the ash tree where he was crouching, Cosimo began to whistle at him and call, "Here, come back here, Ottimo Massimo, come back here, where are you going?" but the dog did not obey, did not even turn; he ran on and on through the field until nothing could be seen but a distant dot like a comma—his tail— and even that vanished.

In the ash tree Cosimo was wringing his hands. He was used to the dog's escapes and absences, but now Ottimo Massimo was vanishing into this field where he could not follow, and the flight linked to the anxiety he had felt a short time ago and filled him with a vague sense of expectation, of waiting for something to appear in that field.

He was brooding over these thoughts when he heard steps under his oak tree, and saw a gamekeeper passing, whistling, hands in pockets. The man had a very careless distracted air for one of those terrible gamekeepers of the preserve, and yet the badge on his uniform was that of the ducal retainers, and Cosimo flattened himself against the trunk. Then the thought of the dog overcame his fear; he called down to the gamekeeper: "Hey, you, Sergeant, have you seen a dog around?"

The gamekeeper looked up. "Ah, it's you! The flying hunter with the sliding dog! No, I've not seen the dog. What have you caught this morning?"

Cosimo recognized one of his keenest adversaries, and said: "Oh, nothing, the dog escaped from me and I had to follow him as far as this . . . my gun's unloaded."

The gamekeeper laughed. "Oh, do load it, and fire it, too, whenever you like; it doesn't matter now!"

"Why not now?"

"Now that the Duke is dead, who cares about trespassing here?"

"Oh, he's dead, is he? I didn't know that."

"He's been dead and buried for three months. And there's a row on between the heirs of his first two marriages and his new widow."

"He'd a third wife, had he?"

"He married when he was eighty, a year before he died; she was a girl of twenty-one or so. It was a mad thing to do, a wife who never even spent a day with him, and is only now beginning to visit his estates, which she doesn't like."

"What, she doesn't like them?"

"Oh, well, she installs herself in a palace, or a castle, and arrives with her whole court, as she always has a group of admirers around her, and after three days she finds everything ugly, everything sad, and sets off again. Then the other heirs come forward, rush into that estate and claim rights over it. She says, 'Oh, yes, take it if you like.' Now she's come here to the hunting pavilion, but how long will she stay? Not long, I'd say."

"And where's the hunting pavilion?"

"Down over the field beyond the oak trees."

"Then my dog has gone there . . ."

"He must have gone looking for bones . . . Excuse me, but it makes me think your Lordship doesn't feed him well!"—and he burst out laughing.

Cosimo did not reply, he looked at the uncrossable field, waiting for the dachshund to return.

The whole day long he never came. Next day Cosimo was again on the ash tree looking at the field, as if forced by a turmoil within.

The dog reappeared toward evening, a little dot in the field under Cosimo's sharp eye, becoming more and more visible. "Ottimo Massimo! Come here! Where have you been?" The dog stopped, wagging his tail and looking at his master, and seemed to be inviting him to follow; but then he realized the space Cosimo could not get over, turned back, made a few hesitating paces, and turned again. "Ottimo Massimo! Come here! Ottimo Massimo!" But the dog was running off again and vanished in the distance.

Later two gamekeepers passed. "Still waiting for your dog, your Lordship! But I saw him at the pavilion, in good hands . . ."

"What?"

"But yes, the Marchesa, or rather the widowed Duchess. We call her the Marchesa, as she was the Marchesina as a girl. She's treating him as though he's been with her all the time. He's a lap dog, that one, if you'll allow me to say so, your Lordship. Now he's found a soft billet, he's staying there . . ."

And the two keepers went off grinning. Ottimo Massimo did not return any more. Day after day Cosimo spent on the ash, looking at the field as if he could read something in it that had been struggling inside him for a long time: the very idea of distance, of intangibility, of the waiting that can be prolonged beyond life.

} 21 {

ONE day Cosimo was looking down from the ash tree. The sun was shining, a ray crossed the field, which from pea green went emerald. Down in the blackness of the clump of oaks there was a movement in the undergrowth, and a horse leaped out. On its saddle was a horseman dressed in black, in a cloak—no, a skirt; it wasn't a horseman, it was a horsewoman; she was galloping on a loose rein and she was fair!

Cosimo's heart gave a leap, and he found himself longing for the horsewoman to come near enough for him to see her face, and for that face to be very beautiful. But apart from this waiting of his for her to approach and to be beautiful, there was a third thing he was waiting for, a third branch of hope entwining with the other two, a longing that this ever more luminous beauty might respond to a need he felt to recapture some memory once known and now almost forgotten, a memory of which only a wispy line, a faint color now remained, and that this would make all the rest emerge once more, or rather be rediscovered in something present and alive.

There he sat, yearning for her to come nearer his end of the field, by the two towering pillars with the lions; but the wait was becoming agonizing, for now he realized that the horse-woman was not cutting through the field directly toward the lions, but across it diagonally, so that she would soon vanish into the wood again.

He was just about to lose sight of her, when she turned her horse sharply and cut across the field in another diagonal, which would certainly bring her a little nearer, but would make her vanish just the same on the opposite side of the field.

And now, at that moment, Cosimo noticed with annoyance two brown horses ridden by cavaliers, who were coming out of the woods into the field, but he quickly tried to overcome his annoyance, and decided that these horsemen did not matter, one only had to see how they were tacking to and fro after her, he really must not let them bother him, and yet, he had to admit, they annoyed him.

And then the horsewoman, just before vanishing from the field, turned her horse around again, but in the other direction, farther away from Cosimo . . . No, now the horse was circling and galloping this way, and the move seemed done on purpose to baffle the two followers, who were now in fact galloping away and had not yet realized that she was rushing in an opposite direction.

Now everything was going just as he wanted; the horsewoman was galloping along in the sun, getting more and more beautiful and corresponding more and more to Cosimo's lost memories; the only alarming thing was her continual zigzagging, which never gave him any idea of her intentions. The two horsemen did not understand where she was going either, and in trying to follow her gyrations, covered a great deal of ground uselessly, though always with good will and dexterity.

Now, in less time than Cosimo expected, the woman on horseback reached the edge of the field near him, passed between the two pillars surmounted by lions which seemed almost to have been put there in her honor, turned toward the field and everything beyond it with a wide gesture of farewell, galloped on, and passed under the ash tree. Cosimo could now see her face and body, clearly. She was sitting erect in the saddle, a haughty woman's and at the same time a child's face, a forehead happy to be above those eyes, eyes happy to be under that forehead, nose, mouth, chin, collar, everything about her happy to be with every other part of her, it all, yes all, reminded him of the little girl he had seen on the swing the first day he had spent on a tree: Sinforosa Viola Violante of Ondariva.

This discovery, or rather having brought it from unconfessed hope to the point of being able to proclaim it to himself, filled Cosimo as if with a fever. He tried to call so that she would raise her eyes to the ash tree and see him, but from his throat came only a hoarse gurgle and she did not turn.

Now the white horse was galloping into the chestnut grove, and the hoofs were beating on the cones scattered about the ground, splitting them open and exposing the shiny kernels of nut. The woman guided her horse first in one direction, then in another, with Cosimo at one moment thinking her away and unreachable, at another, as he jumped from tree to tree, seeing her with surprise reappear amid the perspective of trunks, and her way of moving fanned more and more the memory flaming up in his mind. He tried to reach her with a call, a sign of his presence, but the only sound that came to his lips was the whistle of a pheasant, and she did not even hear.

The two cavaliers following her seemed to understand her intentions even less than her route and continued to take wrong directions, getting entangled in undergrowth and stuck in bog, while she arrowed her way ahead, safe and uncatchable. Every now and again she would give some order or encouragement to the horsemen by raising her crop or tearing off a carob nut and throwing it, as if to tell them to go that way. The horsemen would at once rush off in that direction, galloping over the fields and slopes, but she had turned another way and was no longer looking at them.

"It's she, it's she!" Cosimo was thinking, more and more inflamed with hope and trying to shout her name, but all that came from his lips was a long sad cry, like a plover's.

Now, this tacking to and fro, this deceiving of the cavaliers, and the games all seemed to be tending one way, however irregular and wavering. Guessing this aim, Cosimo abandoned the impossible task of following her, and said to himself, "I'll go in a place she'll go to, if it's her. In fact, she can't be going anywhere else." And leaping along by his own routes, he moved toward the abandoned park of the Ondarivas.

In that shade, in that scented air, in that place where even the leaves and twigs had another color and another substance, he felt so carried away by memories of his childhood that he almost forgot the horsewoman, or if he did not forget, he at least began telling himself it might not be her and that this waiting and hoping for her seemed so real that it was almost as if she were there.

Then he heard a sound. Horse's hoofs on the gravel. It was coming down the garden no longer at a gallop, as if the rider wanted to look at and recognize everything precisely. There was no sign of the silly cavaliers; they must have lost all trace of her.

He saw her; she was wandering around the fountains, urns and garden pavilions, looking at the plants which had now become huge, with hanging vines, the magnolias grown into a copse. But she did not see him who was trying to call her with the cooing of hoopoes, the trilling of larks, and with sounds that merged into the close twitter of birds in the garden.

She had dismounted, and was leading the horse by the bridle. She reached the villa, left the horse, entered the portico. Then suddenly she broke into shouts of "Ortensia! Gaetano! Tarquinio! This needs whitewashing, the shutters painting, the tapestries hung! And I want the big table here, the side ones there, the spinet in the middle. The pictures must all be rehung."

Cosimo realized then that the house which to his distracted eyes had seemed closed and empty as always, now, in reality, was open and full of people—servants cleaning and polishing and rearranging, opening windows, moving furniture, beating carpets. So it *was* Viola who was returning, Viola re-establishing herself at Ombrosa, taking possession once again of the villa she had left as a child! And the pulsating joy in Cosimo's heart was not very different from pulsating fear. For her return, the presence of her, unpredictable and proud, under his very eyes, might mean losing her forever, even in his memory, even in that secret place of scented leaves and dappled green light, might mean that he would be forced to flee from her and so flee too from that first memory of her as a girl.

With this alternating heartbeat Cosimo watched her swirling amid the servants, making them move sofas, harpsichords and consoles, then passing hurriedly into the garden and remounting her horse, followed by groups waiting for more orders, then turning to the gardeners, and telling them how to arrange the abandoned flower beds and rescatter on the paths gravel swept away by rain, and put back the wicker chairs, and the swing.

She pointed, with a wave of the arms, at the branch from which this had once been hanging and was now to be hung again, and indicated how long the ropes were to be, and how long its course, and as she was saying all this, her gestures and glance went up to the magnolia tree on which Cosimo had once appeared. And there he was on the magnolia tree, and she saw him again.

She was surprised—very. There was no doubt of that, though her eyes were laughing through her surprise. But she recovered at once and pretended not to care, and smiled with her eyes and mouth, revealing a tooth she had had as a child.

"You!" and then, trying to use as natural a tone as she could, but not succeeding in hiding her interest and pleasure, she went on, "Ah, so you've stayed up there without ever going down?"

Cosimo succeeded in transforming a sparrow's note in his throat into a "Yes, Viola, it's me, d'you remember me?"

"You've never, really never once set a foot on the ground?"

"Never."

Then she, as if she had already conceded too much: "Ah, so you managed it, you see! It couldn't have been so difficult then."

"I was awaiting your return . . ."

"Excellent. Hey, you, where are you taking that curtain! Leave it all here and I'll see to it!" And she began looking at him again. Cosimo that day was dressed for hunting: hairy all over, with his cap of cat's fur and his musket. "You look like Crusoe!"

"Have you read it?" he said at once, to show he was up to date.

Viola had already turned around. "Gaetano! Ampelio! The dry leaves! It's full of dry leaves!" Then to him: "In an hour, at

the end of the park. Wait for me." And she hurried away to
give more orders, on horseback.

Cosimo threw himself into the thick of the wood; he would
have liked it to be a thousand times thicker, a phalanx of
branches and leaves and thorns and bracken and maidenhair, to
plunge and bury himself in and only after being completely
immersed to be able to understand whether he was happy or
mad with fear.

On the big tree at the end of the park, with his knees
tight against a branch, he looked at the time on an old watch
that had belonged to his maternal grandfather, General von
Kurtewitz, and said to himself: She won't come. But Donna
Viola arrived almost punctually, on horseback. She stopped under
the tree without even looking up. She was no longer wearing
her rider's hat or jacket, but a white blouse, decorated with lace,
and a black skirt that was almost nunlike. Raising herself in her
stirrups she held out a hand to him on the branch; he helped
her; she climbed onto the saddle and reached the branch, then,
still without looking at him, rapidly climbed up it, looked about
for a comfortable fork, and sat down. Cosimo crouched at her
feet, and could begin only by saying: "So you're back?"

Viola gave him an ironical look. Her hair was as fair as it
had been when she was a child. "How do you know that?"
said she.

And he, without understanding her little joke: "I saw you
in that field of the Duke's preserve."

"The preserve's mine. It can fill with weeds, for all I care!
D'you know about it? About me, I mean?"

"No . . . I've only just heard you're a widow now . . ."

"Yes, of course I'm a widow," and she slapped her black
skirt, smoothed it out, and began talking very quickly. "You
never know anything. There you are on the trees all day long,
putting your nose into other people's business, and yet you
know nothing. I married old Tolemaico because my family made
me, forced me. They said I was a flirt and must have a husband.
For a year I've been the Duchess Tolemaico, and it was the

most boring year of my life, though I never spent more than a week with the old man. I'll never set foot in any of their castles or ruins or ratholes, may they fill with snakes! From now on I'm staying here, where I was as a child. I'll stay here as long as I feel like it, of course. Then I'll go off. I'm a widow and can do what I like, finally. I've always done what I liked, to tell the truth; even Tolemaico I married because it suited me to marry him. It's not true they forced me to; they wanted to get me married off at any cost, and so I chose the most decrepit suitor I could find. 'Then I'll be a widow sooner,' I said, and so I am, now."

Cosimo sat there half stunned by this avalanche of news and peremptory statements, and Viola was further away than ever; flirt, widow, duchess, she was part of an unreachable world, and all he could find to say was: "And whom d'you flirt with now?"

And she: "There. You're jealous. Be careful, as I'll never let you be jealous."

Cosimo did have a flash of jealousy provoked by this quarrel, then thought at once: What? Jealous? Why admit that I could be jealous of her? Why say, "I'll never let you"? It's as good as saying that she thinks that we . . .

Then, scarlet in the face, he felt a longing to tell her, to ask her, to hear her, but it was she who asked him dryly: "Tell me about you now. What have you done?"

"Oh, I've done things," he began saying. "I've hunted, even boar, but mostly foxes, hares, pheasants and then, of course, thrushes and blackbirds; and then pirates—Turkish pirates—we had a great fight; my uncle died in it. And I've read lots of books, for myself and a friend of mine, a brigand who was hanged; and I've got the whole *Encyclopaedia* of Diderot and have also written to him and he's replied, from Paris; and I've done lots of work, sown crops, saved a wood from fire . . ."

"And will you always love me, absolutely, above all else, and will you do anything for me?"

At this remark of hers, Cosimo, with a catch at the heart, said: "Yes."

"You are a man who has lived on the trees for me alone, to learn to love me . . ."

"Yes . . . yes . . ."

"Kiss me."

He pressed her against the trunk, kissed her. Raising his face, he realized her beauty as if he had never seen it before. "Say, how beautiful you are . . ."

"For you . . ." and she unbuttoned her white blouse. Her breast was young, the nipples rosy. Cosimo just grazed it with his lips, before Viola slid away over the branches as if she were flying, with him clambering after her, and that skirt of hers always in his face.

"But where are you taking me to?" asked Viola as if it were he leading her, not she him.

"This way," exclaimed Cosimo, and began guiding her, and at every passage of branches he would take her by the hand or the waist and show her the way over.

"This way," and they went on to certain olive trees protruding from a cliff, and from the top of these was the sea, of which till now they had glimpsed only a fragment, and even that was half hidden by leaves and branches; but now suddenly they found the sea there facing them, calm and limpid and vast as the sky. The horizon opened wide and high and the blue was stretched and bare, without a sail; and they could count the scarcely perceptible ripples of the waves. Only a very light rustle, like a sigh, ran over the pebbles on the beach.

With eyes half dazed, Cosimo and Viola moved back into the shade of the dark-green foliage. "This way."

In a walnut, at the fork of the trunk, was a hollow, formed from an old ax wound, and this was one of Cosimo's refuges. Over it was stretched a boarskin, and around it were a flask, a tool or two, and a bowl.

Viola flung herself down on the boarskin. "Do you bring other women here?"

He hesitated. And Viola: "If you haven't, you're not much of a man."

"Yes . . . One or two . . ."

She slapped him full in the face. "So that's how you awaited me?"

Cosimo passed his hand over his scarlet cheek and could think of no word to say; but now she seemed to be in a good mood again. "And what were they like? Tell me. What were they like?"

"Not like you, Viola, not like you . . ."

"How d'you know what I'm like, eh, how d'you know?"

She was gentle now, and Cosimo never ceased to be surprised at these sudden changes of hers. He moved close to her. Viola was gold and honey.

"Say . . ."

"Say . . ."

They knew each other. He knew her and so himself, for in truth he had never known himself. And she knew him and so herself, for although she had always known herself she had never been able to recognize it until now.

} 22 {

THE first pilgrimage they made was to the tree where, in a deep incision in the bark, now so old and deformed that it no longer seemed the work of human hands, were carved in big letters: *Cosimo, Viola,* and beneath—*Ottimo Massimo.*

"Up here? Who did it? When?"

"I; then."

Viola was moved.

"And what does that mean?" and she pointed to the words *Ottimo Massimo.*

"My dog. That is your dog. The dachshund."

"Turcaret?"

"Ottimo Massimo, I called him."

"Turcaret! How I sobbed for him, when I realized as I left that they hadn't put him in the carriage! . . . Oh, I didn't care about not seeing you again, but was desperate at not having the dog any more!"

"If it hadn't been for the dog I wouldn't have found you again! He sniffed in the wind that you were near, and didn't rest until he found you."

"I recognized him at once, as soon as I saw him arrive at the pavilion, panting fit to burst . . . The others said, 'And where's this come from?' I bent down to look at his color, his markings. 'But he's Turcaret! The dachshund I had as a child at Ombrosa!' "

Cosimo laughed. Suddenly she wrinkled up her nose. "Ottimo Massimo! What an ugly name! Where d'you get such ugly names from?" And Cosimo's face clouded over.

But for Ottimo Massimo now there was no cloud to mar his happiness. His old dog's heart that had been divided between two masters was finally at peace, after having worked day after day to attract the Marchesa toward the borders of the game preserve, to the ilex on which Cosimo was crouching. He had pulled her by the skirt, or skipped away with some object of hers, off toward the field so that she should follow, and she had exclaimed: "But what do you want? Where *are* you dragging me? Turcaret! Stop it! What a *mad*dening little dog to find again!"

But seeing the dachshund had already brought back the memories of childhood, a nostalgia for Ombrosa. And she had at once begun preparing her move from the ducal pavilion and her return to the old villa with its strange vegetation.

She had returned, Viola had. For Cosimo, now began the best period of his life, and for her too, who would go galloping over the country on her white horse and when she caught sight of the Baron between branches and sky would dismount, climb up the slanting trees and branches, on which she soon became almost as expert as he and could reach him anywhere.

"Oh, Viola, I don't know, I don't know where I could still climb . . ."

"To me . . ." Viola would say quietly, and he felt himself almost in a frenzy.

Love for her was a heroic exercise; the pleasure of it was mingled with trials of courage and generosity and dedication and straining of all the faculties of her being. Their world was a world of trees—intricate, gnarled and impervious.

"There!" she would exclaim, pointing to a fork high in the branches, and they would launch out together to reach it and start between them a competition in acrobatics, culminating in new embraces. They made love suspended in the void, propping themselves or holding onto branches, she throwing herself upon him, almost flying.

Viola's determination in love accorded with Cosimo's, but sometimes clashed with his. Cosimo avoided the refinements of dalliance, the wanton perversities; nothing in love pleased him that was not natural. The republican virtues were in the air; a period was coming which would be both licentious and severe. Cosimo, insatiable lover, was a stoic, an ascetic, a puritan. Always in search of happiness in love, he would never be a mere voluptuary. He reached the point of distrusting kisses, caresses, verbal play—everything that clouded or replaced the wholesomeness of nature. It was Viola who revealed that in its fullness. And with her he never knew the sadness after love, preached by theologians; on this subject he even wrote a philosophic letter to Rousseau, who, perhaps disturbed by it, did not reply.

But Viola was also a refined, spoiled, capricious woman, ever yearning in body and soul. Cosimo's love fulfilled her sensually but left her imagination unsatisfied. From that came quarrels and cloudy resentments. But these did not last long, so varied was their life and world around.

When tired they would go back to their refuges in the thickest press of leaves: hammocks which enwrapped their bodies like furled leaves, or hanging pavilions with curtains flapping in the breeze, or beds of feathers. At such contrivances Donna Viola was very talented. Wherever she happened to be, the Marchesa had the gift of creating around her ease, luxury and elaborate comfort—elaborate in appearance, but accomplished by her with miraculous facility, for everything she wanted had to be carried out at once and at all costs.

On these aerial alcoves of theirs the robins would perch to sing, and between the curtains would flutter butterflies, in pairs, chasing each other. On summer afternoons, when sleep took the two lovers side by side, a squirrel would enter, looking for something to nibble, and stroke their faces with its feathery tail or plunge its teeth into a big toe. Then they would pull the curtains to more carefully; but a family of tree mice began gnawing at the roof of the pavilion and fell down on their heads.

This was the time in which they were discovering each other, telling of their lives, questioning.

"And did you feel alone?"

"I hadn't you."

"But alone before the rest of the world?"

"No. Why? I always had contacts with other people; I picked fruit, pruned trees, studied philosophy with the Abbé, fought the pirates. Isn't it like that for everyone?"

"You're the only one like that, that's why I love you."

But the Baron had not yet realized what Viola would accept from him and what not. Sometimes a mere nothing, a word or a tone of his was enough to loose the fury of the Marchesa.

He might say for example: "With Gian dei Brughi I used to read novels, with the Cavalier I made plans for irrigation . . ."

"And with me?"

"With you I make love. Like picking fruit or pruning . . ."

She would be silent, motionless. At once Cosimo would realize he had unchained her anger; suddenly her eyes would become cold as ice.

"Why, what is it, Viola, what have I said?"

She was far away as if she did not see or hear, a hundred miles from him, her face like marble.

"But no, Viola, what is it, why, listen . . ."

Viola got up; agile, with no need of help, she began climbing down the tree. Cosimo had not yet understood what his mistake could have been, had not had time to think it over, perhaps preferred not to think of it at all, not to understand it, the better to proclaim his innocence. "No, no, you didn't understand, Viola, listen . . ."

He followed her on to a branch lower down. "Viola, don't go, please don't go, not like this, Viola . . ."

She spoke now, but to the horse, which she had reached and taken by the bridle. She mounted and off she went.

Cosimo began to despair, to jump from tree to tree. "No, Viola, do stay, Viola!"

She had galloped away. He followed her over the branches. *"Please*, Viola, I love you!" But he had lost sight of her. He flung himself on uncertain branches, made risky leaps. "Viola! Viola!"

When he was sure of having lost her and could not restrain his sobs, suddenly she reappeared at the trot, without raising her eyes.

"Look, do look, Viola. Look what I'm doing!" and he began banging himself against a trunk with his bare head (which was, in truth, very hard).

She did not even look at him. She was already away.

Cosimo waited for her to return, zigzagging among the trees.

"Viola! I'm desperate!" and he flung himself into empty space, head down, gripping a branch with his legs and hitting himself with his fists all over his head and face. Or he began to break branches in a fury of destruction, and a leafy elm was reduced in a few seconds to a bare stripped bark as if a hailstorm had passed.

But he never threatened to kill himself; indeed he never threatened anything. Emotional blackmail was not for him. He did what he felt like doing and announced it while he was actually doing it, not before.

Then suddenly Donna Viola, unpredictable as her anger, re-appeared. Of all Cosimo's follies which seemed never to have reached her, one had suddenly set her aflame with pity and love. "No, Cosimo, darling, wait for me!" And she jumped from her saddle and rushed to clamber up a trunk, and his arms were ready to raise her on high.

Love took over again with a fury equal to the quarrel. It was, really, the same thing, but Cosimo had not realized it.

"Why d'you make me suffer?"

"Because I love you."

Now it was his turn to get angry. "No, no, you don't love me! People in love want happiness, not pain!"

"People in love want only love, even at the cost of pain."

"Then you're making me suffer on purpose."

"Yes, to see if you love me."

The Baron's philosophy would not go any further. "Pain is a negative state of the soul."

"Love is all."

"Pain should always be fought against."

"Love refuses nothing."

"Some things I'll never admit."

"Oh yes, you do, now, for you love me and you suffer."

Like his outbursts of despair, Cosimo's explosions of uncontainable joy were noisy. Sometimes his happiness reached such a point that he had to leave his love and go jumping off and shouting and proclaiming her wonders to the world.

> "*Yo quiero the most wonderful puellam de todo el mundo!*"

Those sitting on the benches at Ombrosa, idlers or old salts, got quite into the habit of these sudden appearances of his. There he would come leaping through the ash trees declaiming:

> "*Zu dir, zu dir, gunaika,*
> *Vo cercando il mio ben*
> *En la isla de Jamaica*
> *Du soir jusqu' au matin!*"

or:

> *Il y a un pré where the grass grows toda de oro*
> *Take me away, take me away, che io ci moro!*

then he would vanish.

His studies of classic and modern languages, however little pursued, were enough to let himself go in this clamorous expression of his feelings, and the more he was shaken to the roots by intense emotion, the more his language became obscure. They remember here how once, at the Feast of the Patron Saint, when the people of Ombrosa were gathered in the square around the Tree of Plenty and the festoons and the flagpole, the Baron appeared on the top of a plane tree and with one of those leaps of his, which only his acrobatic agility could produce, jumped onto the Tree of Plenty, clambered to the top, shouted: "*Que viva die schöne Venus posterió r!*" let himself slither down the pole almost to the ground, stopped, groped his way up to the top again, tore from the trophy a round rosy cheese, and with another of his jumps returned to the plane tree and fled, leaving the people of Ombrosa bewildered.

Nothing made the Marchesa happier than these exuberances, and they moved her to repay him with demonstrations of love that were even more violent. The Ombrosians, when they saw her galloping along on a loose rein, her face almost buried in the white mane of the horse, knew that she was rushing to a meeting with the Baron. Even in her way of riding she expressed a love force, but here Cosimo could no longer follow her; and her equestrian passion, much as he admired it, was for him a secret reason for jealousy and rancor, for he saw Viola dominated by a world vaster than his own and realized that he would never be able to have her for himself alone, to shut her in the confines of his kingdom. The Marchesa, on her side, suffered perhaps from her inability to be at once both lover and horsewoman; every now and again she was taken with a vague need for her love and Cosimo's to become a love on horseback, a feeling that running over trees was no longer enough for her, a yearning to race along at full gallop on the crupper of her charger.

And in fact her horse, with that racing over countryside all slopes and drops, was getting to be fleet as a roebuck, and

Viola now began urging it up certain trees—old olives, for example, with bent trunks. Sometimes the horse would reach the first fork in the branches, and she got into the habit of tying it up no longer on the ground, but up in the olive. Dismounting, she would leave it to munch leaves and twigs.

And so when some old gossip passing through the olive grove and raising curious eyes saw the Baron and the Marchesa up there in each other's arms, and went off and told people, and added: "The white horse was up on a branch too," he was taken for a lunatic and no one believed him. And once again that time the lovers' secret was saved.

} 23 {

THIS last story shows that the people of Ombrosa, who before had been teeming with gossip about my brother's love life, now, faced with this passion exploding as it were above their heads, maintained a dignified reserve, as if toward something bigger than themselves. Not that they did not criticize the Marchesa's conduct; but more for its exterior aspects, such as that breakneck galloping of hers ("Where can she be going, at such a pace?") and that continual hoisting of furniture on to treetops. There was already an air among them of considering it all just as one of the nobles' ways, one of their many idiosyncrasies. ("All up trees, nowadays; women, men. What'll they think of next?") In fact, times were coming that were to be more tolerant, but also more hypocritical.

Now the Baron would only show himself at rare intervals on the ilexes in the square, and when he did, it was a sign that she had left. For Viola was sometimes away months seeing to her properties scattered all over Europe, though these departures of hers always corresponded to rifts in their relationship when the Marchesa had been offended with Cosimo's not understanding what she wanted him to understand about love. Not that Viola left in this state of mind: they always managed to make it up before, though there remained the suspicion in him that she had decided to take this particular journey because she was tired of him, and he could not prevent her going; perhaps she was already breaking away from him, perhaps some incident on the journey or a pause for reflection would decide her not to return. So my brother would live in a state of anxiety. He would try to go back to the life he had been used to before meeting her, to hunt and fish, follow the work in the fields, his studies, the gossip in the square, as if he had never done anything else (there persisted in him the stubborn youthful pride of refusing ever to admit himself under anyone else's influence); and at the same time he would congratulate himself on how much love was giving him, the alacrity, the pride; but on the other hand, he noticed that so many things no longer mattered to him, that without Viola life had no flavor, that his thoughts were always following her. The more he tried, away from the whirlwind of Viola's presence, to reacquire command of passions and pleasures in a wise economy of mind, the more he felt the void left by her or the fever for her return. In fact, his love was just what Viola wanted it to be, not as he pretended it was; it was always the woman who triumphed, even from a distance, and Cosimo, in spite of himself, ended by enjoying it.

Then all at once the Marchesa would return. The season of love in the trees would resume, but so too would the season of jealousy. Where had Viola been? What had she done? Cosimo longed to know, but at the same time he was afraid of how she might answer his questions. She would reply with hints, and each hint would further arouse his suspicions, and he realized that though she was purposely answering in such a way as to torment him, it could all be quite true nevertheless. In these uncertainties, he would hide his jealousy one minute, and then the next there would be a violent outburst. Viola would never reply the same way—her answers were always different, always unpredictable. One moment Cosimo would think she was more attached to him than ever, and the next he felt he would never be able to arouse her again.

What the Marchesa really did during her travels we at Ombrosa could not know, far as we were from capitals and their gossip. But I happened at that period to make my second journey to Paris in connection with certain contracts in lemons, for many nobles were already taking to commerce, and I was among the first.

One evening, at one of the most brilliant salons in Paris, I met Donna Viola. Her headdress was so splendid and her gown so sumptuous that if I recognized her at once, in fact gave a start at first seeing her, it was because she was a woman who could never be confused with any other. She greeted me with indifference, but soon found a way of taking me aside and asking me, without waiting for any reply between one question and another: "Have you news of your brother? Will you soon be back at Ombrosa? Here, give him this to remember me by," and taking a silk handkerchief from her bosom she thrust it into my hand. Then she quickly let herself be caught up in the court of admirers who followed her everywhere.

"Do you know the Marchesa?" I was asked quietly by a Parisian friend.

"Only slightly," I replied, and it was true; when she stayed at Ombrosa Donna Viola, under the influence of Cosimo's life in the wilds, never bothered to see anything of the local nobility.

"Rarely has such beauty been allied to such a restless spirit," said my friend. "Gossip has it that in Paris she passes from one lover to another, in such rapid succession that no one can call her his own and consider himself privileged. But every now and again she vanishes for months at a time and they say she retires to a convent, to wallow in penance."

I could scarcely avoid laughing at finding the Marchesa's life on the trees of Ombrosa being thought of by the Parisians as periods of penance; but at the same time this gossip disturbed me, and made me foresee times of sorrow for my brother.

To forestall ugly surprises I decided to warn him, and as soon as I returned to Ombrosa went to search him out. He questioned me at length about my journey and the news from France, but I could not tell him anything of politics and literature about which he was not already informed.

Eventually I drew Donna Viola's handkerchief from my pocket. "At Paris in a salon I met a lady who knows you, and who gave me this for you, with her greetings."

Quickly he dropped the basket attached to the rope, pulled up the silk handkerchief and brought it to his face as if to inhale its scent. "Ah, you saw her? And how was she? Tell me, how was she?"

"Very beautiful and very brilliant," I answered slowly. "But they say this scent is inhaled by many nostrils."

He held the handkerchief against his chest as if fearing it might be torn away from him; then turned to me red in the face. "And have you no sword to thrust those lies down the throat of the person who told you?"

I had to confess that it had not even crossed my mind.

He was silent a moment. Then he shrugged his shoulders. "All lies. I alone know she's mine alone," and he ran off on the branches without a word of farewell. I recognized his usual way of refusing to admit anything which would force him out of his own world.

From then on every time I saw him he was sad and impatient, jumping about here and there, without doing anything. If now and again I heard him whistling in competition with the blackbirds, his note was ever more restless and gloomy.

The Marchesa arrived. As always, his jealousy pleased her; she incited it a little, turned it a little into a joke. So back came the beautiful days of love, and my brother was happy.

But now the Marchesa never let pass a chance to accuse Cosimo of having a narrow idea of love.

"What d'you mean? That I'm jealous?"

"You're right to be jealous. But you try to make jealousy submit to reason."

"Of course; so I can do more about it."

"You reason too much. Why should one ever reason about love?"

"To love you all the more. Everything done with reasoning grows in power."

"You live on trees and have the mentality of a notary with gout."

"The most arduous deeds must be undertaken in the simplest states of mind."

He went on mouthing maxims, till she fled; then he ran after her, desperate, tearing his hair.

In those days a British flagship anchored in our port. The Admiral gave a party for the notables of Ombrosa and the officers of other ships that happened to be in port; the Marchesa went; and from that evening Cosimo felt the pangs of jealousy start anew. Two officers of two different ships fell in love with Donna Viola and were seen continually on shore, courting the lady and trying to outdo each other in attentions. One was a flag officer on the British flagship; the other was also a flag officer, but of the Neapolitan fleet. Hiring two sorrels, the two officers would alternate beneath the Marchesa's balconies, and when they met, the Neapolitan would roll at the Englishman an eye so fiery that it should have burned him on the spot, while between the half-shut lids of the Englishman glinted a glance like the point of a sword.

And Donna Viola? What should she do, the minx, but remain hour by hour at home, leaning over the window sill in her peignoir, as if she were newly widowed and just out of mourning! Cosimo, not having her on the trees with him any more, not hearing her white horse galloping toward him, was going crazy, and ended by settling (even he) before that window sill, to keep an eye on her and the two flag officers.

He was plotting a way to prepare some dreadful pitfall for his rivals so they would return immediately to their respective ships, when he noticed that Viola showed signs of encouraging both of them. He began hoping that she was only teasing them, and him too. He continued keeping a close watch on her nevertheless, and was ready to intervene the minute she showed any sign of preferring one to the other.

Along, one morning, comes the Englishman. Viola is at the window. They smile at each other. The Marchesa lets fall a note. The officer catches it in the air, reads it, bows, blushes, and spurs away. A rendezvous! The Englishman was the lucky one! Cosimo swore he wouldn't let him get through that night undisturbed.

At that moment along comes the Neapolitan. Viola throws him a note too. The officer reads it, puts it to his lips and kisses it. So he thought he was the chosen one, did he? What about the other, then? Against which was Cosimo to act? Donna Viola must surely have fixed an appointment with one of them; on the other she must have just played one of her tricks. Or did she want to make fun of them both?

As for the place of the meeting, Cosimo settled his suspicions on a pavilion at the end of the park. This had been done up and furnished by the Marchesa a short time before, and Cosimo was gnawed with jealousy at the thought of the times when she had loaded the treetops with sofas and curtains; now she was concentrating on places he could never enter. "I'll watch the pavilion," said Cosimo to himself. "If she's arranged a meeting with one of the two officers, it can only be there." And he hid in the foliage of a horse chestnut.

Shortly before dusk, the sound of a galloping horse is heard. It is the Neapolitan. Now I'll provoke him! thinks Cosimo, takes his catapult and hits him on the neck with a handful of squirrel's dung. The officer shakes himself, looks around. Cosimo comes out on his branch, and as he appears in the open, sees the English officer dismounting beyond a hedge and tying his horse to a stake. "Then it's him; perhaps the other was just passing here by chance." And down comes a load of dung on the Englishman's nose.

"Who's there?" says the Englishman, and makes to cross the

hedge, but finds himself face to face with his Neapolitan colleague, who has also dismounted and is also saying, "Who's there?"

"I beg your pardon, sir," says the Englishman, "but I must ask you to leave here at once!"

"I'm here with full right," exclaims the Neapolitan. "It's I who must ask your Lordship to leave!"

"No right can be more than mine," replies the Englishman. "I'm sorry, but I cannot allow you to stay."

" 'Tis a question of honor," says the other, "and I rely upon that of my House: Salvatore di San Cataldo di Santa Maria Capua Vetere, of the Navy of His Majesty of the Two Sicilies!"

"Sir Osbert Castlefight, third of the name!" the Englishman introduced himself. " 'Tis on *my* honor that I demand that you vacate the field."

"Not before *I* have put you out with this trusty sword!" and he draws it from its sheath.

"Sir, you wish to fight!" exclaims Sir Osbert, and puts himself on guard.

They fight.

"This is where I wanted you, colleague, and for many a day," and the Neapolitan makes a thrust.

And Sir Osbert, parrying: "I've been following your movements for some time, sir, and was awaiting this!"

Equals in skill, the two officers threw themselves into assaults and feints. They were at the height of their fury when: "Stop in heaven's name!" exclaimed a voice. On the steps of the pavilion had appeared Donna Viola.

"Marchesa, this man . . ." said the two officers in one voice, lowering their swords and pointing to each other.

And Donna Viola: "My dear friends! Sheath your blades, I beg you! Is this the way to alarm a lady? I had chosen this pavilion as the most silent and most secret place in my park, and scarcely have I dozed off than I hear the clash of arms!"

"But, Milady," said the Englishman, "was I not invited by you?"

"You were here awaiting *me*, Signora . . ." said the Neapolitan.

From Donna Viola's throat came a laugh light as a flutter of wings. "Ah, yes, yes, I had invited you . . . or you. Oh, I get so confused. Well, sirs, what are you waiting for? Do come in, please . . ."

"Milady, I thought the invitation was for me alone. I am disappointed. May I offer my respects and request leave to withdraw."

"I too wish to say the same, Signora, and bid farewell."

The Marchesa laughed. "My good friends . . . My *good* friends . . . I'm so scatterbrained . . . I thought I had invited Sir Osbert at one time . . . and Don Salvatore at another . . . No, no, excuse me; at the same time, but in different places . . . Oh, no, how can that be? . . . Well, anyway, seeing that you are both here, why can we not sit down and hold civilized converse?"

The two lieutenants looked at each other, then looked at her. "Are we to understand, Marchesa, that you are pretending to accept our attentions merely in order to make fun of both of us?"

"Why so, my good friends? On the contrary, quite on the contrary . . . Your assiduity can scarcely leave me indifferent . . . You are both such dear people . . . And that is my worry . . . If I choose the elegance of Sir Osbert I shall lose you, my passionate Don Salvatore . . . And by choosing the fire of the officer of San Cataldo, I would have to renounce you, sir. Oh, why ever . . . why ever . . ."

"Why ever what?" asked the two officers in one voice.

And Donna Viola, lowering her eyes: "Why ever could it not be both at the same time?"

From the horse chestnut above came a crash of branches. It was Cosimo, who could retain his calm no longer.

But the two flag officers were too confused to hear this. They both stepped back a pace. "That never, Madame."

The Marchesa raised her lovely face with its most radiant smile. "Well, then, I shall give myself to the first of you who, to please me in all things, declares himself ready to share me with his rival!"

"Signora."

"Milady."

The two officers bowed coldly to Viola, then turned to face each other, held out their hands and shook.

"I was sure you were a gentleman, Signor Cataldo," said the Englishman.

"I never doubted your honor, Sir Osberto," exclaimed the Neapolitan.

They turned their backs on the Marchesa and marched off toward their horses.

"My friends . . . Why so offended . . . Silly boys . . ." Viola was saying, but the two officers already had their feet in the stirrups.

It was the moment for which Cosimo had long been waiting, enjoying in anticipation the revenge he had prepared, when the two would get a most painful surprise. Now, however, seeing their virile attitude in bidding farewell to the immodest Marchesa, Cosimo suddenly felt reconciled with them. Too late! Now it was too late to remove his appalling devices for revenge! A second's thought, and Cosimo had generously decided to warn them. "Stop!" he called from the tree. "Don't mount!"

The two officers raised startled heads. "What are you doing up there? What d'you mean by this? Come down!"

Behind them was heard Donna Viola's laugh, one of her bird's wing laughs.

The two were looking perplexed. So there was a third, who seemed to have been present at the whole scene! The situation was becoming more complicated than ever.

"Anyway," said they to each other, "we two remain in complete agreement!"

"On our honor!"

"Neither of us two will agree to share Milady with anyone else!"

"Never on our lives!"

"But if one of us two should decide to accept . . ."

"In that case, still agreed! We would accept together!"

"That's a pact! And now, away!"

At this new dialogue, Cosimo began gnawing his thumb with rage for having tried to prevent his own revenge. "Let it be, then!" he said to himself, and drew back into the leaves. The two officers leaped into their saddles. Now they'll yell, thought Cosimo, and stopped his ears. Double shrieks rang out. The two flag officers had sat on two porcupines hidden under the trappings of their saddles.

"Betrayed!" They flew to the ground in an explosion of screams and hops and writhing and they looked as if they were going to put the blame on the Marchesa.

But Donna Viola, more indignant than they, shouted up: "You malicious, monstrous monkey!" She rushed toward the trunk of the horse chestnut and rapidly vanished from the sight of the two officers, who thought she had been swallowed up by the earth.

Up in the branches Viola was facing Cosimo. They looked at each other with flaming eyes, and their rage gave them a kind of purity, like archangels. They seemed just about to tear each other to pieces, when, "Oh, my darling!" exclaimed the woman. "That's, yes, that's how I like you. Jealous, implacable! . . ." Already she had flung an arm around his neck and they were embracing and now Cosimo could remember nothing more.

She was in his arms, then took her face from his, as if some thought had struck her, and said: "But that pair, too, how much they love me. Did you see? They're even ready to share me between them . . ."

Cosimo felt for a second like flinging himself at her, then he pulled himself up on the branches, tore the leaves with his teeth, and banged his head against the trunk. "They're vermin . . ."

Viola had moved away, her face immobile like a statue's. "You've a lot to learn from them!" She turned and climbed quickly down the tree.

The two suitors had quite forgotten their past differences, and were now absorbed in patiently helping to pick out each other's quills. They were interrupted by Donna Viola. "Quick! Into my carriage!" They all vanished behind the pavilion. The carriage moved off. Cosimo was left on the horse chestnut, hiding his face in his hands.

Now began a time of torment for Cosimo, and also for the two ex-rivals. And for Viola, could it be called a time of joy? I believe the Marchesa tormented others because she wanted to torment herself. The two noble officers were always underfoot, inseparable, under her windows, or in her salon, or on long bouts in the local tavern. She would flatter them both and ask them to compete in constant new proofs of love, which every time they declared themselves ready to do; and by now they were even ready to halve her with each other, not only that, but to share her with anyone else, and once they had begun rolling down the slippery slopes of concessions, they could no longer halt, each urged by the wish to succeed thus in moving her and obtaining the fulfillment of her promises, and each at the same time tied in a pact of solidarity with his rival, and devoured too by jealousy and by the hope of supplanting him, and, I fear, by the pull of the obscure degradation into which they felt themselves sinking.

At every new concession torn from the naval officers, Viola would mount her horse and go to tell Cosimo about it.

"Say, d'you know the Englishman is ready to do this and this ... And the Neapolitan too ..." She would shout as soon as she saw him gloomily perching on a tree.

Cosimo would not reply.

"This is absolute love," she would insist.

"Absolute shit, that's what you all are!" screamed Cosimo, and vanished.

This was now their cruel way of loving each other, and from it they could find no way out.

The English flagship was about to weigh anchor. "You're staying, aren't you?" said Viola to Sir Osbert. Sir Osbert did not report on board and was declared a deserter. In a spirit of solidarity and emulation, Don Salvatore did the same.

"They've deserted!" announced Viola triumphantly to Cosimo. "For me! And you ..."

"And I?" screamed Cosimo with such a ferocious look that Viola did not dare say another word.

Sir Osbert and Salvatore di San Cataldo, deserters from the navies of their respective Majesties, now spent their days at the tavern, playing dice, pale, restless, trying to encourage each other, while Viola was at the peak of her discontent with herself and with all around her.

She took her horse, went toward the wood. Cosimo was on an oak. She stopped underneath, in a field.

"I'm tired."

"Of those?"

"Of you all."

"Ah!"

"They've given me the greatest proofs of love . . ."

Cosimo spat.

". . . But that's not enough for me."

Cosimo lowered his eyes to meet hers.

And she: "Don't you think that love should be an absolute dedication, a renunciation of self?"

There she was in the field, lovely as ever, and the coldness just touching her features and the haughtiness of her bearing would have dissolved at a touch, and he would have had her in his arms again . . . Anything would have been all right for Cosimo to say, anything to show he was ready to give in: "Tell me what you want me to do, I'm ready"—and once more there would have been happiness for him, happiness without a cloud. But he said: "There can be no love if one does not remain oneself with all one's strength."

Viola shrugged in irritation, which was also a shrug of weariness. And yet she could have understood him still, as in fact she did understand him then and had on the tip of her tongue the words, "You are as I want you," and she would be back with him again . . . She bit her lip. And said: "Be yourself by yourself, then."

"But being myself then has no sense." That is what Cosimo wanted to say. Instead of which he said: "If you prefer those vermin . . ."

"I will not allow you to despise my friends!" she shouted, still thinking: All that matters to me is you, and it is only for you that I do all I do!

"So, I'm the only one to be despised."

"What a way you think!"

"It's part of me."

"Then good-by. I leave tonight. You won't see me again."

She hurried to the house, packed her bags, and left without even a word to the officers. And she kept her word, never returned to Ombrosa. She went to France, and there a succession of historical events stood in her way when she was longing for nothing but to return. The Revolution broke out, then the war; first the Marchesa took an interest in the new course of events (she was in the entourage of Lafayette), then emigrated to Belgium and from there to England. In the London mists, during the long years of wars against Napoleon, she would dream of the trees of Ombrosa. Then she remarried—an English peer connected with the East India Company—and settled at Calcutta. From her terrace she would look out over the forests, the trees even stranger than those of the gardens of her childhood; every moment it seemed that she could see Cosimo appearing through the leaves. But it would be the shadow of a monkey, or a jaguar.

Sir Osbert Castlefight and Salvatore di San Cataldo remained linked in life and death, and launched into a career of adventure. They were seen in the gambling houses of Venice, in the Faculty of Theology at Göttingen, in Petersburg at the Court of Catherine II. Then trace was lost.

Cosimo remained for a long time wandering aimlessly around the woods, weeping, ragged, refusing food. He would sob out loud, as do newborn babes. The birds which had once fled at the approach of this infallible marksman would now come near him, on the tops of nearby trees or flying over his head, and the sparrow called, the goldfinch trilled, the turtle dove cooed, the thrush whistled, the chaffinch chirped and so did the wren; and from their lairs on high issued the squirrels, the tree mice, the field mice, to add their squeals to the chorus, so that my brother moved amidst this cloud of lamentation.

Then a destructive violence came over him; every tree, beginning from the top, leaf by leaf, he quickly stripped till it was bare as in winter, even if it usually shed no leaves at all. Then climbing back to the peaks he would break off all the smaller branches and twigs till he left nothing but the main wood, would go farther up and with a penknife begin to strip off the bark, and the stricken trees could be seen showing the whites of ghastly wounds.

In all this frenzy of his there was no resentment against Viola, only remorse at having lost her, at not having known how to keep her tied to him, at having wounded her with a pride unjust and stupid. For, he understood now, she had always been faithful to him, and if she took a pair of other men about with her it merely meant that it was Cosimo alone she considered worthy of being her only lover, and all her whims and dissatisfactions were but an insatiable urge for the increase of their love and the refusal to admit it could reach a limit, and it was he, he, he, who had understood nothing of this and had goaded her till he lost her.

For some weeks he kept to the woods, alone as never before; he had not even Ottimo Massimo, for Viola had taken the dog with her. When my brother showed himself at Ombrosa again, he had changed. Not even I could delude myself any longer; this time Cosimo really had gone mad.

} 24 {

IT HAD always been said at Ombrosa that Cosimo was mad, ever since he had jumped onto the trees at the age of twelve and refused to come down. But later, as happens, this madness of his had been accepted by all, and I am not talking only of his determination to live up there, but of the various oddities of his character; and no one considered him other than an original. Then in the full spate of his love for Viola there were those burblings in incomprehensible languages, particularly the ones during the Feast of the Patron Saint, which some considered as sacrilege, interpreting his words as heretical cries, perhaps in Punic, the tongue of the Pelasgians, or as a profession of Socinianism, in Polish. Since then began the rumor—"The Baron's gone mad"—and the conventional added, "How can someone go mad who's always been mad?"

In the midst of these different pronouncements, Cosimo really had gone mad. If before he went about dressed in furs from head to foot, now he began to adorn his head with feathers, like the American aborigines, bright-colored feathers of hoopoes or greenfinch, and apart from those on his head he scattered feathers all over his clothes. He ended by making himself jackets all covered with feathers, and imitating the habits of the various birds, such as the woodpecker, drawing worms and insects from the tree trunks and boasting of what riches he had found.

He would also make speeches in defense of birds, to the people who gathered to listen and banter under the trees; and from marksman he became barrister to the feathered tribe, and declared himself now a tomtit, now an owl, now a redbreast, and would wear suitable camouflaging and make long prosecution speeches against human beings, who did not know how to recognize birds as their real friends, speeches which were accusations in the form of parables against all human society. The birds also realized this change in his ideas, and came close to him, even if there were people listening beneath. Thus he was able to illustrate his speeches with living examples, which he pointed out on the branches around.

Because of this particular quality of his, there was much talk among the hunters of Ombrosa of using him as a decoy, but no one ever dared fire on the birds perching near him. For even now when he was more or less out of his senses the Baron still im-

pressed them: they quizzed him, yes, and often under his trees
he had a retinue of urchins and idlers jesting at his expense; yet
he was also respected, and always heard with attention.

His trees were now hung all over with scrawled pieces of paper
and bits of cardboard with maxims from Seneca and Shaftesbury,
and with various objects: clusters of feathers, church candles,
crowns of leaves, women's corsets, pistols, scales, tied to each
other in a certain order. The Ombrosians used to spend hours
trying to guess what those symbols meant: nobles, Pope, virtue,
war? I think some of them had no meaning at all but just served
to jog his memory and make him realize that even the most uncommon ideas could be right.

Cosimo also began to write certain things himself, such as
The Song of the Blackbird, *The Knock of the Woodpecker*, *The
Dialogue of the Owls*, and to distribute them publicly. In fact,
it was at this very period of dementia that he learned the art
of printing and began to print some pamphlets or gazettes (among
them *The Magpie's Gazette*), later all collected under the title,
The Bipeds' Monitor. He had brought into a nut tree a typog-
rapher's table and chase, a press, a case of type, and a crock of
ink, and he spent his days composing his pages and pulling his
copies. Sometimes spiders and butterflies would get caught between type and paper, and their marks would be printed on the
page; sometimes a lizard would jump on the sheet while the ink
was fresh and smear everything with its tail; sometimes the
squirrels would take a letter of the alphabet and carry it off to
their lair thinking it was something to eat, as happened with the
letter Q, which because of its round shape and stalk they mis-
took for a fruit, so that Cosimo had to begin some of his articles
with Cueer and end them with C.E.D.

All this was very fine, of course, but I had the impression that
at the time my brother had not only gone mad, but was getting
imbecilic too, which was more serious and sadder, for madness is
a force of nature, for good or evil, while imbecility is a weakness
of nature, without any counterpart.

In winter, though, he seemed able to reduce himself to a kind of lethargy. He would hang on a bough in his lined sleeping bag, with only his head out, as if from a huge nest, and it was rare if, in the warmest hours of the day, he made more than a few hops to reach the alder tree over the Merdanzo torrent, for his daily duties. He would stay in the bag desultorily reading (lighting a little oil lamp in the dark), or muttering to himself, or humming. But most of the time he spent sleeping.

For eating he had certain mysterious arrangements of his own, but he would accept offerings of minestrone or ravioli when some kind soul brought these up to him on a ladder. In fact, a kind of superstition had grown up among the local peasants that an offering to the Baron brought luck—a sign that he aroused either fear or good will, and I think it was the latter. That the reigning Baron of Rondò should live on public charity seemed improper to me; and above all I thought of what our dead father would have said if he had known. As for myself, till then I had nothing to reproach myself with, for my brother had always despised family comforts and had signed that power of attorney by which, after giving him a small allowance (which he spent almost entirely on books) I had no more duties toward him. But now, seeing him incapable of getting himself food, I tried making one of our lackeys in livery and white wig go up a ladder to him with a quarter of turkey and a glass of Bordeaux on a salver. I thought he would refuse from one of those mysterious principles of his, instead of which he accepted at once and most willingly; and from then on, every time it crossed my mind, we would send a portion of our viands up to him on the branches.

Yes, it was a sad decline. Then luckily there was an invasion of wolves, and that gave Cosimo a chance to show his best qualities again. It was an icy winter, snow had even fallen in our woods. Packs of wolves, pushed out of the Alps by famine, fell on to our coasts. Some woodman ran into them and rushed back in terror with the news. The people of Ombrosa, who from the days of the guardians against fires had learned to unite in moments of danger, began to take turns as sentries around the town, to prevent the famished beasts from getting nearer. But no one dared go beyond the houses, particularly at night.

"What bad luck the Baron isn't what he used to be!" they were saying at Ombrosa.

That hard winter had not been without effect on Cosimo's health. He was dangling there crouched in his pelt like a chrysalis in its cocoon, his nose dribbling, looking muzzy and vague. The alarm went up about the wolves and people passing beneath called up: "Ah, Baron, once it would have been you keeping guard from your trees, and now it's we who are guarding you."

He remained with his eyes half closed, as if he did not understand or did not care about anything. Then, suddenly he raised his head, blew his nose and said, hoarsely: "Sheep. For the wolves. Put some on the trees. Tied."

People were crowding about beneath to hear what nonsense he would bring out and to jeer. Instead he rose from the sack, puffing and coughing, and said: "I'll show you where," and moved off among the branches.

Onto some walnuts or oaks, between woods and cultivated land, in positions chosen with great care, Cosimo told them to bring sheep or lambs, which he himself tied to branches, alive, bleating, but in such a way that they could not fall down. On each of these trees he hid a musketful of grapeshot. He then dressed himself up like a sheep: hood, jacket, breeches—all of curly sheepskin. And he began to wait out the night on the open trees. Everyone thought this was the maddest thing he had ever done.

That very night, though, down came the wolves. Sniffing the scent of sheep, hearing the bleating and then seeing them up there, the whole pack stopped at the foot of the trees and howled with famished fangs bared and clawed against the trunk. And now, bounding over the branches, along came Cosimo, and the wolves, seeing that cross between sheep and man hopping up there like a bird, were transfixed. Until *"Bum! Bum!"* and they got a couple of bullets in the throat. A couple—for Cosimo carried one gun with him (and recharged every time) and had another on every tree ready with a bullet in the barrel; so every time he fired, two wolves were stretched on the frozen ground. He exterminated a great number like that and at every shot the pack tacked to and fro in confused flight, while the other men with guns ran to where they heard the cries, and their shots did the rest.

Cosimo had many a tale in many a version to tell afterward about this wolf hunt, and I could not say which was the right one. For example: "The battle was going quite well when, as I was moving toward the tree with the last sheep on it, I found three wolves which had managed to climb up on to the branches and were just killing it off. Half blinded and stunned by fever as I was, I nearly got up to the wolves' snouts before they noticed me. Then, seeing this other sheep walking on two feet along the branches, they turned on it, baring fangs still red with blood. My gun was unloaded, as after all that firing I had run out of powder, and I could not reach the gun on that tree as the wolves were there. I was on a smaller, rather weak branch, but above me was a stronger one within arm's reach. I began walking backward on my branch, retreating slowly away from the main trunk. And slowly, following me, came a wolf. But I was hanging on to the branch above by my hands, and moving my feet on that other one; really I was hanging from above. The wolf, deceived, moved forward and the branch bent beneath it, while with a jump I yanked myself on to the branch above. Down the wolf went with a little bark like a dog's, broke its back on the ground and killed itself."

"And what about the other two wolves?"

". . . The other two were stock-still, staring at me. Then suddenly I took off my sheepskin jacket and hood and threw them at the wolves. One of the two, seeing this white ghost of a sheep flying toward them, tried to seize it in his teeth, but as he was expecting a heavy weight and that was just an empty skin, he lost his balance and also ended by breaking claws and neck on the ground."

"There's still one left."

". . . There's still one left—but as my clothes had suddenly been so lightened by throwing away that jacket, a fit of sneezing came over me, to shake heaven and earth. At this sudden unexpected eruption, the wolf got such a shock that he fell from the tree and broke his neck too. . . ."

Thus my brother on his night of battle. What is certain is that the fever he caught as a result, ailing as he already was, very nearly proved fatal. For some days he lay between life and death, tended at the expense of the Commune of Ombrosa, in sign of gratitude. He was put into a hammock, and surrounded by doctors going up and down on ladders. The best doctors available were called into consultation, and some gave enemas, some leeches, some mustard plasters, some fomentations. None spoke any more of the Baron of Rondò as mad, but all as one of the greatest brains, one of the outstanding phenomena of the century.

That while he was ill. When he recovered, things changed. Once again, as always before, some said he was wise, some that he was mad. But in fact he was never taken by these vagaries again. He went on printing a weekly paper, no longer called *The Bipeds' Monitor* but *The Reasonable Vertebrate*.

} 25 {

I'M NOT sure if at that time a Lodge of Freemasons was already founded at Ombrosa; I myself was initiated into Masonry much later, after the first Napoleonic Campaign, together with a great part of the local upper bourgeoisie and petty nobility, and so I cannot tell when my brother's first relations were with the Lodge. In this connection I will cite an episode which happened more or less at the time I am describing, and which various witnesses would confirm as true.

One day two Spaniards, passing travelers, arrived at Ombrosa. They went to the house of a certain Bartolomeo Cavagna, a pastry cook, a well-known Freemason. They declared themselves, it seems, as brethren of the Lodge of Madrid, so that he took them one night to a meeting of the Ombrosian Masons, which then met by the light of torch and flare in a clearing in the middle of the woods. All this comes from hearsay and speculation; what is certain is that next day, as soon as the two Spaniards came out of their inn, they were followed by Cosimo, who had been watching for them, unseen from the trees above.

The two travelers entered the courtyard of a tavern outside the town gate. Cosimo perched himself on an arbor overhung with wisteria. At a table was sitting a customer waiting for the pair; his face could not be seen, shaded as it was by a black hat with a wide brim. Their three heads, or rather their three hats, nodded over the white square of the tablecloth; and after some confabulation the hand of the unknown man began to write on a narrow piece of paper something dictated by the other two and which, from the order in which the words were set one below the other, appeared to be a list of names.

"Gentlemen, good day to you," said Cosimo. The three hats went up, showing three faces with eyes staring at the man on the trelliswork. But one of the three, the one with the wide brim, dropped his at once, so low that he touched the table with the tip of his nose. My brother just had time to catch a glimpse of features which did not seem unfamiliar to him.

"*Buenos días!*" exclaimed the two. "But is it a local habit here to introduce oneself to strangers by dropping from the sky like a pigeon? Perhaps you would be good enough to come down and explain!"

"Those high up are clearly seen," said the Baron, "though others trail in the dust to hide their faces."

"May I say, *Señor*, that none of us are under an obligation to show our faces, just as none of us are to show our rumps."

"For certain kinds of persons, of course, it is a point of honor to hide the face."

"Which, for instance?"

"Spies, to name one!"

The two companions started. The bent man remained motionless, but his voice was heard for the first time. "Or, to name another, members of secret societies . . ." he said slowly.

This remark was open to various interpretations. So Cosimo thought and so he said out loud. "That remark, sir, is open to various interpretations. Did you say 'members of secret societies,' hinting that I am one myself, or hinting that you are, or that we both are, or that neither of us are, or did you say it because whichever way it's taken the remark is useful in terms of my reply?"

"*Cómo, cómo, cómo?*" exclaimed the man with the wide-brimmed hat confusedly, and in his confusion he forgot to keep his head down, and raised it enough to look Cosimo in the eyes. And Cosimo recognized him; it was Don Sulpicio, the Jesuit, his enemy from the days at Olivabassa!

"Ah! So I was not mistaken. Down with the mask, Reverend Father!" exclaimed the Baron.

"You! I was sure of it!" exclaimed the Spaniard, and took off his hat and bowed, disclosing his tonsure. "Don Sulpicio de Guadalete, *Superior de la Compañia de Jesús.*"

"Cosimo di Rondò, Freemason!"

The two other Spaniards also introduced themselves with slight bows.

"Don Calisto!"

"Don Fulgencio!"

"Also Jesuits?"

"*Nosotros también!*"

"But has not your order recently been dissolved by order of the Pope?"

"Not as a respite to libertines and heretics of your stamp!" exclaimed Don Sulpicio, unsheathing his sword.

They were Spanish Jesuits, who after the disbandment of the Order had gone into hiding and were trying to form an armed militia all over the countryside, to combat Theism and the new ideas.

Cosimo put his hand on the hilt of his sword. A number of people had formed a ring around. "Be good enough to descend, if you wish to fight *caballerosamente*," said the Spaniard.

Nearby was a wood of nut trees. It was the time of the crop and the peasants had hung sheets from one tree to another, to gather the nuts they beat down. Cosimo rushed on to a nut tree, jumped into the sheet, and managed to keep upright and prevent his feet from slipping on the cloth of this hammock-like support.

"You come up a span or two, Don Sulpicio, as I've come down farther than I usually do!" and he, too, drew his sword.

The Spaniard also jumped onto the outstretched sheet. It was difficult to keep upright, as the sheet tended to fold up like a sack around their bodies, but so heated were the two contestants that they managed to cross swords.

"To the Greater Glory of God!"

"To the Glory of the Great Architect of the Universe!"

And they set on each other.

"Before I plunge this blade into your gullet," said Cosimo, "give me news of the Señorita Ursula."

"She died in a convent!"

Cosimo was disturbed by this news (which, however, I think was made up on the spot) and the ex-Jesuit profited by this devilish trick. He swung out at one of the knots tied to the branches of the nut tree and sustaining the sheet on Cosimo's side, and cut it clean through. Cosimo would have fallen had he not quickly flung himself on to the sheet in Don Sulpicio's part and seized a rope. In his leap his sword pierced the Spaniard's guard and plunged into his stomach. Don Sulpicio slumped, slithered down the sheet on to the side where he had cut the knot, and fell to the ground. Cosimo pulled himself back on to the nut tree. The other two ex-Jesuits raised their companion—whether dead or just wounded was never known—hurried off and were never seen again.

A crowd formed round the blood-spattered sheet. And from that day my brother had the reputation of being a Freemason.

Due to the Society's secrecy I never got to know more. When I entered it, as I said, I heard Cosimo spoken of as an old-time brother whose relations with the Lodge were not quite clear, and whom some defined as inactive, some as a heretic who had switched to another sect, some even as an apostate; but his past activities were always mentioned with great respect. He may even have been that legendary Master "Woodpecker Mason," to whom was attributed the foundation of the Lodge called "East of Ombrosa," and the description of the first rites of that Lodge seem to show his influence; suffice it to say that the neophytes were blindfolded, made to climb a tree, then dropped on the end of a rope.

It is certain that the first meetings of Freemasons with us took place at night in the midst of the woods. So Cosimo's presence would have been more than justified, whether he was the person who received from correspondents abroad the volumes of the Masonic Constitutions, or whether it was someone else who had been initiated, possibly in France or England, who introduced the rites into Ombrosa too. It is possible, though, that Masonry had existed here for some time unknown to Cosimo, and that one night, moving about the trees in the wood, he happened by chance on a clearing where there was a meeting of men with strange vestments and instruments by the light of candles, and he stopped up there to listen and then intervened and confused them by some unexpected remark, such as: "If you put up a wall, think of what's left outside!" (a phrase which I often heard him repeat), or another one of his, and the Masons, recognizing his superior insight, made him a member of their Lodge, with special duties, and he brought in a great number of new rites and symbols.

The fact is that for the whole period my brother had anything to do with it, the open-air Masonry (as I will call it to distinguish it from that which was later to meet in a closed building) had

a much richer ritual, in which a part was played by owls, telescopes, pine cones, hydraulic pumps, mushrooms, little Cartesian
devils, cobwebs, Pythagorean tables. There was also a certain
show of skulls, not only of humans, but also of cows, wolves
and eagles. Such objects and others, such as the trowels, rulers
and compasses of the normal Masonic liturgy, were found at that
time hanging on to branches in strange juxtapositions, and also
attributed to the Baron's madness. Only a few persons hinted
that this rebus now had a more serious meaning; but anyway, no
one was ever able to trace a clear distinction between the earlier
and later symbols, or exclude the possibility that from the first
they had been esoteric symbols of some other secret society.

For long before Cosimo joined the Masons, he had been in
various associations and confraternities of trades and professions,
such as St. Crispin's or the Shoemakers', the Virtuous Coopers',
the Just Armorers' or the Conscientious Capmakers'. As he
made on his own nearly everything he needed to live with, he
knew a great variety of trades, and could boast himself a member
of many guilds, which on their part were pleased to have with
them a member of a noble family, of unusual talents and proved
disinterest.

How this passion which Cosimo always showed for communal
life fitted in with his perpetual flight from society, I have never
properly understood, and it remains not the least of his singu-
larities of character. One would say that the more determined
he was to hide away in his den of branches, the more he felt
the need to create new links with the human race. But although
every now and again he flung himself, body and soul, into organiz-
ing a new fellowship, suggesting detailed rules and aims, choosing
the aptest men for every job, his comrades never knew how far
they could count on him, where they could meet him, and when
he would be suddenly urged back into the bird side of his nature
and let himself be caught no more. Perhaps, if one tried, one
could take these contradictory impulses back to a single impulse.
One should remember that he was just as contrary to every kind
of human organization flourishing at the time, and so he fled

from them all and tried experiments with new ones. But none of these seemed right or different enough from the others. From this came his constant periods of utter wildness.

What he had in mind was an idea of a universal society. And every time he busied himself getting people together, either for a definite purpose such as guarding against fire or defending from wolves, or in confraternities of trades such as the Perfect Wheel-wrights or the Enlightened Skin Tanners, since he always got them to meet in the woods, at night, around a tree from which he would preach, there was always an air of conspiracy, of sect, of heresy, and in that atmosphere his speeches also passed easily from particular to general, and from the simple rules of some manual trade moved far too easily to a plan for installing a world republic of men—equal, free and just.

So Cosimo did little more in Masonry than to repeat what he had done in the other secret or semi-secret societies of which he had been a member. And when a certain Lord Liverpuck, sent by the Grand Lodge of London to visit his brethren on the continent, came to Ombrosa while my brother was Master, he was so scandalized by Cosimo's unorthodoxy that he wrote to tell London that this Ombrosa Masonry must be some new Masonry of the Scottish rite financed by the Stuarts to use propaganda against the Hanoverian throne, for a Jacobite restoration.

After this came the incident I have described, of the two Spanish travelers who introduced themselves to Bartolomeo Cavagna as Masons. Invited to a meeting of the Lodge, they found it all quite normal, in fact they said it was just like the Orient of Madrid. It was this which roused the suspicion of Cosimo, who knew only too well how much of the ritual was his own invention; that is why he tracked down the spies, unmasked them and triumphed over his old enemy, Don Sulpicio.

Anyway, my opinion is that these changes in liturgy were a personal need of his own, for he could just as easily have taken the symbols of every trade, except that of mason, he who had never wanted nor built nor inhabited any houses with walls.

} 26 {

OMBROSA was also a land of vines. I have never mentioned this, as in following Cosimo I have always had to keep to vegetation with high trunks. But there were vast slopes of vines, and in August under the festooned leaves the rosy grapes swelled in clusters of thick juice that was already wine-colored. Some vines were on arbors. I mention this because as Cosimo became older he had got so small and light and learned so well how to move without throwing all his weight in one place that the crossbars of the pergolas held him. He could thus pass on to the vines, and by supporting himself on the poles called *scarasse*, could do work, such as pruning in winter, when the vines are like bare hieroglyphics, or in summer thin out the heavy foliage or look for insects, and then in September help with the vintage.

For the vintage the entire population of Ombrosa would come out into the vineyards for the day, and everywhere the green of vines was dappled with the bright colors of skirts and tasseled caps. Muleteers loaded basket after full basket into the panniers and emptied them in the vats; other basketfuls were taken by the various tax collectors, who came with squads of bailiffs to levy dues for the local nobles, the Government of the Republic of Genoa, the clergy and other tithes. Every year there was some row or other.

The question of what parts of crops to allot around was the major reason for the protests set down in the "books of complaints," at the time of the French Revolution. Books like these were also filled up at Ombrosa, just to try it, even if here they were no use at all. This had been one of Cosimo's ideas. At that time he no longer felt any need to attend the meetings of the Lodge and hold discussions with those old stick-in-the-muds of Masons. He was on the trees in the square and all the people from the beaches and countryside around came crowding beneath to get him to explain the news, for he received newspapers by post and also had certain friends who wrote to him, among them the astronomer Bailly, who was later made mayor of Paris, and other club members. Every day there was something new: Necker, and the Tennis Court, and the Bastille, and Lafayette on his white horse, and King Louis disguised as a lackey. Cosimo would explain and act everything out, jumping from branch to branch, and on one branch he would be Mirabeau at the tribune, and on another Marat at the Jacobins, and on yet another King Louis at Versailles putting on the Phrygian cap to please the housewives who had come marching out from Paris.

To explain what "books of complaints" were, Cosimo said: "Let's try and make one." He took a school notebook and hung it on the tree by a string; everyone came there and wrote down whatever they found wrong. All sorts of things came out; the fishermen wrote about the price of fish, and the vineyard men about those tithes, and the shepherds about the borders of pastures, and the woodmen about the Commune's woods, and then there were all those who had relatives in prison, and those who had got lashes for some misdeed, and those who had it in for the nobles because of something to do with women; it was endless. Cosimo thought that even if it was a "book of complaints" it need not be quite so glum, and he got the idea of asking everyone to write down what they would like most. And again everyone went to put down their ideas, sometimes rather well. One wrote of the local cakes, one of the local soup; one wanted a blonde, one a couple of brunettes; one would have liked to sleep the whole day through, one to go mushrooming all the year round; some wanted a carriage with four horses, some found a goat enough; some would have liked to see their dead mother again, some to meet the gods on Olympus. In fact, all the good in the world was written down in the exercise-book, or drawn— since as many did not know how to write—or even painted in colors. Cosimo wrote too—a name—Viola. The name he had been writing everywhere for years.

It was a fine exercise-book-full, and Cosimo called it "Book of Complaints and Contents." But when it was all written from cover to cover there was no assembly to send it to, so there it remained hanging on the tree by a string, and when it rained it began to blotch and fade, and the sight made the hearts of the Ombrosians tighten at their present plight, and filled them with desire to rebel.

In fact, all the causes of the French Revolution were present among us too. Only we were not in France, and there was no revolution. We live in a country where causes are always seen but never effects.

At Ombrosa, though, we had some exciting times all the same. The Republican army warred against the Austro-Sardinians almost under our noses. Massena at Collardente, Laharpe on the Nervia, Mouret on the coast road—and Napoleon was then only a general of artillery, so that those rumbles we heard fitfully reaching Ombrosa on the breeze were made by the man himself.

In September they began preparing for the vintage again. And now they seemed to be preparing something secret and terrible.

Counsels of war from door to door:

"The grapes are ripe!"

"Ripe! Yes, indeed!"

"Ripe as ripe! They need picking!"

"We'll go and get 'em!"

"We're all ready. Where will you be?"

"In the vineyard beyond the bridge. And you? And you?"

"In Count Pina's."

"I in the vineyard by the mill."

"Have you seen the number of bailiffs? They seem like blackbirds dropping to pick the grapes!"

"But they won't peck this year!"

"If there are so many blackbirds, we're just as many hunters!"

"Some of us daren't come! Some are running away."

"Why is it so many people don't like the vintage this year?"

"They wanted to put it off here. But now the grapes are ripe!"

"They're ripe!"

Next day, though, the vintage began silently. The vineyards were crowded with chains of people under the festoons, but no song went up. A call or two, a shout of "You here too? It's ripe!" a movement of groups, a touch of gloom—even in the sky, which was not entirely overcast, just rather cloudy—and if a voice struck up a song it soon faded off, not taken up by the chorus. The muleteers were taking the panniers full of grapes to the vats. In other years the dues for the nobles, the bishop and the government were set aside beforehand; this year, though, they seemed to have been forgotten.

The tax collectors, come to draw the tithes, were nervous, did not know quite what to do. The more time passed, the less happened. The more they felt something must happen, the more the bailiffs realized they had to do something but the less they understood what it was.

Cosimo was walking along the pergolas with his cat's tread. He was carrying some scissors and cutting off a bunch here and a bunch there, haphazardly, offering them to the men and women vintaging below, and saying something to each in a low voice.

The chief of the bailiffs could bear the tension no more. He said: "Eh, well, now, then, what about these tithes?" Scarcely had he said this than he had already regretted it. Through the vineyards rang a deep note, part bellow, part hiss; it was a vintager blowing on a conch shell and sounding the alarm all over the valley. From every hillock similar sounds replied. The vintagers raised up their shells like trumpets, and Cosimo, too, from the top of a pergola.

A song went along the rows of vines; first broken, discordant, so it was difficult to understand. Then the voices fused, harmonized, took up the tune and sang as if they were running, flying along, and the men and women standing stock-still half hidden among the vines and each pole's vine cluster and grape seemed to run, and the grapes to be vintaging themselves, flinging themselves into the vats and treading themselves down. And the air, the clouds, the sun, all became unfermented juice; and now the song began to be understood, first the notes and then some of the words, which went: "*Ça ira! Ça ira! Ça ira!*" And the young men pounded the grapes with their bare red feet—"*Ça ira!*"— and the girls thrust their sharp dagger-like scissors into the thick greenery, wounding the twisted stalks of the grape clusters— "*Ça ira!*"—and clouds of gnats flew above the heaps of fruit ready for the press—"*Ça ira!*" And it was then that the bailiffs lost control of themselves and called: "Stop that! Silence! Enough of this row! Whoever sings we shoot!" And they began firing rounds in the air.

In reply came a rumble of gunfire that seemed to come from regiments lined in battle order on the hills. All the muskets of Ombrosa exploded, and from the top of a high fig tree Cosimo sounded the charge on a conch shell. All over the hillsides people moved. It was impossible to distinguish now between vintage and crowd: men, grapes, women, sprigs, clippers, festoons, *scarasse*, muskets, baskets, horses, barbed wire, fists, mule's kicks, shins, teats—all singing "*Ça ira!*"

"Here are your tithes!" It ended with the bailiffs and tax collectors being thrust head over heels into the vats full of grapes, their legs sticking out kicking wildly. And they returned without having gathered a thing, smeared from head to foot with grape juice, and with pips, husks, stalks, stuck all over their muskets, powder pouches and mustaches.

Then the vintage turned into a fête, with all convinced of their having abolished feudal privileges once and for all. Meanwhile we nobles and petty squires had barricaded ourselves in our houses, armed to the teeth and ready to sell our skins dear. (I, in truth, did no more than keep my nose inside our gates, above all to avoid giving the other nobles a chance to say I was in agreement with that Antichrist of a brother of mine, reputed the worst agitator and Jacobin in the whole area.) But that day, once the troops and tax collectors had been flung out, no one else was hurt.

Everyone was deep in preparing celebrations. They even put up a Tree of Liberty, just to follow the mode from France; only they weren't quite sure what it was like, and then there were so many trees in our parts that it was scarcely worth while putting up a false one. So they dressed up a real tree, an elm, with flowers, clusters of grapes, festoons and placards: *"Vive la Grande Nation!"* From the very tip my brother, in a tricolor cockade on his cat's-fur cap, delivered a lecture on Rousseau and Voltaire, of which not a single word could be heard, as the whole population was twirling round beneath singing *"Ça ira!"*

The gaiety was short-lived. Troops came in great strength. Genoese, to exact dues and guarantee territorial neutrality, and Austro-Sardinians too, as the rumor had got around that the Jacobins of Ombrosa intended to proclaim the place annexed to the "Great Universal Nation," that is, to the Republic of France. The rebels tried to resist, built a barricade or two, shut the town gates . . . But no, more than that was needed! The troops passed into the place on every side, set up block-posts on every country lane, and those with the reputation of agitators were imprisoned, except for Cosimo, who would have needed a devil to catch him, and a few others with him.

The trial of the revolutionaries was hastily set up, but the accused succeeded in showing that they had nothing whatsoever to do with it and that the real leaders were the very ones who had decamped. So everyone was freed, particularly as with all those troops stationed at Ombrosa no more unrest was to be feared. A garrison of Austro-Sardinians stayed too, as a guarantee against any possible enemy infiltration, and in command of these was our brother-in-law, D'Estomac, the husband of Battista, emigrated from France in the suite of the Comte de Provence.

So I found my sister Battista underfoot again, with what reaction I leave you to imagine. She installed herself in the house, with husband, horses, orderlies. And every evening she would spend describing the last executions in Paris; she even had a model of a guillotine, with a real blade, and to explain the end of all her friends and relations-in-law she would decapitate lizards, centipedes, worms and even mice. So we would spend our evenings. I envied Cosimo living his days and nights out in the open, hidden in some wood.

} 27 {

SO MANY and so incredible were the tales Cosimo told about his activities in the woods during the war that I cannot really accept outright any one version. So I leave the word to him, and just faithfully report some of his stories.

"In the woods there used to patrol scouting parties from both the opposing armies. From up on the branches, at every step I heard crashing through the undergrowth, I would strain my ears to guess if they were Austro-Sardinians or French.

"A little Austrian lieutenant, with very fair hair, was in command of a patrol of soldiers in perfect uniforms—queues and tassels, tricorns and gaiters, crossed white bands, muskets and bayonets—and making them march along in double file, trying to keep them in step on the rough paths. Ignorant of what the woods were like, but certain of carrying out his orders punctiliously, the little officer was proceeding according to the lines traced on the map, banging his nose continually against tree trunks, the troops slipping with their hobnailed boots on the smooth stones or gouging their eyes out with brambles, but conscious always of the supremacy of the imperial arms.

"Magnificent soldiers they were. I waited for them at a clearing, hidden on a pine. In my hand I had a heavy pine cone which I dropped on the head of the last man in the file. The soldier threw up his arms, his knees buckled and down he fell among the ferns of the undergrowth. No one noticed and the platoon continued its march.

"I caught up with them again. This time I threw down a rolled-up porcupine on the head of a corporal. The corporal's head sagged and he fainted. This time the lieutenant saw what happened, sent two men to fetch a stretcher, and pressed on.

"The patrol, as if on purpose, went and got entangled in the thickest juniper bushes in the whole wood. And a new ambush was ready there too. I had collected some caterpillars in a piece of paper, the hairy, blue sort, whose touch makes the skin swell worse than a nettle, and poured a hundred or so down on them. The platoon passed, vanished in thick bushes, re-emerged scratching themselves, with hands and knees covered with little red bubbles, and marched on.

"Splendid troops, a splendid officer! The whole wood was so strange to him that he could not distinguish what was unusual about it, and proceeded with his decimated cadres, but proud and indomitable as ever. Then I had recourse to a family of wild cats; I launched them by their tails, after swinging them in the air a bit, which goaded them to a frenzy. There was a lot of noise, especially feline, then silence and truce. The Austrians were tending their wounded. Then the patrol, white with bandages, started off on the march again.

" 'The only thing is to try and take them prisoners!' said I to myself, hurrying to get ahead of them, and hoping to find a French patrol to warn of the enemy approach. But the French had not been giving any sign of life on that front for some time.

"While I was getting over a slippery place, I saw something move. I stopped, and pricked up my ears. I heard a kind of bubbling stream which then ran on into a continual gurgle and I began distinguishing the words: '*Mais alors . . .'cré-nom-de . . . foutez-moi-donc . . . tu m'emmer . . . quoi. . . .*' Squinting into the half-darkness, I saw that the soft vegetation below was composed chiefly of hairy busbies and flowing mustaches and beards. It was a squadron of French hussars. Having been soaked with damp during the winter campaign, toward spring all their hats were sprouting with mildew and moss.

"In command of this outpost was Lieutenant Agrippa Papillon, of Rouen, poet, and volunteer in the Republican Army. Convinced of the general goodness of nature, Lieutenant Papillon told his soldiers not to crunch the pine needles, the chestnut cones, the twigs, the leaves, the snails which stuck on to his men as they crossed the wood. And the patrol was already so fused with surrounding nature that it needed my well-trained eye to spot them at all.

"Amid his bivouacking soldiers, the officer-poet, with long hair in ringlets framing his gaunt face under the cocked hat, was declaiming to the woods: 'O Forest! O Night! Here I am in your power! Could a tender tendril of your maidenhair fern, clasped to the ankles of these doughty soldiers, not hold the destiny of France? O, Valmy! How far away you are!'

"I came forward. 'Pardon, citoyen.'

" 'Who is it? Who's there?'

" 'A patriot of these woods, citizen officer.'

" 'Ah! Here? Where?'

" 'Right over your nose, citizen officer.'

" 'So I see! Who is it? A bird-man, progeny of the Harpies! Are you a creature of mythology?'

" 'I am Citizen Rondò, progeny of humans, I assure you, on father's and mother's side, citizen officer. In fact my mother was a brave soldier in the Wars of Succession.'

" 'I understand. O Times, O Glory! I believe you, citizen, and I am anxious to hear the news which you appear to have come to announce.'

" 'An Austrian patrol is penetrating your lines!'

" 'What d'you say? To battle then! 'Tis the hour! O Stream, gentle stream, ah, soon you will be stained with blood! On, On! To arms!'

"At the lieutenant-poet's command the hussars began gathering up arms and equipment, but they moved in such a scatterbrained and sluggish way, stretching, spitting, swearing, that I began to have doubts of their military efficiency.

" 'Citizen officer, have you a plan?'

" 'A plan? To march on the enemy!'

" 'Yes, but how?'

" 'How? In closed ranks!'

" 'Well, if you will allow me to give advice, I would keep the soldiers halted, in open order, and let the enemy patrol entrap itself!'

"Lieutenant Papillon was an accommodating fellow and made no objections to my plan. The hussars, scattered about the wood, could be scarcely distinguished from clumps of verdure, and the Austrian lieutenant was certainly the man least adapted to see the difference. The imperialist patrol was marching along according to the itinerary traced out on the map, with every now and again a brusque 'To the right!' or 'To the left!' So they passed under the noses of the French hussars without noticing them. Silently the hussars, producing only natural sounds such as the rustles of leaves and the flutter of wings, arranged themselves for an encircling maneuver. I kept sentry for them from above and made whistles and stoats' cries to signal the enemy troop movements, and the short cuts ours had to take. The Austrians, all unawares, were caught in a trap.

"Suddenly they heard a shout from a tree. 'Halt there! In the name of liberty, equality and fraternity. I declare you all prisoners!' And between the branches appeared a human ghost brandishing a long-barreled hunting gun.

" 'Urrah! Vive la Nation!' And all the bushes around sprouted French hussars, with Lieutenant Papillon at their head.

"Deep oaths resounded from the Austro-Sardinians, but before they had a chance to react they were disarmed. The Austrian lieutenant, pale but head high surrendered his sword to his enemy colleague."

"I became quite a useful auxiliary to the Republican Army, but preferred to go about things alone, with the help of the animals of the forest, like the time when I put an Austrian column to flight by tipping a nest of wasps on their heads.

"My reputation spread to the Austro-Sardinian camp, exaggerated to such a point that the woods were said to be packed with armed Jacobins, hidden on top of every tree. Wherever they went, the royal and imperial troops were on the *qui-vive;* at the slightest plop of chestnuts dropping from their husks and the faintest squirrel's squeak, they already felt themselves surrounded by Jacobins, and changed their route. In this way, just by provoking almost imperceptible rustles and sounds, I caused the Piedmontese and Austrians' columns to deviate and succeeded in leading them by the nose wherever I wanted.

"One day I got a column of them to a thick prickly copse and made them all lose their way. In the copse lived a family of wild boar. Driven from the mountains by the boom of cannon, the boars were descending in droves to take refuge in the woods lower down. The lost Austrians were marching along without being able to see a hand's-breadth in front of their noses, and suddenly hairy boars sprung up everywhere under their feet, emitting piercing cries. Snouts thrust out, they flung themselves between the knees of every soldier, pushing them all head over heels and stamping on the fallen in an avalanche of pointed hoofs, and piercing their stomachs with tusks. The entire battalion was routed. I and my comrades, from our perch on the trees, followed them with musket fire. Those who managed to get back to camp said either an earthquake had suddenly opened the thorny ground under their feet, or that they'd been attacked by a band of Jacobins sprung from the bowels of the earth, as these Jacobins were nothing but devils, half man and half beast, who lived on the trees or in the midst of bushes.

"As I said, I preferred to carry out my coups alone, or with a few comrades from Ombrosa who had taken refuge with me in the woods after that vintage. With the French army I tried to have as little to do as possible, as we know what armies are, every time they move there's some disaster. But I had taken rather a liking to that outpost of Lieutenant Papillon and was rather worried about what might happen to them. For the immobility of the front threatened to be fatal to the squadron under the poet's command. Moss and lichen were growing on the troopers' uniforms, and sometimes even heather and fern; the tops of the busbies were nested in by screech owls, or sprouted and flowered with lilies of the valley; their thigh boots clotted with soil into campact clogs. The whole platoon was about to take root. Lieutenant Agrippa Papillon's yielding attitude toward nature was sinking that squad of brave men into a fusion of animal and vegetable.

"They had to be awakened. How, though? I had an idea and went to Lieutenant Papillon to propose it. The poet was declaiming to the moon:

"'O Moon! round as a muzzle, like a cannon ball whose thrust from gunpowder is exhausted and continues to rotate slowly and silently through the sky! When will you burst on us, O Moon, raising a high cloud of dust and sparks, submerging enemy armies and thrones, and opening a breach of glory for me in the compact wall of my fellow citizens' distrust of me! O Rouen! O moon! O fate! O convention! O frogs! O girls! O life!'

"And I: '*Citoyen . . .*'

"Papillon, annoyed at my constant interruptions, said sharply: 'Well?'

"'I only wanted to suggest, citizen officer, a way of rousing your men from a lethargy which is getting dangerous.'

"'I wish to heaven there were, citizen. Action is what I yearn for, as you see. And what might this way of yours be?'

"'Fleas, citizen officer.'

"'I'm sorry to disillusion you, citizen. There are no fleas in the Republican Army. They've all died of famine as a result of the blockade and high cost of living.'

"'I can supply some, citizen officer.'

"'I don't know if it's sense or a joke you're making. Anyway I will report the matter to Higher Command, and we shall see. Citizen, my thanks for your help to the republican cause! O glory! O Rouen! O fleas! O moon!' and he went off raving.

"I realized I had to act on my own initiative. So I collected a lot of fleas, and as soon as I saw a French hussar I'd shoot one at him with a catapult, trying to aim accurately enough to get it into his collar. Then I began to sprinkle the whole unit, in handfuls. It was a dangerous mission, for had I been caught in the act, no reputation of mine as a patriot would have saved me. They would have taken me prisoner, dragged me off to France and guillotined me as an emissary of Pitt. Instead of which my intervention was providential. The itching of the fleas quickly kindled in the hussars a human and civilized need to scratch themselves, search themselves, delouse themselves. They flung away their mossy clothes, their packs and knapsacks covered with mushrooms and cobwebs, washed, shaved, combed, in fact reacquired a perception of their individual humanity and regained the sense of civilization, of enfranchisement from the ugly side of nature. They were spurred, too, by a stimulus to activity, a zeal, a combativity long forgotten. The attack, when it came, found them pervaded by this new zest: the Armies of the Republic overcame the enemy resistance, broke through the front, and advanced to the victories of Dego and Millesimo . . ."

} 28 {

OUR sister and the emigré D'Estomac escaped from Ombrosa just in time to avoid capture by the Republican Army. The people of Ombrosa seemed to have returned to those days of the vintage. They raised the Tree of Liberty, this time more in conformity to French example, that is, a little like a Tree of Plenty. Cosimo, it goes without saying, climbed onto it, with a Phrygian cap on his head; but he soon got tired and left.

There was some rioting around the palaces of the nobles, a few cries of "Aristó, aristó, string 'em up. Ça ira!" Me, what with my being my brother's brother and our always having been nobles of little account, they left in peace. Later on, in fact, they came to consider me as a patriot too (so that, at the next change, I was in trouble myself).

They set up a *municipalité*, a *maire*, in the French style; my brother was nominated to the provisional junta, although many did not agree with this, considering him to be out of his wits. Those of the old régime laughed and said that the whole lot were a cageful of lunatics.

The sittings of the *junta* were held in the former palace of the Genoese governor. Cosimo would perch on a carob which was the same height as the windows and follow the discussion from there. Sometimes he intervened to protest and give his vote. It is an acknowledged fact that revolutionaries are greater sticklers for formality than conservatives. They found Cosimo objectionable and his system of attendance unworkable, said that it lessened the decorum of the assembly, and so on. When the Ligurian Republic was set up in place of the oligarchic Republic of Genoa, my brother was not elected to the new administration.

Cosimo, by the way, had at that time written and published a *"Constitutional Project for a Republican City with a Declaration of the Rights of Men, Women, Children, Domestic and Wild Animals, Including Birds, Fishes and Insects, and All Vegetation, whether Trees, Vegetables, or Grass."* It was a very fine work, which could have been a useful guide to any government; but which no one took any notice of, and it remained a dead letter.

Most of his time, however, Cosimo still spent in the woods, where the sappers of the French Army were opening a road for the transport of artillery. With their long beards flowing under their busbies and merging into their leather aprons, the sappers were different from all the other troops. Perhaps this was due to the fact that they did not leave behind them all that trail of disaster and destruction (like other troops), but had the satisfaction of doing things that remained and the ambition to carry them out as best they could. Then they had so many stories to tell. They had crossed nations, seen sieges and battles; some of them had even been present at the recent great events in Paris—the storming of the Bastille and the guillotinings—and Cosimo used to spend his evenings listening to them. On putting away their spades and stakes they would sit around a fire, smoking short pipes and digging up old memories.

By day, Cosimo used to help the surveyors mark out the track. No one was better fitted to do so than he; he knew all the places where the road could pass with the gentlest gradients and the lowest loss of trees. And he always bore in mind not so much the needs of the French artillery as of the population of those roadless parts. At least one advantage would come from all the passage of brutal and plundering soldiery—a road made at their expense.

This was no bad thing at the time, either; for by then, the occupation troops, particularly since they had changed their name from republican to imperial, were a pain in the neck to all. And all went to the patriots to complain—"Just see what your friends are doing!" And the patriots would fling up their arms and raise their eyes to the sky, and reply: "Oh, well! Soldiers! Let's hope it all blows over!"

The Napoleonic troops would requisition pigs, cows, even goats, from the stalls. And as for taxes and tithes, they were worse than before. On top of everything, conscription started. This having to go as a soldier, no one could understand round our way; and the called-up youths would take refuge in the woods.

Cosimo did what he could to help out. He would watch over cattle in the woods when the peasant owners sent them into the wilds for fear of a roundup; or he would guard clandestine loads of wheat on their way to the mill or olives to the press, so that the Napoleonic troops should not get a part; or show the youths called to the service caves in the woods where they could hide. In fact, he tried to defend people against hectoring, although he never made any attacks against the occupying troops, in spite of the armed bands which were beginning to wander around the woods making life difficult for the French. Cosimo, stubborn as he was, refused ever to retract, and having been a friend of the French before, went on thinking he must be loyal to them, even if so much had changed and all was so different from what he expected. Then one should also remember that he was no longer as young as he used to be, and did not put himself out much now, for either side.

Napoleon went to Milan to get himself crowned, and then made a few journeys through Italy. In every town he passed people gave him a great welcome and took him to see the

local sights. At Ombrosa they also put in the program a visit to
the "patriot on the treetops," for, as often happens, none of us
bothered much about Cosimo, but he was very famous in the
world outside, particularly abroad.

It was not a chance encounter. Everything was arranged
beforehand by the municipal committee for the celebrations, so
as to make a good impression. They chose a fine big tree. They
wanted an oak, but the one most suitably placed was a walnut, so
they tricked this up with a few oak branches, and hung it with
ribbons in the French tricolor and the Lombard tricolor, cockades
and frills. In the middle of all this they perched my brother,
dressed in gala rig but wearing his characteristic cat's-fur cap,
with a squirrel on his shoulder.

Everything was set for ten o'clock and a big crowd was waiting
around the tree, but of course Napoleon did not appear till
half-past eleven, to the great annoyance of my brother, who as he
got older was beginning to suffer from bladder trouble and had to
get behind the trunk every now and again to urinate.

Came the Emperor, with a suite all shimmering epaulettes.
It was already midday. Napoleon looked up between the branches
toward Cosimo and found the sun in his eyes. And he began to
address a few suitable phrases to Cosimo: "*Je sais très bien de
vous, citoyen . . .*" and he shaded his eyes, "*parmi les forêts . . .*"
and he gave a little skip to one side so that the sun did not
come right into his eyes, "*parmi les frondaisons de notre luxuri-
ante . . .*" and he gave another skip the other way as Cosimo's
bow of assent had bared the sun on him again.

Seeing Bonaparte so restless, Cosimo asked politely: "Is there
anything I can do for you, *mon Empereur?*"

"Yes, yes," said Napoleon, "keep over that side a bit, will
you, to shade the sun off me. There, that's right, keep still
now. . . ." Then he fell silent as if struck by some thought, and
turned to the Viceroy Eugène. "All this reminds me of something . . . something I've seen before."

Cosimo came to his help. "Not you, Majesty; it was Alexander
the Great."

"Ah, of course!" exclaimed Napoleon. "The meeting of Alexander and Diogenes!"

"You never forget your Plutarch, *mon Empereur,*" said Beauharnais.

"Only that time," added Cosimo, "it was Alexander who asked Diogenes what he could do and Diogenes asked him to move . . ."

Napoleon gave a flick of the fingers as if he had finally found the phrase he was looking for. Assuring himself with a glance that the dignitaries of his suite were listening, he said in excellent Italian: "Were I not the Emperor Napoleon, I would like to be the citizen Cosimo Rondò!"

And he turned and went. The suite followed with a great clinking of spurs.

That was all. One might have expected that within a week Cosimo would have been sent the cross of the Legion of Honor. My brother did not care a rap about that, but it would have given us pleasure in the family.

} 29 {

YOUTH soon passes on earth, so imagine it on the trees, where it is the fate of everything to fall: leaves, fruit. Cosimo was growing old. All the years, all the nights spent in the cold, the wind, the rain, under fragile shelters or nothing at all, surrounded by air, without ever a house, a fire, a warm dish . . . He was getting to be a shriveled old man, with bandy legs and long monkey-like arms, hunchbacked, sunk in a fur cloak topped by a hood, like a hairy friar. His face was baked by the sun, creased as a chestnut, with clear round eyes among the wrinkles.

The army of Napoleon was put to rout at the Beresina. The British fleet landed at Genoa. We spent the days waiting for news of reverses. Cosimo did not show himself at Ombrosa; he was crouching in a pine tree in the woods overlooking the Sappers' Road, where the guns had passed toward Marengo, and looking toward the east, over the deserted surface on which only shepherds with their goats or mules loaded with wood were to be seen. What was he waiting for? Napoleon he had seen, he knew how the Revolution had ended, there was nothing to expect now but the worst. And yet there he was, eyes fixed, as if at any moment the Imperial Army would appear round the bend, still covered with Russian icicles, and Bonaparte on horseback, his unshaven chin sunk in his chest, feverish, pale . . . He would stop under the pine tree (behind him a confusion of smothered steps, a clattering of packs and rifles on the ground, exhausted soldiers taking off boots by the roadside, unwinding rags round their feet) and he would say: "You were right, Citizen Rondò; give me the constitutions you wrote out, give me your advice to which neither the Directorate nor the Consulate nor the Empire would listen; let us begin again from the beginning, raise the Tree of Liberty once more, save the universal nation!" These were surely the dreams, the aspirations, of Cosimo.

Instead, one day, three figures came limping along the Sappers' Road from the east. One, lame, was supporting himself on a crutch; another's head was wrapped in a turban of bandages; the third was the halest, as he only had a black patch over one eye. The filthy rags they wore, the tattered braid hanging from their chests, the cocked hats without cockades but with a plume still on one of them, the high boots rent all the way up the leg, seemed to have belonged to uniforms of the Napoleonic Guard. But they had no arms; or, rather, one was brandishing an empty scabbard; the second had a gun barrel on his shoulder, like a stick with a bundle on it. They came on singing: "*De mon pays . . . De mon pays . . . De mon pays . . .*" like a trio of drunks.

"Hey, strangers," shouted my brother at them, "who are you?"

"What an odd bird! What are you doing up there. Eating pine kernels?"

And the second: "Who wants pine kernels? Famished as we are, d'you expect us to eat pine kernels?"

"And the thirst! We got that from eating snow!"

"We are the Third Regiment of Hussars!"

"To a man!"

"All that's left!"

"Three out of three hundred; not bad!"

"Well, I've made it and that's enough for me!"

"Ah, it's too early to say that, you're not home yet with a whole skin!"

"A plague on you!"

"We are the victors of Austerlitz!"

"And the botched of Vilna! Hurrah!"

"Hey, talking bird, tell us where there's a tavern around here!"

"We've emptied the wine barrels of half of Europe but can't get rid of our thirst!"

"That's because we're riddled with bullets, and the wine flows straight through us!"

"You know where you're riddled!"

"A tavern that would give us credit!"

"We'll come back and pay another time!"

"Napoleon will pay!"

"Prrr . . ."

"The Czar will pay! He's coming along behind. Hand him the bills!"

Cosimo said: "There's no wine around here, but farther on there's a stream and you can quench your thirst."

"May you drown in the stream, you owl!"

"If I hadn't lost my musket in the Vistula River I'd have shot you down by now and cooked you on the spit like a thrush!"

"Wait a bit, will you: I'm going to get my feet in that stream, they're burning."

"You can wash your behind in it, for all I care."

But all three of them went to the stream, to take off their boots, bathe their feet, wash their faces and clothes. Soap they got from Cosimo, who was one of those people who get cleaner as they get older, as they are seized by a self-disgust which they did not notice in youth; so he always took soap around with him. The cool water cleared the fumes of alcohol a little in the three. And as the drunkenness passed, they were overwhelmed by the gloom of their state and heaved a sigh; but in their dejection the limpid water became a joy, and they splashed about in it, singing: *"De mon pays . . . De mon pays . . ."*

Cosimo had returned to his lookout post on the edge of the road. He heard galloping and a squadron of light horse appeared, raising dust. They were in uniforms he had never seen before; and under their heavy busbies could be seen fair-skinned faces, bearded and rather gaunt, with half-closed green eyes. Cosimo doffed his cap to them. "What good wind, sirs?"

They stopped. *"Sdrastvuy!* Say, *batjuska,* how long more before we get there?"

"Sdrastvujte, soldiers," said Cosimo, who had learned a bit of every language and Russian too. *"Kuda vam?* to get where?"

"To get wherever this road goes to . . ."

"Oh, this road goes to so many places. Where are you going?"

"V Pariz."

"Well, there are better routes to Paris."

"Niet, nie Pariz. Vo Frantsiu, za Napoleonom. Kuda vedjot eta doroga?"

"Oh, to so many places: Olivabassa, Sassocorto, Trappa . . ."

"Tchto? Aliviabasse? Niet, niet."

"Well, if you want to, you can get to Marseilles . . ."

"V Marsel . . . da, da, Marsel . . . Frantsia . . ."

"And what are you going to do in France?"

"Napoleon came to war on our Czar, and now our Czar is chasing Napoleon."

"And where do you come from?"

"Iz Charkova. Iz Kieva. Iz Rostova."

"What nice places you must have seen! And which d'you like more, here or in Russia?"

"Nice places, ugly places, all the same to us, we like Russia!"

A gallop, a cloud of dust, and a horse pulled up, ridden by an officer, who shouted at the Cossacks: "*Von! Marsh! Kto vam pozvolil ostanovitsja?*"

"*Do svidanja, batjuska!*" said the troopers to Cosimo, "*Nam pora . . .*" and spurred away.

The officer had remained there at the foot of the pine tree. He was tall, slim, with a noble and sad air; he was holding his bare head raised toward a sky veined with clouds.

"*Bonjour, monsieur,*" he said to Cosimo. "So you know our language?"

"*Da, gospodin ofitser,*" replied my brother, "but not more than you do French, all the same."

"Are you an inhabitant of this country? Were you here while Napoleon was about?"

"Yes, *monsieur l'officier.*"

"How did that go?"

"You know, *monsieur,* armies always loot, whatever the ideas they bring."

"Yes, we too do a lot of looting . . . but we don't bring ideas . . ."

He was sad and worried, though a victor. Cosimo liked him and tried to console him. "You have won!"

"Yes. We fought well. Very well. But perhaps . . ."

Suddenly yells broke out, rifle fire, a clash of arms. "*Kto tam?*" exclaimed the officer. The Cossacks returned, dragging over the ground some half-naked corpses, and holding something in their hands, their left hands (the right were grasping wide curved scimitars, bared and—yes—dripping with blood), and this something was the hairy heads of those three drunken hussars. "*Frantsuzy! Napoleon! All dead!*"

The young officer barked out a sharp order, and made them take the things away.

"You see . . . War . . . For years now I've been dealing as best I can with a thing that in itself is appalling; war . . . and all this for ideals which I shall never, perhaps, be able to explain fully to myself . . ."

"I too," replied Cosimo, "have lived many years for ideals which I would never be able to explain to myself; but I do something entirely good. I live on trees."

The officer's mood had suddenly changed from melancholy to nervous. "Well," he said, "I must be moving on." He gave a military salute. "*Adieu, monsieur* . . . What is your name?"

"*Le Baron Cosime de Rondeau*," Cosimo shouted after his departing figure. "*Proshtchajte, gospodin* . . . And yours?"

"*Je suis le Prince Andrej* . . ." and the galloping horse carried off the surname.

} 30 {

I HAVE no idea what this nineteenth century of ours will bring, starting so badly and getting so much worse. The shadow of the Restoration hangs over Europe; all the innovators—whether Jacobins or Bonapartists—defeated; once more absolutism and Jesuitry have the field; the ideals of youth, the lights, the hopes of our eighteenth century—all are dust.

Such thoughts I confide to this notebook, nor would I know how to express them otherwise; I have always been a balanced man, without great impetus or yearnings, a father, a noble by birth, enlightened in ideas, observant of the laws. The excesses of politics have never shocked me much, and I hope never will. And yet within, how sad I feel!

It was different before. My brother was there. I used to say to myself, "That's his business," and get on with my life. For me the sign of change has not been the arrival of the Austro-Russians or our annexation to Piedmont or the new taxes or anything of that kind, but just the fact of never seeing him,

when I open the window, balancing there up above. Now that
he is no longer here I should be interested in so many things:
philosophy, politics, history. I follow the news, read books, but
they befuddle me. What he meant to say is not there, for he
understood something else, something that was all-embracing,
and he could not say it in words but only by living as he did.
Only by being so frankly himself as he was till his death could he
give something to all men.

I remember when he fell ill. We realized it because he brought
his sleeping bag on to the great nut tree in the middle of the
square. Before, the places where he slept he had always kept
hidden, with his wild beast's instinct. Now he felt the need to be
always seen by others. It tore at my heart; I had always thought
that he would not like to die alone, and perhaps this was a first
sign. We sent a doctor up on a ladder; when he came down he
made a grimace and raised both arms.

I went up the ladder myself. "Cosimo," I began, "you're
past sixty-five now, can you stay up here any longer? What you
wanted to say you've said now. We've understood. It's meant a
great effort of will on your part, but you've done it, and now
you can come down. For those who have spent all their lives on
the sea, too, there comes a time for landing."

No use. He made a sign of disagreement with one hand. Now
he could scarcely speak. Every now and again he would get up,
wrapped in a blanket to the top of his head, and sit on a branch
to sun himself a little. More than that he did not move. An
old peasant woman, an old mistress of his perhaps, went up
and did for him, and brought him hot food. We kept the
ladder leaning against the trunk, since there was constant need of
going up to help him, and also since some still hoped that he
might suddenly take it into his head to come down. (It was
others who hoped so; I knew what he was like.) On the square
below there was always a circle of people who kept him company, chatting among themselves and sometimes making a
remark to him too, though they knew that he no longer wanted
to talk.

He got worse. We hoisted a bed onto the tree, and succeeded in fixing it in balance; he got into it quite willingly. We felt a twinge of remorse at not having thought of it before; but in truth he had never rejected comfort; though on trees, he had always tried to live the best he could. So we hurriedly took up other comforts: screens to keep the draught off, a canopy, a brazier. He improved a bit, and we brought him an armchair and lashed it between two branches. He began to spend his days on it, wrapped in his blankets.

One morning, though, we saw him neither in bed nor in the armchair. Alarmed, we raised our eyes. He had climbed onto the top of the tree and was sitting astride a very high branch, wearing only a shirt.

"What are you doing up there?"

No reply. He was half rigid, and seemed to stay up there by a miracle. We got out a big sheet of the kind used to gather olives, and twenty or so of us held it taut beneath, as we were expecting him to fall.

Meanwhile the doctor went up; it was a difficult climb, and two ladders had to be tied together end to end. When he came down he said: "Let the priest go up."

We had already agreed to try a certain Don Pericle, a friend of his, a priest of the Constitutional Church at the time of the French, a Freemason before it was forbidden to the clergy, and readmitted to his offices by the Bishop a short time before, after many ups and downs. He went up with his vestments and ciborium, followed by an acolyte. He spent a short time up there. They seemed to discuss something. Then he came down.

"Has he taken the Sacraments then, Don Pericle?"

"No, no, but he says it's all right, for him it's all right." And I never managed to get more out of him.

The men holding the sheet were tired. Cosimo was still up there, motionless. The wind came up, it was westerly, the tip of the tree quivered, we stood ready. At that moment a balloon appeared in the sky.

Some English aeronauts were experimenting with balloon

flights along the coast. It was a fine big balloon decorated with fringes and flounces and tassels, with a wickerwork basket attached. Inside it were two officers in gilt epaulettes and peaked caps, gazing through telescopes at the landscape beneath, watching the man on the tree, the outstretched sheet, the crowd, strange aspects of the world. Cosimo had raised his head too and was looking fixedly at the balloon.

And then suddenly the balloon was caught in a gust of westerly wind; it began running before the wind, twisting like a trout and going out to sea. The aeronauts, undaunted, busied themselves reducing—I think—the pressure in the balloon, and at the same time unrolled the anchor to try and grip some support. The anchor flew silvery in the sky attached to a long rope, and following the balloon's course obliquely it began passing right over the square, more or less at the height of the top of the nut tree, so that we were afraid it would hit Cosimo. But little did we guess what we were to see with our own eyes a second later.

The dying Cosimo, at the second when the anchor rope passed near him, gave one of those leaps he so often used to do in his youth, gripped the rope, with his feet on the anchor and his body in a hunch, and so we saw him fly away, taken by the wind, scarce braking the course of the balloon, and vanish out to sea . . . .

The balloon, having crossed the gulf, managed to land on the other side. On the rope was nothing but the anchor. The aeronauts, too busy at the time trying to keep a lookout, had noticed nothing. It was presumed that the dying old man had disappeared while the balloon was flying over the bay.

So vanished Cosimo, without giving us even the satisfaction of seeing him return to earth a corpse. On the family tomb there is a plaque in commemoration of him, with the inscription: "Cosimo Piovasco di Rondò—Lived in trees—Always loved earth —Went into sky."

Every now and again as I write I interrupt myself and go to the window. The sky is empty, and for us old folk of Ombrosa, used to living under those green domes, it hurts the eyes to look out now. Trees seem almost to have no right here since my brother left them or since men have been swept by this frenzy for the ax. And the species have changed too; no longer are there ilexes, elms, oaks; nowadays Africa, Australia, the Americas, the Indies, reach out roots and branches as far as here. What old trees exist are tucked away on the heights; olives on the hills, pines and chestnuts in the mountain woods; the coast down below is a red Australia of eucalyptus, of swollen India rubber trees, huge and isolated garden growths, and the whole of the rest is palms, with their scraggy tufts, inhospitable trees from the desert.

Ombrosa no longer exists. Looking at the empty sky, I ask myself if it ever did really exist. That mesh of leaves and twigs of fork and froth, minute and endless, with the sky glimpsed only in sudden specks and splinters, perhaps it was only there so that my brother could pass through it with his tomtit's tread, was embroidered on nothing, like this thread of ink which I have let run on for page after page, swarming with cancellations, corrections, doodles, blots and gaps, bursting at times into clear big berries, coagulating at others into piles of tiny starry seeds, then twisting away, forking off, surrounding buds of phrases with frameworks of leaves and clouds, then interweaving again, and so running on and on and on until it splutters and bursts into a last senseless cluster of words, ideas, dreams, and so ends.

Books by Italo Calvino
available in Harvest paperback editions
from Harcourt Brace & Company

The Baron in the Trees
The Castle of Crossed Destinies
Cosmicomics
Difficult Loves
If on a winter's night a traveler
Invisible Cities
Italian Folktales
Marcovaldo, or The seasons in the city
Mr. Palomar
The Nonexistent Knight and *The Cloven Viscount*
t zero
Under the Jaguar Sun
The Uses of Literature
The Watcher and Other Stories